North & South
CONTINUES

By
Mary Jo Schrauben

Copyright © 2013 Mary Jo Schrauben

2nd Edition, December 2013

All rights reserved.

ISBN: 1482795701
ISBN-13: 978-1482795707

Dedications

This continuation is dedicated to all period drama enthusiasts who long for that simpler and more innocent time.

For my mom, Joanne. I will see her again.
Ellie May, my sunshine. I miss her so much.

I would also like to give thanks to the
Holy Father who directs all my ways and brings
many blessings to my life.

Acknowledgment

To my wonderful friend and second pair of eyes, Lina Papadopoulou. Located in Athens, Greece, she is a professional Greek to English translator. To contact, please email her at lina.papadopoulou@gmail.com.

Contents

	Introduction	*i*
Chapter One	Her Mr. Thornton	1
Chapter Two	The Black Leather Gloves	16
Chapter Three	A Battle Won With A Miracle	29
Chapter Four	Outwood Station	45
Chapter Five	Expressed But Not Said	58
Chapter Six	Afternoon Reunions	73
Chapter Seven	Man or Machine	86
Chapter Eight	Dismantling the Machine	102
Chapter Nine	True Vision and True Blindness	118
Chapter Ten	Evil Intent	130
Chapter Eleven	Change of Plan	146
Chapter Twelve	Coming Home With Me	162
Chapter Thirteen	Parting & Revelations	180
Chapter Fourteen	A Thundering Storm	196
Chapter Fifteen	Choices & Sacrifices	212
Chapter Sixteen	Tears of Sorrow and Joy	230
Chapter Seventeen	Always	248
	Epilogue	256

Introduction

Dear Readers –

It was a few years back when I first heard about the miniseries of Elizabeth Gaskell's classic, *North & South* that was made for television. On reading the online reviews, virtually all of which were positive, I had to see it without delay.

It being quite late at night, I endeavored to find the entire four episodes—233 minutes worth—available online to download in short ten to twelve minute segments each. Once I started watching, the characters captivated me, endearing each into my heart. I could not stop.

Several hours later (slow internet connection), I reached that breathtaking reunion of John and Margaret at the train station. The used tissues piled up as I replayed the scene repeatedly; it was the most sincere and genuinely romantic four minutes and fifty seconds I had ever viewed in my lifetime. I have yet to see one to come even remotely close to replacing it.

As most viewers, my heart sank when the credits began to roll right after. I wanted more of John Thornton and Margaret Hale's story! That day (for it was daylight when I finished), I went out for the sole purpose of finding and purchasing my own copy. It remains the top on my list as the most "DVD Worthy" movies in my vast collection.

Some time after, I learned of a new writing genre called Fan Fiction. This is where amateur, fiction authors write continuations of their favorite characters in literature, movie, and television productions. Inspired, I authored a rough draft of *John & Margaret – Coming Home With Me* on a period drama blog. After its completion, I posted the story in it's entirety on a Fan Fiction site where readers are able to read and then write reviews. Except for the mention of the grammatical errors, out of over hundred reviews, **all were positive**. Here is a few that made me beam with pleasure:

> My goodness - I'm only a third of the way through and this is amazing. I can clearly picture their faces and hear their voices through their lines, especially Margaret and Mrs. Thornton. – GRock87

> This is one of the best books and TV series and your story has done it justice! I have never read a fan fiction from this story or time period worded like books back then and so true to the original characters. I love the references you made to the TV miniseries and that you continued the story, in my opinion, as the original author would've. Amazing work! I hope you continue to write like this because your writing is extraordinary! My favorite story I've read on here. :-) – Force319

What a beautifully written story. You definitely succeeded in writing a worthy sequel that's rich with emotion and evokes such vivid pictures. Thank you so much! – Jareya

What a wonderful way to spend a lazy Saturday afternoon - reading your story straight through! You did an amazing job of having our favorite characters express themselves in the next stage of their lives and I loved the dialog between them. The last chapter was indeed "icing on the cake" and just absolutely a satisfying way to end. Great job and thanks for sharing your skill and talent in such an entertaining way! – Kandern

This story is absolutely fantastic! You are an amazing writer, and I think you should seriously consider publishing this :) I'm a big fan of North and South and I think that you have the characters down pat. I'm so sad that it's over, but it was an excellent ending to an excellent story. Well done! This definitely deserves more reviews than it does. – Son

The above review got me thinking. I do love writing, especially the dialogue. There was so much more I wanted to add to my Fan Fiction. Moreover, I have read many of the other attempts to continue with their story and found that the true essence of the characters were rarely captured, leaving me either extremely dissatisfied or disappointed.

With self-publishing hitting an all time high in the Fan Fiction genre, I set upon publishing my continuing story of John and Margaret; thereby, making it much improved, with an enriched plot adding more twists and turns, tears, deep sighs and smiles. As I finished the last chapters, I knew that I had done well by the number of used tissues, once again, littering the floor and me sobbing out, "Oh my…they're gonna love that!"

I hope you enjoy my laborious, work of love.

With warmest regards,

Mary Jo Schrauben

Chapter One
Her Mr. Thornton

The rhythmic clanging of the train's steel disks on the tracks could not keep pace with Margaret's racing heart as she gazed out of the window at the passing landscape.

Her lips still tingled from the warm mouth of the man who sat next to her. His arm rested along her back, confining her in his private space, thigh touching thigh and his hand lightly possessing hers. With this closeness, she experienced no unease. This is where she should be.

Outwardly, her countenance gave the appearance of poised serenity, but the enormity of what had occurred approached as an incoming thunderstorm, gaining in intensity as each moment came and went.

Margaret welcomed this unexpected storm. With that first flash of resplendent light, came the thunder in the form of Mr. Thornton. His power took control of all her senses and caused the beat of her heart to echo loud in her ears. The thundering Mr. Thornton had become *her* Mr. Thornton.

Such as they were, moments before, sitting together on the bench when the announcement came of her train's departure. The fear of being parted from him gave way to impulse and she rushed back to her cabin. The guilt of sending Henry back alone, along with any hopes he may have had for a future with her, dissolved when she observed Mr. Thornton's gratified expression upon seeing her standing resolute behind him. When he asked if she was coming home with him, a light smile and handing over her satchel gave him her answer.

In the cabin, he secured her bag over head as she took her seat expecting him to take the seat across from her. Her elation bounded when he did not. He sat close, not hesitant to reconnect by seeking a kiss. She gladly submitted to this fresh and extraordinary tenderness from him.

Imprudent as the decision may have been to board the northbound train, Margaret believed unreservedly, that in this, she would not suffer regret.

Regret had been a constant companion ever since that day she refused him, slowly growing until she comprehended with great despondency that the man she rejected became the man she loved.

Margaret necessitated passing many hours perplexed on how she could have come to love this man given their tumultuous backstory. This question remained unanswered but she determined on when it started—when he vehemently asserted his love.

From their first encounter at Marlborough Mill, to the day after the riots, she knew her mind; Mr. Thornton was arrogant, wild and not to be esteemed. She had been certain that he could not have any misgivings on her feelings towards him. Even the burden of this knowledge did not prevent him from paving an unconventional path to her doorstep to ask her to be his wife.

Margaret became stupefied as she grasped his real purpose for calling on her that morning. The atmosphere in the room had previously been made uneasy with the conversation about the Irish workers and she had expected his swift departure soon after. However, he did not leave as anticipated.

When she comprehended what he was about to ask, she stopped him from speaking any further and reproached him for not being a gentleman. His anger flared demanding a reason why she found him offensive. Tempered, she was obliged to impart that his distorted obligation and belief that he could have her as a possession, resulted in her swift rejection.

His reaction became assertive, overwhelming her with his advancing presence and harsh tone that had her nervously backing away and emphasizing her dislike of him.

A mulled impasse had Margaret at the window and him on the other side of the room. It was in that short span of time that she apprehended what he said. He exposed his feelings for her so passionately that the words got lost in the confrontation. It never entered her mind that Mr. Thornton could come to love her legitimately. Could she have been mistaken about his motivation in asking her?

One minute we talk of the color of fruit, the next of love. How does that happen?

Margaret caught her breath at the dejection in his voice. She had her answer. It subdued her into awareness that Mr. Thornton did not express himself as an ordinary man. With this new understanding, the unpleasantness of his visit did not have her thinking less of him; in its stead, the wheel of discord stopped, switched gears, and went into reverse.

She sighted his gloves seconds after the door closed shut. In picking them up, she knew that she did not have the courage to rush after the owner. Clutching the gloves to the center of her chest, her eyes watered and head bowed. How much hurt and humiliation he must be feeling, she thought. She should have been kinder. In reviewing her words and actions, and then his, she wished she had done everything differently.

Fingering the soft leather in her hand, she withdrew back to the one time when Mr. Thornton's hand held hers. Like pulling on gloves on a cold, blustery day, she could not forget how warm and comforting his skin wrapped around hers felt. For some unexplainable reason, it pained her to know that his hand would most likely remain down by his side when it came to her.

A seed was sown in her heart that day. Its growth began when she started to view Mr. Thornton in a new light. He no longer seemed the tyrannical tradesman, but a man capable of feeling love and experience pain. Resolved, she vowed to make a considerable effort not to be opposed to his beliefs, but attempt to understand them from his point of view.

This gave her hope that, given an opening, she could find goodwill with him. Unfortunately, each time they crossed paths, the wall of disregard he built around his shattered heart prevented any sort of reconciliation from happening. The incident at the train station made the wall all but impenetrable.

It soon became clear that he longed for her to be gone from his life. His future seemed set on Miss Latimer, but the last visit to the Thornton house had Margaret thinking that perhaps, not entirely.

Mr. Thornton's manner upon learning of her departure did not appear to be one of relief but one of remorse. When she gifted her father's Plato to him, he had such a manifestation of warm regard for his lost friend; it touched her deeply. Such as they were, unified for the briefest of moments. Then he repeated his previous statement.

So you are going. And never come back.

Lifting her eyes to his, she wished him well. She expected him to say something in return but he turned and walked away. For the first time in their acquaintance, she wished he had not.

It seemed inconceivable that, in spite of everything, he may hold some affection for her. She found herself searching for further confirmation. At that time, the reason why she sought that unsolicited acknowledgement from him baffled her.

Upon leaving the residence, she turned to address him a final time but he had gone. Hannah Thornton, who noticed her searching for him, informed her that he left to address an urgent business matter. Margaret nodded, spoke her farewells, and walked out into the snowy air believing that she would never see the Thornton's again.

The door closing behind her set off an unexplained sadness within her. She wanted that opportunity to take his hand in friendship and hear the warmth in his voice he had once greeted her with on that night of the dinner gathering so long ago.

Stepping up into the cab, she found she could not bear to look behind fearing that the threatening tears would come. She had no explanation for the sudden rush of emotion. Certainly, she had found little joy in Milton.

That elusive explanation would come shortly after her arrival at her Aunt Shaw's home on Harley Street, as the buried feelings for him began to surface. Margaret now discerned what she wanted to hear that last day—Mr. Thornton asking her to stay. If she had known her true feelings and he asked, she unambiguously believed that she would have, gladly withstanding the worst of Mrs. Thornton's disapproval.

Now, three months settled in London, she found herself reestablished into a higher-class bracket and given a new role to play as an unattached heiress. This afforded much interest in the populace. She disliked it all and longed for an escape.

Word spread like wildfire of her unexpected fortune, causing her to become inundated with attention and invitations. The majority of those invitations she did not accept. She detected the insincerity of the people who sent them. Did they honestly desire her company or her newly acquired wealth? Since most were practically strangers, she suspected it was the latter. Previously, they did not take much notice of a poor clergyman's daughter. When eligible men called, Edith was the one to descend the gilded staircase, not the inconspicuous cousin from the South.

After Edith's marriage and Aunt's departure on an extended tour abroad, Margaret gladly returned to Helstone to content herself to a quiet life as a reclusive devoted daughter.

Henry Lennox's surprise visit and subsequent proposal interrupted her solitude. Any sensible young woman of meager prospects would have accepted gratefully. She considered herself sensible in every way but admitted guilt to her impracticability for believing that *mutual deep affection* is a requirement for a binding union.

Her unexpected prosperity and her recent unhappiness was the result of this belief. If she had accepted Mr. Thornton, she would be his wife, and Mr. Bell would not have had to secure her future by signing over the majority of his fortune in her name.

Mr. Bell's generosity made marriage no longer essential for her survival, and she allowed it to circulate that she did not seek any consideration. This did not prevent the flood of masculine opportunists from staging their interest and trying to sway her to reconsider. Their attempts went unacknowledged. Her focus remained on the North and its muddled array of vivid characters, one in particular, Marlborough Mill's towering master.

Time would have her trying to bury the memory of Mr. Thornton to avoid the longing. As a phantom in the night, he often returned to haunt her. His ghostly appearances intensified her desire to see him in the flesh, but a valid reason to return to Milton could not be found.

Margaret resolved to suffer in her heart, but she hoped that each new day would bring word of Mr. Thornton either in writing or by word. After months, those hopes faded.

Then, as a thunder clap in a cloudless sky, word came unexpectedly.

Henry Lennox could not have known the chill that struck Margaret when he informed her of the certain loss of her tenant. As she calmly buttered her toasted bread, the shock of what she heard began to register.

Mr. Thornton had failed.

Her appetite vanished, leaving an upset in the pit of her stomach. How could this have happened? The strike set back many of the factories financially, but certainly not to the degree where it would bring about bankruptcy.

Deep concern rushed in to take over the initial shock. What will become of the workers and their families? Would other mills fall? The more pressing question on her mind, what will happen to Mr. Thornton?

Frustration settled in from not knowing. Fear of having her secret affection revealed kept her from asking. Her sex made her helpless to take any action. Yanking at the bars and begging to be freed, Margaret felt imprisoned by society's restraint.

But it's his spirit I fear for. Remember after his father died, he struggled for years to build everything up again. He raised his family from poverty. How much worse to be brought low a second time.

Her mouth dropped and fingers flew up to touch the parted lips as she recalled what her father said. Would this break his spirit?

"Margaret dear, are you well?" her Aunt Shaw asked.

She blinked out of her gaze. "What…Aunt?"

"Are you well?" she repeated. "You went rather pale."

"I am well. Preoccupied, that is all."

Margaret glanced at Henry. By the look on his face, she guessed that he knew the subject of that preoccupation. Pushing back on her chair, she rose from the table, which he politely hurried to follow.

"Please don't get up, Henry," she said as she waved him down. "If you will excuse me."

"Of course. Margaret, about this afternoon?"

"Oh, the outing. I think not, Henry. I would like to write to Mr. Bell."

"Perhaps next week then?"

"Perhaps."

Back in the solitude of her room, she sat down at her desk and pulled out a blank page hoping that writing that letter would engage her plagued thoughts elsewhere. A paragraph in, the tears started to drop on the paper causing the ink to bleed. Despairingly, she threw the pen down and dropped her head into the palms of her hands.

Suppressed frustration gave way. She cried for Mr. Thornton, for Nicholas and Mary Higgins, and the other laborers who must find means to survive once again.

Spent emotionally, she sought the softness of her bed where she closed her eyes to stop the cascade of tears. Shivering against the chill of the room, she pulled the bed's coverlet over. The warmth soon had her relaxed and drifting off into a white void.

A familiar authoritarian voice, low and laced heavily with

longing, cut through the quiet.

Come back to me, Margaret. I need you.

Her ghostly self ran toward the sound. After a short distance, she became disoriented and stopped, calling out his name. Only silence followed.

Movement caused her head to turn sharply to see a barely visible figure of a man in the distance. Relief lighted her facial features as she moved forward only to witness the white fog thicken and engulf his silhouette until it vanished.

"John, come back. I'm here!"

Lids flashed open as she sat up in the bed. Did she say that aloud?

A soft knock came at her door. "Margaret, are you all right?"

Pushing herself up from the bed, she rushed to the door opening it a crack. "Oh, Edith," replied she, somewhat embarrassed, "I believe I had a bad dream."

"I thought it may have been something like that. I never heard you speak so abruptly." She paused then asked, "Who is John?"

Margaret tensed. "Thank you, Edith." Bypassing the question, she added, "I will be right down."

She went to close the door but the dream emboldened her to stick her head out from behind it. "Edith, do you know where Henry has gone?"

"He is still here. I'll get him."

"Oh, wait…"

Edith could not be delayed. Her cousin's resolve to see her married to her brother-in-law had been evident before she had a chance to unpack her bags upon her return.

It was apparent that Henry's affections and wishes had not wavered since her refusal long ago in Helstone. Margaret's anxiety heightened when she found herself alone with him, dreading to have to refuse him a second time. Her strategy was avoidance and to be careful not to encourage him.

Sighing, she stepped out into the hallway, closing the bedroom door behind her. Sadly, that approach did not seem to work with Mr. Thornton, and the timing of his offer was most unfortunate. Under different circumstances and with more time to understand him, she wondered if Mr. Thornton and she could have parted on friendlier terms.

How different things might have been if the strike ended sooner and the violence never occurred. The workers would be safe, including Boucher. And if Mr. Thornton speculated in Mr. Watson's scheme, Marlborough Mill would be functioning and—

Margaret's insides vibrated as her mind sparked. Adrenaline fueled the spark causing sudden excitement to radiate throughout her frame. Of course! She was looking at it completely wrong. She could make a far more significant contribution than a charitable basket!

Seeking Henry became a priority. Eagerness to bring her sudden brainstorm into fruition overruled any restraint in going to him. Her justification to return to Milton had come!

The two came upon each other on the second floor landing. She allowed no time for him to imagine any other purpose for her needing him but for his help and to arrange travel north to Milton as soon as possible. Henry replied that he would gladly be of service in any way and when he inquired for what purpose, she spoke confidently that she wanted to help Mr. Thornton reestablish Marlborough Mill with the windfall from Mr. Bell's investment.

"Let me look into Thornton's holdings and debts—"

"Henry," she interrupted softly, "this isn't something that I might want to consider. It is something I insist upon. I wish to leave immediately."

His brows drew in. "Thornton, he's a proud man, Margaret. He may not accept this business proposal from a woman. I should go alone."

From his comment, she received the distinct impression that Henry did not like the idea. Not because it was not a sound business venture, but because it would unite Mr. Thornton and her again. Possibly the enthusiasm she expressed caused him to pause. In either case, he pressed that he should travel north alone to represent her interests.

She thanked him for his concern but declined his offer. She assumed that would end the discussion but he considered another reason she should stay in London. Soon, she took offense at his belittling persistence. She was not a pet to be trained how to sit and stay.

Holding up her hand, she silenced him in mid-speech to tell him that she would go with him or she would engage another counselor who would honor his client's wishes without impertinent superiority.

Visibly shaken by her uncharacteristic crossness, Henry apologized profusely and endeavored to redeem him further by saying that he would make sure that they leave on the earliest scheduled train out in the morning.

Back in her room, she sat at her desk to start drafting the letters Henry instructed she would need to authorize certain transactions. The partially written letter to Mr. Bell was still lying where she had left it. It is because of him that she felt rejuvenated and no longer helpless. She decided that it was more important to write him first.

As she wrote about Henry aiding her with her new venture, she found herself comparing him to Mr. Thornton. The two men were direct opposites. Mr. Thornton would not have yielded easily and descend into courteous submissiveness as Henry often demonstrated.

The pen stilled as a troubling thought occurred. How can it be that she found Mr. Thornton imperfect traits to be preferable to Mr. Lennox's unimpeachable ones?

Dipping her pen in the inkwell, she poised the pen to begin to write while still pondering the question. Moving the pen over to the bottom of Mr. Bell's ruined, tear-stained letter, she wrote her conclusion—she loved one and not the other.

True to his word, they were traveling north on the earliest train. Excitement mixed with nervous anticipation knotted her stomach. Mr. Thornton's reaction in seeing her again weighed heavily on her mind.

Margaret spent a restless night trying to prepare for the reunion. She had no illusions that the meeting would be nothing more than a polite conference with the main focus on the business of a silent partnership. Henry would be present and possibly Mrs. Thornton as the immovable matriarch. There would be no opportunity to be alone with him.

In all probability, their history dictated that the general atmosphere of the reunion would be strained. Her feelings would remain hidden and she would have to content herself to seeing him for a short time and then return to London.

The nightly preparation did not concentrate on the meeting itself, but on having to leave him after. The event had yet to happen, but she could feel the pain from it acutely.

It was of some consolation that a connection would be established even if it were in the form of an investment in Marlborough Mill. Mr. Thornton, no doubt, would be grateful that the connection would be distant, as well as, minimal. He made it quite clear that his affections for her had dissolved. She could not reproach him for it after all that transpired. When their purpose concluded, a handshake in mutual agreement would be all that she could hope for before going separate ways.

Margaret's eyes dropped to her lap. The dream the previous day with him calling out for her with such yearning was precisely that, a dream.

Margaret was unhappily surprised to find that the factory's yard abandoned and its doors closed. Henry applied to the solicitor to have the building unlocked. He left with the man to discuss details in the upper office, leaving her below.

Walking the deserted floor, she came upon Mrs. Thornton. Showing herself unpleasant in behavior, she charged Margaret of having joy in seeing the place vacant, which she calmly rebuffed. Then the mother's demeanor changed abruptly to anxiety. Her son had disappeared.

He left the previous day without leaving any word. Mrs. Thornton's steady voice faltered when she emphasize that she did not know where he had gone. This news caused Margaret's concern to heighten to a level of foreboding. She sensed that this was uncharacteristic of Mr. Thornton. Her head dropped to peer at the floor, certain that the fear she had for him must surely be visible on her face.

The mother's countenance turned to indicate that she did not consider Margaret entirely blameless in her son's mysterious disappearance.

"I've seen the struggle that my son has fought inwardly for months, Miss Hale. It weighed on him cruelly ever since the strike and your...the other events that have occurred."

She did not miss the accusatory glare Mrs. Thornton gave her. There could be no question that the events she alluded to were the refusal and the encounter at the station with her in the arms of a perceived lover.

In spite of the woman's rude undertones, Margaret wanted to reiterate what she said not moments before that she knew *now* the man she refused and explain about Frederick, but Mrs. Thornton's expression, marred with clear disdain for her, kept her from speaking. In its stead, Margaret nodded her understanding and politely excused herself and left without disclosing the reason for coming back to Milton.

Outside, while waiting in the carriage for Henry to finish with the solicitor, she became convinced that Mrs. Thornton's distress about her son caused her to strike out impolitely. For that reason, she would not allow herself to think unkindly about her. She empathized wholeheartedly.

Margaret did not remember much after that, lunching with Henry and the limited conversation, the return to the railway station and the boarding and departure back to London. The noonday past in a blur brought on by worried tension of Mr. Thornton's whereabouts and welfare. It occupied every corner of her thoughts. So much that she jumped a little off her seat when Henry took up her hand.

"I'll come back, Margaret, and speak to him when he returns. I will handle everything," he assured.

What he did not say is that he would handle everything without her. Her chance to see Mr. Thornton had come and gone. Depression settled in to mingle with her unease. She gave him a forced smile, pulled her hand from his, and rested it on her lap as she turned her head back to look out the window.

The morning left her in such low spirits traveling back to London that she battled to hide the tears that constantly threatened. Questions kept flooding her mind causing her privately to cry out for answers.

The train came to an unexpected stop. Henry casually informed her of a delayed due to a passing train going in the opposite direction. Grateful for an escape from the cabin, she stepped out, welcoming a respite from her troubled thoughts.

Glancing up her eyes focused on the approaching train directly in front of her. Brushing a tendril of hair away from her face, unblinking eyes locked on a man inside one of the cabins.

The tall, phantom materialized right before her. Her legs carried her forward to put the stilled train better into view. A state of astonishment took over causing her to stop then stare at the apparition. She could not acknowledge him in any other way.

She became transfixed as he opened the door to allow other passengers' to exit. A fleeting look as he was closing the door caught her in his sight and disbelief registered on his face as well.

Margaret watched, unmoving, as he approached. In an instant, she found herself standing nervously before him on the boardwalk, barely able to breathe; to her, this could not be happening.

His low voice broke the stunned quiet by asking her where she was going.

In dazed obedience to answer his question, she spoke, "To London. I…I've been to Milton."

He nodded and a slight grin formed. "You'll not guess where I've been."

Her eyes followed his fingers as he reached inside his

waistcoat's pocket, pulled out a rose, and held it out for her to take.

"To Helstone! I'd thought those had all gone."

"I found it in the hedgerow. You have to look hard." John paused then asked, "Why were you in Milton?"

"On business. Well, that is, I have a business proposition." Margaret started to quake and put herself into motion to rationalize it. "Oh dear, I need Henry to help me explain."

Taking light hold of her lower arm, he spoke to her decisively, "You don't need Henry to explain."

Mesmerized by his unassailable but gentle tone she found herself directed to a bench. Sitting beside him, she became conscious of his arm behind her and him leaning and listening closely as she tried to put the reason into words.

As she spoke, an overwhelming range of emotions in seeing him caused her to avoid direct eye contact and timidly fumble with the rose he given her.

Having explained the basic premise of the proposed investment, she glanced up to catch his reaction while clarifying that he would be under no obligation for he would be doing her a service.

The tendered expression on his face stole her breath and quickened her pulse. Softened, heavily lashed eyes studied her intensely causing her finishing words to stagger and trail off. Suddenly feeling awkward, her focus went down to her lap.

His hand appeared into view and took hold of hers. Her lips parted as its reassuring warmth jolted her into the realization that the phantom was flesh not spirit. Mr. Thornton was here with her now! She felt light headed with emotions. This was more than what she hoped for—his hand taking hers. It was in his eyes and manner, full of tenderness and manly attention, that stirred her heart to pound erratically.

Her fingers tentatively moved to thread with his when the deluge of suppressed feelings erupted. Unable to utter a sound she took up his hand and placed it to her lips. This small gesture revealed everything that was in her heart to say.

Coyly she raised her eyes to see his adoring look as he moved to fuse his lips with hers. What followed numbed all thoughts, and flooded her body with new sensations of touch. That first physical love gave the confirmation that would define the rest of her life.

As his mouth moved over hers in his silent but powerful declaration of his affection, she knew that she never wanted to be far from him again. ଘ

Chapter Two
The Black Leather Gloves

Margaret lost interest in the passing scenery and turned her head enough to glance shyly at the man next to her. She caught only the lower half of his face. He must have noticed her looking because his mouth upturned into a grin. A wave of awkwardness of what to say or how to act caused her to bow her head to stare at his hand clasping hers.

The same hand moved up to direct her face up to his. His arresting blue eyes met hers causing her lose her breath.

She never had been this close to him. Previously, his eyes seemed to cast a stormy indigo that often matched his mood. In the light of the cabin, his facial features changed considerably; his face became softened and youthful. Believing him handsome before, she now clearly saw that he was striking as well.

"What are you thinking?" he asked while his thumb glided over her slightly opened mouth.

His touch coupled with his voice exuded warmth which she had yet to familiarize herself with.

"Your black leather gloves," she answered.

"My gloves? I mislaid them some time ago."

"No, you didn't…I mean, I have them." His questioning look invited her to continue. "You left them behind that day," sounding apologetic she clarified, "the day I refused you."

He took in a deep intake of breath. Margaret knew she was stirring up unpleasant memories.

"I had every intention of returning them but they seem to have found a place in my bedside table." She looked down a little embarrassed with the confession. "It doesn't make any sense me keeping them. I believe that I didn't like you at that time."

"You had me convinced."

"I never wanted to cause you pain, John. I wanted to take back many of my actions and words."

He took her hand into his. "That is the first time you called me by my Christian name."

"I daresay you grow tired of hearing Mr. Thornton, Mr. Thornton."

"From your lips, it is a caress no matter what context it is said. As for those two days, I have regrets as well. Can we put it behind us, Miss Hale?" he asked, putting emphasis on her formal name.

"Gladly, and if you are asking for permission, I give it."

John leaned in close. "Maggie," he crooned while smoothing his jaw softly across her cheek, "why keep the gloves?"

He watched for her reaction and became pleased by what he saw; she beamed. In his dreams, he addressed her affectionately in that manner. Speaking it for the first time in reality gave him the confirmation of their togetherness. Margaret was now *his* Maggie.

Recovering from the intimacy of his question, she found her voice to answer.

"I confess I am a miserable thief who is not sorry. There must have been something wanting. Then in London," she said wistfully with her head bowing, "when I realized what I'd done in refusing you, I found myself clinging to the gloves as if they were a priceless treasure. That is when I knew."

"You loved me?"

She nodded. "I wanted to return to Milton and to you."

"Now, that is irony working," he spoke with amusement. "Which brings up the next question. Mind you, I'm not fishing for compliments, merely understanding."

"Ask me anything and I will be truthful."

"What changed?"

She rested her head on his shoulder, "I found that you had all the qualities of the man I needed from the start. Unfortunately—"

"You said you were going to be truthful," he snickered.

Raising her head, she looked at him with forged annoyance. "Would you allow me finish, Mr. Thornton?"

"I'd like to hear you get yourself out of this one, Miss Hale."

"As I was saying…unfortunately, you disguised these qualities exceedingly well. I believe it is unconsciously done." Laying her head back on him she continued, "They only began to reveal themselves after it was too late. You captured my attention but all too slowly captured my heart."

"Someday you'll have to tell me of these qualities because I don't know them myself."

"If you like, I will speak of one now."

"And what is that?"

Tilting her head up, his neck turned down, brought their faces close that breathing mingled.

"Your passion is often mistaken for anger or ungentlemanly behavior. I find that it is excusable now, at least in my eyes."

"If that be the case, I am, indeed, a deeply passionate man."

"After this day, I can confir—"

John did not allow her finish as he took her mouth heartily, trailing up he kissed the bridge of her nose and then her forehead whereon he rested his head, satisfied in providing the passion she just accused him of having.

Margaret released a deep gratifying sigh as muscles relaxed throughout her body. Only minutes before this man had her feeling shy and awkward. That had all gone.

Arm around her waist, he squeezed her closer to his side, enough that his fingers were able to touch the buttons on her coat. He locked her intimately to himself, which she cared not if the key was lost forever.

His head cradled hers and she heard him whisper her name against her forehead as if to test the sound of it again.

As a child, she disliked Frederick calling her Maggie but hearing it from John, in his low, soothing baritone voice; he sanctified her as his cherished own.

Breaking the respite, he asked her when her feelings had changed for him.

"I believe when I handed over father's Plato and thought I'd never see you again. There was such a sharp feeling of loss in leaving you." Her face took on a pained expression. "It continued and then after some weeks in London I began to understand that it wasn't only my father that I was mourning but the loss of the man I loved as well."

Her admission struck at his heart and his entire being. She could not have known how seeing her for what he believed to be the last time, had crippled him emotionally.

John tried to keep in control but the turmoil raging inside tore at him. As Margaret and her aunt readied themselves to leave, he slipt away to battle his emotions privately. He would not watch her go!

Only seconds later did his resolve shatter. Like a powerful magnet, the ache of never seeing her beautiful face again brought him to stand rigidly on the large delivery dock.

Agonizingly, he watched her walk to the waiting carriage; frustration chewed at him because he could only see the back of her. So much so, that as she climbed into the carriage he willed her to look back at him. He needed her to see him and give him a shard of hope that she cared even the slightest. He vowed that if she turned, he would find some way to have a part in her life.

When that did not happen and the carriage disappeared into the snowy distance, the complete emptiness without her settled in as a starvation, leaving a big part of him empty.

The numbness he felt was not from the cold, snowy air, but from the shock of her sudden departure from his life. Needing to come to terms with this new reality, he stepped down from the raised platform and mechanically followed the wheeled tracks into the greyish-white nothingness that was blanketing the deserted industrial square.

Now, he learned that it had been the same for her but perhaps, not with as much intensity.

Margaret pulled out of his embrace and affirmed, "Your mother once accused me of not knowing the man who I refused, and I said that she was right. I suffered because of it." Her hand gingerly reached up and touched his rough, whiskered face. "I over-idealized the South and held the North in contempt for not being the same. I reserved much of that contempt for you because you defended it so."

John's eyes fixated on hers not believing what he was hearing.

Dropping her hand, she concluded, "I was mistaken about everything."

"Margaret, look at me." When she would not he made her by placing his hand on her far cheek and directing her attention back to him. "Your world collided with mine, not mine with yours until this morning when I placed myself there in Helstone. If I had taken the time to learn about where you came from, I would have understood and been gentler…kinder. I am the one who is at fault here." He got a faraway look and muttered, "It would have been different if I'd seen it from your prospective."

"We are here now," she said softly, "and by God's grace been given another chance. I am determined to not let it pass me by." Her eyes rose demurely to his. "That is why I am on this train with you."

"You'll have me?"

Her delicate lips curved up into a modest smile. "I daresay, Mr. Thornton, that you know the answer."

"I do, Miss Hale, but I'll ask for it all the same." His eyes focused on her lips to watch for her reply.

"Then, yes…I accept."

John's chest pounded out his elation. Looking deeply into her eyes, he brought her face forward and shared his joy by joining their mouths. He wound his arm her waist, while his other hand moved up and found the back of her head, pressing it more into his possession, kissing her powerfully.

Every nerve under his skin registered every contact with her from the cool tips of the pins that held her hair in place, soft brush of eyelashes, and the smooth pearl buttons of her striped over coat.

Before Margaret Hale came into his life, he was a rock, solidly built and unbreakable. Pleasant feelings rarely surfaced. From the first moment his iced-blue eyes fell upon her face, she began chipping away at him.

John's hands slipt to the sides of her arms as he broke to see if what he was feeling had been imagined. Moisture filled eyes roamed her face and then down her frame. Hoarsely he asked, "Are you real?"

Her mouth went to answer but no words came out. He drew her back into his arms and confessed, "I needed you, Maggie."

As God breathed life into man, this woman breathed life back into him. In the span of less than an hour, he experienced more exhilaration, harmony, contentment, and being wanted as a man than he had in years. The magnitude of all these joys crashed down upon him crushing the remaining pieces of rock into dust.

Margaret choked with emotion at his assertion. It was the same voice in her dream. She pressed her ear to his waistcoat, clearly hearing his strong heartbeat pounding underneath.

"I'm here," she barely whispered, thinking of him disappearing in the white void, "I'll not lose you again."

His chest expanded with a huge breath and then exhaled, but he remained silent. She sensed that something changed in him. As if a weight had been lifted.

Pure happiness of having the love of the man of her dreamscape, struck her. Thinking of the disappearing phantom, she needed to reconfirm that he was genuine. Lifting her face, she lightly kissed the underside of his jaw. The unshaved roughness of his skin on her sensitive lips told her positively that he was indeed not a figment of her imagination.

John tilted his head to look down at her. "I need a shave," he declared with a tinge of humor.

"I find I like this unkempt look and feel."

"You do?"

"I do," she confirmed. "You will find there is much I find agreeable about you that you may have believed otherwise."

His eyes held hers as a finger trailed down the curve of her neck. "More of those qualities or are we talking physical attributes?"

"You are fishing," she accused smiling.

"Perhaps, this time. I do have the most attractive bait at my disposal."

"Fred took me fishing once, I don't know if I like being compared to the bait that was used."

His grin found her mouth for a kiss and then they both contented a rest from conversation.

She spent many minutes lavishing in the feel of John's encompassing arms and would have slumbered there in the warmth but a startling reflection brought her out of her peaceful state. She drew out of his embrace and looked up at him with wide unblinking eyes.

"John, I mentioned Fred but what you don't know…I need to explain to you about that night at the railway station. The man who I was with—"

"Your brother."

"You know about Frederick! How?"

"Higgins asked after you after the last shift. He thought you might have gone to Spain to live with him. He mentioned him being in Milton at that time of your mother's passing." John fingered a stray tendril away from her forehead. "I wanted to wait until you were comfortable enough to speak of him yourself."

"He was in danger, and it had to be a secret."

"Higgins said as much."

"When I was questioned about that man's death, I was frighten he would be found out. I can only imagine what you thought of me. Yet you knew I was being dishonest but you still—"

"Loved you very deeply," he finished with sincerity.

"You were extremely convincing in having me believe otherwise."

"I'd admit I lashed out. He was in your arms and I was not. And when you lied for him, I imagined that you must be in love." Shaking his head he lamented, "My anger and jealousy was for him. As for you, I simply wanted to get you out of my head."

"You had every right to speak to me as you did. I saw you as a tradesman and not…" With down casted eyes, she changed her thinking, "No, as a friend of father's, I should have trusted you."

A look of incredulous crossed his face and then his temper flared. Grabbing hold of her arms, he commanded her attention.

"Maggie, hear what I have to say," he said with gentled vehemence in his voice. "You had no reason to trust me! I'll not allow you to reproach your conduct. It is as it should have been as a loving sister protecting her brother."

He dropped his hands from her arms and turned his face away from her. She had not been alarmed at his anger; again, she knew it was his way to show other emotions.

A sigh of resignation came from him and he reached over and took her hand in apology.

"Your brother is fortunate to have you as his sister."

Margaret knew he was comparing her to Fanny. Running her palm up and down his arm she soothed, "Like yourself, Fanny disguises her true feelings. She loves you, John, really, never question that." He nodded.

Wanting to tell him everything, she volunteered to relate the history of her brother's troubles—the mutiny, his return to see his dying mother, the scuffle with Leonards, and her assurance that Frederick had nothing to do with his death.

John listened intently to the details of her brother's history. He saw relief come over her face as she unburdened herself. It was good to see that she unreservedly gave him her trust and respect; it could only strengthen their bond.

As she spoke, the uneasiness of guilt caused him to run his fingers in his hair. What she must have suffered during that time, he thought. The hardship of the imminent death of her mother and the anxiety of bringing the brother back. His conduct added to that suffering. John turned to speak when he noticed her eyes filling with tears, his words were then lost.

He never saw her cry, not even after the deaths of her parents. He assumed the remembrance of that frightful time and sadness of lost loved ones brought the tears on. A fierce protectiveness rushed over him wishing that he could have been the shelter she ran to for comfort and security. But instead he had been her adversary, harsh and cold.

"John, please allow me to say this for I have wanted for a long time to do so." With tears falling, her fingers once again laced with his as she drew his hand to her chest. "By not disclosing my deception you not only saved me but my brother as well. He was able to escape. We are grateful to you."

Her tears were of gratitude directed towards him! He still did not believe that he deserved her. Taking out a handkerchief from a side pocket, he wiped the streaming tears on her face.

"Maggie, don't make excuses for my conduct. Not knowing he was your brother, if I had been sure you would have turned to me, I daresay, I'd thrown him in jail myself. I am ashamed of my foolhardy assumptions and set out to be indifferent. Forgive me for believing the worse."

"I will never believe that you would have placed any person in prison unless it was justified, and, yes, I can forgive you," she assured with glistening eyes, "if you'll forgive me for pilfering your gloves."

John's face transformed as a full smile crossed it. "The gloves are yours as well as my whole heart."

Bring his hand to her cheek, she replied, "They are fitted for these hands and will be returned but as for your heart, I selfishly claim it as mine."

He took charge of the physical connection and brought the back of her hand up to his lips.

"And, John, I am quite relieved to find that you have teeth and they are not rotting away. I could get used to seeing that handsome smile of yours more often."

His masculine laughter echoed in the cabin and before he could respond, she said in a matter-in-fact tone, "What is that strange sound. I've certainly never heard it before in my life."

After a moment, he controlled himself, placed his hand behind the nape of her neck, and drew her face close to his. "That sound, Miss Hale, is the sound of a man who found happiness in his life. Can you guess what caused it?"

"Fanny's marriage and departure from your residence?"

A resurgence of boisterous laughter sounded.

Margaret could not believe those words came from her. Undoubtedly, provoked by the lighthearted mood, she wanted to unearth more of this jovial side of him. That aside, decorum dictated that she should not have been so cheeky at Fanny's expense.

"I should not have said that," she absently murmured.

Shaking his head in humored incredulity, he lifted her face to capture her attention. "I assure you that what you said is not to be a foundation for guilt. I admit that Fanny's leaving could be considered the third cause for my current happiness."

"What is the second?" she questioned.

"There could be no question on the first but the second is you being in my arms and me kissing you with all this passion you say I have," he said with an enticing grin, "from which I intend to take full advantage of."

She felt her cheeks flush and her palms flew up to cover them.

"Ah, is this the first blush from her? I question why it is only making an appearance now."

"I do not understand what you mean."

"A blush provoked by mere words of your new lover and not by his intimate embraces." Moving his mouth close to her ear he asked in a half-whisper, "Why the words and not the actions?"

Margaret's mouth opened and her head dropped to the side to hide her face. Certainly, John's ardor should have had her face incessantly flaming all shades of red. Did he think that she was accustomed to being embraced and kissed? Perhaps he believed that Henry and she had been more acquainted.

Her head snapped up. "You are mistaken if you believe that I have been…forthcoming with other men. I…I have not," she stuttered.

John guiltily chuckled and took her into his arms. "I am a brute for teasing and making you uneasy. You'll have to forgive me again for my behavior, Maggie."

She pulled back and spoke boldly, "You listen to me closely, John Thornton. I have never been intimate with a man before in my life as I have been with you this day."

Feeling deservingly reprimanded he went to speak his regrets but she move her hand to his mouth to silence him.

"The only account I can make for the lack of maidenly modesty is that when you take me in your arms," moving her hand away from his lips she rested it on his shoulder and raised herself up to whisper in his ear, "is that it must be as natural of an occurrence as me breathing."

Made speechless by her words, he went still as she ran her soft lips down his jaw line. Her other hand ran up his shirted chest as her face nuzzled into his neck, her warm breath teasing the hairs under his collar.

John, swallowing hard, cleared his throat and moved her away.

Margaret's sweet innocent moves became master over him. She easily could break down his carefully guarded defenses. He imagined her moving her dainty mouth to his and her hand sliding to the inside of the open part of his shirt. She would not, of course, but the thought evoke stirrings that forced him to take her shoulders and created space between their bodies, while giving her a sincere look of apology.

Suddenly, light feminine laughter resonated inside the cabin. John's brow rose not imagining what could have brought this on. As delightful he found the sound to be, his curiosity needed to be satisfied. Crossing his arms before him, he gave her an authoritarian look that demanded a straight answer.

"What is this all about?"

Margaret looked at him to answer but, to John's surprise, she burst out again with more reverberation.

"No, this cannot be possible," she exclaimed, eyes twinkling with merriment.

"I am not used to being laughed about," he said trying to stay serious, but her sweet mirth began to grab hold of his buoyant side.

Waving a hand, she indicated that she could not answer under her present condition. He sat back in defeat and resigned himself to wait for her healthy bout to dissipate.

The wait was not unpleasant. Far from it. He found himself captivated by her animated face and child-like struggle to regain her equanimity. Grinning broadly, he grasped the extent of what he was witnessing, Margaret Hale losing her composure in the most pleasing of ways. It greeted him like a cooling fresh breeze on a sweltering day. He savored this never seen side of her.

Margaret gained control back. "John, you were blushing," she revealed.

"What!"

"You did, I saw it plain as the nose on your face."

He harrumphed, "I've been accused of many things but never blushing. And after?"

"I'm sorry, John, but it's your intimidating posture. Remember, I'm, well, immune."

His lip twitched upward but his face recoiled in mock disgust. "Smiles, laughter, and blushing…what will you do to me next?"

Her amusement now suppressed she answered, "Humility perhaps? It is something I have recently discovered."

John nodded in agreement. "Aye, add it to my list as well. I found it the day I learned you were protecting your brother."

The cabin went silent in shared understanding for a moment before he cut in on the quiet.

"Your discoveries in my character could jeopardize my reputation as an inhuman master. Once out, I won't get a decent day of labor out of my workers. Will you keep my secret?"

"Yes, as long as you don't hide them from me."

"That is easily done since you are the motivation behind me producing such emotions. I am further relieved that you find some part of me handsome and not entirely an unsightly ogre."

"An ogre in spirit, perhaps, but not unsightly," she said. His brows drew in causing her to smile, "There, you see, I can tease as well."

John's face lightened. Before he could say anything, she wrapped her arm around his.

"I have always found you handsome, John Thornton, even with your tough exterior," she assured. "Would you be surprised to know that I was envious of the attention Miss Latimer was receiving from you?"

"You, jealous?"

"Yes, I felt it profoundly at Fanny's wedding."

"Even back then?"

"Is that hard for you to believe?"

Moving in close, a hair's breath away from her lips, he spoke, "Then, yes, but now, I'm a believer."

He closed the gap between their mouths and kissed her reverently in his newly established faith. ଔ

Chapter Three
A Battle Won With A Miracle

A number of unscheduled delays made the trip back to Outwood Station longer than usual. Daylight since faded into a chilled, star-filled night. The arrival into the railway station was fast approaching.

John's desire was for the train to continue and not stop. Inside the cabin was their idyllic and tranquil world in which he never wanted to escape.

The woman to who was that morning an unrealized cherished dream was now sleeping in the crook of his arm and shoulder. It was likely that the next time she would be sleeping close to him would be on their wedding night. He knew that was a long time off and he wanted to savor what he held at that moment.

Her palm, which had rested on his chest, fell to his hip as her determination to stay awake became unsuccessful, resulting in a deep sleep where even the shrilling of the train's whistle could not stir her.

John luxuriated in the experience of his arm wrapped around her back and hand holding the small curve of her waist. His fingers spread out to allow a more complete access to her waistline as he absorbed the warmth and fresh feel of her. He did not believe that he would ever have the opportunity to hold her closely and yet, here he was.

Before she fell asleep, they conversed about the mounting

feelings and truths they each kept secretly inside. Together they relived the events and powerful feelings of the past days that compelled John to journey south to Helstone and Margaret north to Milton. Finishing his narrative on his morning venture to her childhood home, he noticed her stifling a yawn.

"I'm boring you."

"Certainly not. I slept very little last night, and I find myself exhausted. The last thing I want to do is sleep but find I am fighting it."

"What kept you from sleeping?"

"I was in such a state in seeing you. I had to get the speech right so I spent most of the night practicing what I might say." Her eyes dropped as her face flushed. "It was all very childlike but I was determined to find the words."

"Did you?"

Shaking her head. "I worked on it until early and must have drifted asleep."—a smile appeared—"My poor pillow, I'm afraid I took all my frustrations out on it. I discovered that there is no proper way to adequately voice my true feelings when leaving you again."

Confused, his brows drew in. "We're not talking about seeing me for the first time after all these months, but leaving me after the meeting?"

Nodding, she confirmed, "I didn't know my heart before, but this time I did. I knew that saying goodbye would be the hardest part of our meeting," she said sadly. "I was certain that the wrong words would have me visually tearful, or worse, falling where I stood from the heartache." His brow rose as her eyes lifted up to his face. "It would have been completely out of the realm of proper decorum."

His crooked smile appeared. "Decorum be damned. I would have caught you and welcomed your tears on my breast."

"I daresay, knowing that would have made quite a difference in curing my insomnia."

He lifted his hand and ran his thumb over her jaw line moving to the underside of her graceful neck never imagining her having a sleepless night because of him. Lord knew he had many because of her.

"So, you practiced hard for me. You must have had one speech that would've pass muster."

"Yes, but I only dare to speak it to you in my dreams," she admitted. "There could be no mistaking its message."

His eyebrows rose in surprise, "You dreamt of me?"

Margaret took up his hand and confirmed, "Yes, you crept in quite subtly."

"I'm ready for it."

"What…you want to hear it?"

"You cannot fear my response now. Let us see if my answer will match the one in your dream."

She pondered, giving him a look of suspicion that perhaps he was up for some mischief. He was about to give her a reprieve when she decisively she sat up tall in her seat and produced her hand.

"Mr. Thornton, I was very pleased to have opportunity to see you again."

John did not miss her emphasis on the word *very* and decided to play the expected part; he ignored her hand—mirroring a similar occasion—crossed his arms and coolly nodded once in acknowledgement.

Her brows rose at his actions but continued in a more honeyed tone, "Since I have concluded that I was mistaken in my refusal of your proposal, you'll find my door opened to you to ask it of me again…if you so choose. I assure you that the answer will be quite the opposite." She paused, then added a firm but sweetened, "I bid you a good-day."

John fought not to grin. He understood why she would have never given the speech. He could see the jaws dropping and those in earshot rush to start the tongues a-wagging.

A woman would never ask for another chance. A man's general humiliation and disgrace of the first refusal would render any possibility of the woman broaching the subject again unthinkable. It was up to the man to instigate the reprisal of the matter, which was a rare occurrence. However, given the scenario, he knew what his reply would be.

His expression serious he answered, "Miss Hale, I believe that the only possible answer I can give you is this."

He uncrossed his arms, reached for her waist, drew her to his chest, and kissed her hungrily.

Breathless, she pulled her head back to catch it. After a moment of composure, she gave him a contrived frown. "You wouldn't have dared."

"Wouldn't I? This being a dream, I allowed my actions speak my answer which could only be interpreted as an undeniable yes to the invitation."

"If your mother was—"

"Oh, was my mother present in your dream?"

"No. I could never imagine that."

They both smiled together at the thought.

After a moment, she gave him a sideways glance and asked, "If she had been there what would you have said then?"

He did not miss the slight tremor in her body when imagining his mother's reaction. Perhaps she was thinking more about the future event of informing his mother of their engagement. In that regard, she was justified to feel anxious. His mother did not struggle to conceal her objection to Margaret even to him.

Wanting to distract her from any apprehension, he released her from his embrace and spoke analytically.

"My answer, if my mother had been present, would have to be more discreet and no taking you into my arms." She emphatically nodded in agreement.

After a few seconds of further thoughtfulness, a shadow of a grin emerged to verify that he had the answer. His face was vacant of all emotion except for his eyes, which warmly locked on hers, taking up her hand politely, he spoke.

"Miss Hale, I will take your invitation into careful consideration as I accompany you back to London to retrieve my gloves. I believe you have them in your possession." He lowered his face giving her a mischievous grin as he added, "On the train, when we are alone, I'll give you my answer which I guarantee you, will be agreeable to us both."

A small lift of her mouth was detected but she crossed her arms and shook her head.

"After she took a broom to me and swept me out the door, she would box your ears good and lock you in your room without supper." A glint in her eyes had her adding, "She would not have approved the price of a ticket solely to retrieve a pair of gloves."

Their mingled laughter filled the space. By and by, the laughter muted and Margaret was able to voice her trepidation about informing his mother.

He imagined that she must believe that every person feared Hannah Thornton. She wasn't too far off. His mother was a force that few could approach casually. Adoringly he took her face once again in his hands and was descending to her pursed mouth but stopped a fraction from it.

"No person, including my mother, can keep you from me from this day forward." Feeling deeply the intensity of his statement, he added a firm, "This I vow to you, here and now."

Margaret's mouth relaxed into a slight smile queuing him to close the minuscule gap between them. Her body melted into his. All thoughts of speeches, gloves and his mother evaporated away.

Time stilled as he deepened the intensity of his kiss. Briefly, he lifted his mouth to shift his head in the other direction to allow them both to breathe, and then he recaptured her open mouth.

He stopped and opened his eyes to find her staring wide-eyed at him. The luminous beauty of her had him wanting more but he took pause, waiting for a sign for him to continue.

It did not take long. She breathed the words that had him descending again to take her petal soft lips.

"Please…don't stop."

Margaret never expected kissing would be like this and it was in her mind as a young girl to assume it would be an unpleasant part of courtship.

Edith and she imagined it to be equivalent to placing ones lips on a freshly caught fish—cold and slimy. Even after Edith informed her that the act was extremely agreeable, the fish stayed with her. Enjoying it was not something she considered.

Earlier, sitting on the bench and receiving that first taste of physical contact from John she deduced—rather quickly—that she had been mistaken in her innocent assessment. His touch excited her and in no way comparable to anything unpleasant.

As his intimacy intensified upon familiarity, she found herself appreciating his skill to take passionate control of all her senses. Helpless to resist, Margaret yielded to his attentions and wished that she had the confidence to reciprocate. It was in the back of her mind to wonder where on this earth did men learn such power over women.

When he stopped, mentally she begged him to continue. She became embarrassed when she realized that she, involuntarily, voiced that desire from which he hurried to comply.

Soon his firm lips began to soften and masterfully brought her heart rate down to a steadier pace. Her mouth felt pleasingly sensitive and wondered if his was feeling the same. Pulling away, her eyes focused in on that part of his face.

"Only you know that my bark is worse than my bite," he told her. "You can kiss me back. I promise you, I will not bite."

She blinked in surprise. "I am not afraid it's only that I am, well, unpracticed," she said shyly, feeling her insecurities rise.

He grinned. "It isn't difficult, Maggie."

"I am aware of that. What I meant is, what if you do not like the manner of my return?"

John crossed his arms and let out a grunt of doubt. "Highly unlikely. The chances of me not liking any kiss from you is impossible. And since I am the only man you'll be allowed to kiss from now on, you might as well start this practicing." Seeing her still disinclined, he lowered his face to hers. "Miss Hale, I have issued you a challenge but if you are not up for it, I will understand."

Margaret stiffened at his preposterous taunt. She mirrored his stance by crossing her arms and giving him a look that told him that her qualms were dissolving.

His challenge was about to be accepted.

John grinned knowing that any other young woman would have no scruple to label him as an ungentlemanly provocateur. Miss Latimer would have surely voiced a contrived transgression from him because it was expected.

Not Margaret Hale. She would not be falsely affronted; he would stake his life on it. The woman had a calm, inner courage and resolve about her that he admired from the moment he made her acquaintance.

As much as he wanted to have her kiss him, John did not over-romanticize his purpose in his goading. He wanted her to feel she could let down all precautions around him including societal restraint. It was important she felt secure to speak or act freely when they were alone together. As he predicted, she did precisely that.

Without giving him any warning, arms still crossed, she kissed him on the lips so quickly that he wasn't even able to blink. It took a couple of seconds to register what she did.

"And you call that a kiss?"

"I recall you said that you would like *any* kiss from me? That was any kiss."

John dropped his head to hide his full smile but his voice-feigned annoyance. "I did not think I was obliged to define what a proper kiss entails." Looking up he projected, "Be assured, Miss Hale that when—"

Margaret's small hands framed and lifted his face, which silenced his voice. Without any hesitation and with all womanly gracefulness she raised her lips to his.

She still was not familiar with the amount of pressure she should apply but by the low utterance coming from his throat, she could not help think that she was doing well and when she felt him smile on her lips, she became decidedly pleased with her first…second attempt.

"There…I believe, judging from the look on your face, I am the victor," Margaret said. "And, John, that is Maggie to you," she finished with triumphant sweetness.

Affected, he cleared his throat. "That was a challenge I did not mind admitting defeat. I look forward to being pleasantly conquered in the next."

"I will be ready," she said, lifting her palm to his upper jaw, loving the freedom to touch and feel him without restraint.

Taking her hand into his he brought the palm to his lips. She followed every move he made and adored him. This man was not the man of her dreams; this man was indescribably better.

Placing her hand to his side he spoke, "Now, about these gloves. Shall we purchase tickets for the next train back to London?"

Margaret determined that she loved his dry humor, edged with stern seriousness. John's wit was of the kind that kept a person guessing whether laughter or a perplexed nod would be adequate. She did neither for she knew how to reply.

She wrapped her arms around his waist and rested her head under his chin. "Setting the subject of your gloves aside, I surmised that overall your answer is a yes to you once again finding me to be in your good favor."

"It definitely wasn't a no!"

The way he answered, with amused certainty, made her smile. "I'm glad of it," she sighed.

She allowed her tired body to relax. His hand smoothed up and down her back lulling her into drowsiness. Margaret's lids were heavy and nearly closed, but the feel his breath on her forehead compelled her to open them.

"In the end, it was your actions that said everything to me," he half-whispered with feeling.

She nodded to acknowledge that she knew what he spoke of—her bringing his hand to her lips while sitting on the bench.

"If you hadn't done that, seeing you again,"—pausing to change his thought—"I talked once of not wanting to claim you as my possession because of my true feelings. It was you who possessed me. If you had not acted as you did and got back on that train, I daresay, I would have come after you," he acknowledged with a low steady voice, "I was always yours."

Her eyes started to moisten and she went to raise her head to speak but he put his hand on her head to keep her from moving.

"No more talk, Love. Are you comfortable?"

Margaret allowed a soft sigh to escape, tightened her hold on him, and closed her eyes. The cabin went quiet except the recurring beat of wheels on the tracks.

John was exhausted too. He was accustomed to exhaustion and often he found himself slumped uncomfortably in places other than a bed because of it. In the past months, he hardly slept with the strain of seeing the slow death of the mill and the despondent workers left in its wake. Feeling her slow and steady breathing, this time he would not succumb to sleep.

He relished in her light floral fragrance, and soft silky feel of her hair, pulled up in her usual style. He never saw her with her hair down. Allowing his lips to kiss and linger on the top of her head, he imagined her long soft tresses down and free for him to entangle his fingers in.

A faint shadow of a smile appeared as he realized that he would eventually be able to compare the real thing to his imagination. Touching and holding her went beyond his every expectation. She was his and he could only begin to believe it with her warm form slumbering in his arms.

Currents of impatience invaded his body as his thoughts turned to her becoming his wife and their first night together. He would have to build up a wall of constraint against the long interval he would have to endure before he could make her completely his. His consolation was that their time would come and that she would be worth the wait.

In the meantime, he would bask in making new discoveries about her. Thus far, the time spent with her revealed many new sides of her.

 Moreover, the liberties they taken, it seemed as if they had been engaged for months. The remarkable chance reunion gave them a temporary pass on controlled etiquette. He knew that the miraculous realm, such as they were in, would disappear and reality would come back into view as soon as they stepped off the train.

 Lifting his head, he turned to peer out of the window into the night. His look turned serious as his mind began to focus on what lay ahead for them. Beyond this extraordinary day, he needed to start thinking of her reputation and their mutually established good names.

 He must look to the future, but he could not help reliving of the remarkable, sometimes painful, journey of the recent past.

 John recollected how he came to be in Helstone that morning. The day before the last, after packing the last of the ledgers in his office, he began to feel caged-in with nowhere to go.

 His mind did not focus on what was to come after he walked out of that emptied space. No, he became infatuated with the recent discovery that the man at the station had been her brother.

 When first learning he was overjoyed and relieved. It was her brother! Then reflection brought his spirits down low and severe regrets invaded.

 Do you not realize the risk that you take in being so indiscreet? Have you no explanation for your behavior that night at the station? You must imagine what I must think.

 I'm aware of what you must think of me. I know how it must have appeared, being with a stranger so late at night. The man you saw me with…the secret is another person's and I cannot explain it without doing him harm.

 After this, his deepest regret is that he did not trust his first instinct upon seeing her with the strange man. That instinct was to believe that Margaret Hale could not be so reckless and there was a plausible explanation. His jealousy crushed that gut feeling immediately.

 His self-loathing at his treatment of her carried throughout the day to mix with his sense of worthlessness. For the first time in over a decade and a half, he had no occupation or purpose. Suddenly thrust into idleness, it left him vulnerable to the dark emotional storm that was starting to engulf him.

Knowing the truth of the matter, the revelation made his love for her all consuming and his longing to see her overpower any sense. Because of this, he boarded the last train to London. His mind was so preoccupied with the need to take action that he bypassed stopping by the house to inform his mother or to pack.

On the train, he thought it best he did not stop. His mother would have attempted to thwart his course of travel; his motivation would have been clear. On this occasion, he did not give her unbendable logic a chance to overrule the pressing need to see Miss Hale and admit his wrongdoing regarding the brother. With each blast of the train's whistle, his resolve was drowned out and his courage to face her faded.

He had no reason to believe that she wouldn't accept his apology but he could not bear seeing her turn her back and him having to walk away from her. By the time he stepped off the train he found that his impetuous excursion was for naught. A letter would have to suffice; his meager hopes would have to remain on any reply.

With no more trains traveling back that late in the evening, he stayed at the closest inn with every intention to return to Milton on the first train out. The next morning, standing at the ticket window, he glanced behind the clerk and saw the destination listed for the train about to leave. One of the stops, Hampshire, was where the little town of Helstone was located. Instantly, his course changed.

He didn't question his reasoning for traveling further south. He found that he desired to seek some sort of solace in the place he knew she loved and was the happiest.

In the cabin, he stared out window, taking interest in the scenery. The further south he traveled, the more he started to appreciate the beauty of the countryside. This is what Margaret left behind.

Standing on the edge of the property in sight of the

parsonage's cottage where she once lived, he imagined her as a little girl playing and skipping about. He could not help but smile at the thought of being a father and having a little girl. His smile faded. Looking up at the pristine blue sky, he willed the sudden rush of emptiness to go away.

The warm sun invited him to peel off his jacket and tossed it over his shoulder as he walked along the bushed fence line. A flash of color caught his eye; he squinted and walked towards it. Off to the side, behind a non-flowering shrub was the source.

Plucking the yellow hedge rose from the bush and taking in its fragrance, he saw her face. She could have been standing right in front of him, smiling with the sunlight highlighting her hair and face. John pocketed the bloom feeling it somehow kept him linked with her and to this place.

Now he understood.

In the quaint town, every sight, sound, and smell reminded him of her. Within a half hour of walking he could finally empathize with her grief and anguish in leaving the South and relocating to the unsightliness of an industrial town with its towering smoke stacks billowing out greyness and stench. The stark contrast must have been like heaven and hell.

He found that he did not want to leave and would have stayed but years of duty and the vision of his mother's worried expression propelled him to depart on the earliest afternoon train.

John knew that his failure had her most anxious about what it would do to him and he was feeling guilty about leaving the night before without leaving word. It turned out to be an impulse decision he would by no account regret.

It was harrowing to reflect on the past two days. The impact of the series of decisions he made struck him like crashing waves on a seaside wall.

What if the compulsion to leave for London never occurred? One second was all it took to see the name of Hampshire on the schedule, and it was only mentioned by Mr. Hale in passing. If he hadn't looked up, he would now be back in Milton, alone. He could have stayed in Helstone and taken a later train. In any of these cases, she would not be with him now.

John shudder caused Margaret to stir. Tenderly, he whispered soothing words in her ear—a masculine lullaby—sending her back into sleep. Running his lips over her cheek his eyes started to moisten as his buried emotions started to surface. How he loved her.

Peering once again out into the night, it occurred to him that the timing had to be perfect for their reunion to have happened. He could not wrap his mind around the phenomenon that led to the beautiful woman who was now, so willingly, with him. His recourse was to accept it with all his heart and never take it and her for granted.

It was as if their history together was never tainted. Erased was the past by the first touch of his hand on hers, and the present, moved forward with the freshness of new purpose of shared living.

Furthermore, he was engraving her deeper into his heart with sides of her character never seen—her musical laughter and quick wit, her adventurous spirit and innocent boldness. Oh, how he wanted her securely and permanently fixed with him forever!

But marrying her right away was out of the question. The spontaneous events of this day could irrevocably harm them both; he must keep sharp.

He considered her traveling alone with Henry Lennox, a man to whom he had no regard for until this day when he conceded his defeat and said goodbye to Margaret.

There had been no impropriety in him escorting her because the circumstances were vastly different. Lennox was a business associate, brother of her cousin's husband, and a close acquaintance. Although, John knew that Lennox wanted more from her by observing his demeanor at the exposition.

You must tell them how the London break is suiting Miss Hale. Don't you think Thornton? Doesn't Miss Hale look well?

The stab cut deep. Lennox knew Thornton was the man he

needed to do battle with for Margaret's affections. He was certain that Lennox would win.

It seemed that with Margaret living in London and he, wounded back in Milton, Lennox would have the clear advantage and most definitely come up victorious. John expected their betrothal announced at some length. He avoided the posts because it would bring a quick and painful death to any hopes, no matter how small.

John could relate with Lennox's pain of seeing her choose another man. He remembered his own anguish and hurt when witnessing her in the arms of an unknown man that night. Lennox was now where he had been. Yes, he empathized wholeheartedly with what his past rival was probably feeling at that moment.

Where acquaintance and friendship crossed over to an entirely new level of intimacy between a man and a woman was where he found himself and his Maggie.

He made a mental note to be sure to call Margaret by her formal name in public. Society frowned upon casual addresses in public, which alluded to a more intimate familiarity between a couple. His mother, most of all, would acknowledge it as such.

No observer could mistake his affection towards Miss Hale while sitting on the bench. Innocent social contact was elevated when she taken up his hand and kissed it. He soared to new heights of awareness, emotionally and physically.

His hand gently cupped her cheek, asking her, preparing her. As she lowered his hand, her eyes lifted to his, innocently inviting him to draw closer. His mind could not believe it was happening, and his chest drummed loud jubilance of her accepting his mouth on hers. He finally was able to demonstrate his complete devotion.

Margaret likened their intimacy as effortless as breathing but for him, sitting on that bench, it was like drinking life-sustaining water. Her lips were silky-smooth and her receptive response intoxicated him to continue. He drank her in, as a dying man in a desert, giving him will to live. In those few moments all the pain, doubt, stress and depression drifted away as a feather in the wind.

His world was no longer dark and filled with such promise and light. A few moments in time, that he would treasure forever.

A train whistle blew and the announcement of the London train's departure broke his joy. She, without a word, rose and rushed away from him. The hues all darken in his life again. He thought she was ashamed and took her leave because of it.

John chided himself for his indiscretion. He should not have kissed her, in its stead, appealed to her to allow him be in her life again.

Dejected, with heart plummeting, he gotten up not knowing what he should do. He found himself at his cabin's door with head bowed, not allowing himself to see her leave in the reflection of the cabin's window. He could not bear her not looking back at him a second time.

Rubbing his forehead in frustration, he weighed disparagingly that perhaps this was for the best. Currently he had nothing to offer her but himself. If he did not deserve her before, he definitely did not deserve her now.

He determined long ago that only Margaret Hale could bring worth into his stormy grey life. Shaking his head, he quickly decided he was not willing to a martyr his life away. He would make her look back this time!

John felt a surge of determination. There must be something between them or she would not have partaken so readily of his affections. He would not rest until he found out exactly what that was. He would move to London to be near her and do what ever was necessary to become successful again. First, he had to convince her to wait for him and prayed that she would say yes. Lifting his head to see if she departed, his heart leaped to find her standing behind him in the window's reflection.

His heart started to thunder in his chest as he turned and asked, "You going home with me?"

She did not say a word but handed him her bag instead. That was all that he needed to answer his question. She furthermore answered his other question; which was yes, she would wait for him. Once again, he found that the life sustaining joy was back.

In the cabin, John saw in her enlightened face a new calm confidence as they kissed tenderly. After their lips parted, her eyes briefly met his as she gave him a soft reassuring smile. He saw no regret, only certainty and promise. She then turned to look out the window.

He bowed his head and smiled to himself thinking of the remarkable chance reunion that occurred. Minutes before, two trains going in the opposite directions came to a stop within the same short span in time to reunite two misapprehended passengers to a life altering understanding.

To John, it would be the miracle of his life. ଔ

Chapter Four
Outwood Station

Margaret shifted in her sleep and John accommodated her by moving to allow her to rest more comfortably on his shoulder. Tilting his head back to rest on the seat, he closed his eyes to ease some of the fatigue that was settling in. A long night was still ahead of him.

The nearer the train drew to Outwood Station the more his body became tense and on edge. He learned to utilize this condition to his advantage; it kept him sharp and alert within the trade industry where hard-edged men were its rulers.

He could not apply the same to the situation that he currently found himself. Margaret was a completely different matter and his brain raced to plan for when they both stepped off the train together.

John's analytical mind reviewed the past hours and found he had no regrets within the confines of the cabin but felt apprehension of his inability to manage the scene better while on the outside. He must not take for granted than nobody noticed her embarking alone with him after the intimate display on the bench. It was unfortunate as well, that they were to be arriving late into the station. This certainly added to his unease.

He thought about Lennox, back in London, explaining why Margaret had not returned with him. No matter what his account, he envisioned her aunt's main assumption was to think the worse; her niece eloped with a downtrodden, northern manufacturer.

It would not be long before that assumption traveled beyond the confines of the aunt's walls to burn the ears of gossipmongers. To get married so soon after, innocent as it may be, would lead to a great scandal. No, before any vows, he was going to court Margaret Hale properly.

Her reappearance in his life changed much of his plans that he previously worked out. It was on his mind to rent the grander house out and he and his mother take up residence in the still vacant house on Crampton street where the Hale's had resided. With Margaret back in Milton, this was no longer an option for obvious reasons. He would not allow her to return to the place she experienced much sadness and loss.

No, the larger residence would have to be maintained. Still having in his possession two of the fluff alleviating machines, he could sell one, giving allowance for another year with full staff.

John decided that she will stay in Fanny's room and he would move to the unused storage space adjacent to his office at Marlborough Mill. This should quash some of the rumors that would sure to start circulating upon their return.

While Margaret's occupancy would be a vast improvement over his sister, he knew his mother would not think it so. She would have to adjust and hope that the largeness of the house would afford enough space to allow a peaceful habitation between the two women. With time, Margaret would win her over; he was sure of it. Placing the two women under the same roof seemed like the best way to help bring that about.

In the interim, he considered that he might start a search for a more suitable home for his future wife. After seeing the serene countryside she loved, he did not think she could be content in a house attached to a mill's loud industrial square. Her happiness and health was his priority and relocating to a less urbanized location seemed a good place to start.

Then he remembered and his shoulders slumped; a country cottage will have to wait. Raising his hand to rub his tired eyes, John realized that he could not secure a property without taking out another loan. Only until he was free and clear of all outstanding debts would he even consider such a major purchase. He would fulfill his financial obligations, but it would take time.

It was the issue of time that he surmised would become problematic between Margaret and him; she will not understand why he would not want her money to pay off the debts sooner. What's more, she had yet to learn, and it pained him considerably, was that their engagement would be a long one as well.

She would have no qualms in handing all her fortune over to him. Most men would seize the pile and run with it without a second thought. He was determined not to take advantage of her generous nature at this point in the relationship. It was another reason he did not want to rush into marriage. If he, a failed manufacturer, were to wed a heritress suddenly, it would paint him to be the worse of opportunist.

For John, it went deeper. He did not want reveal to her a painful aspect of his past that was the main motive why he would not make use of her wealth.

Margaret was in the same position his mother had been when his father wed her; she was an heir to a fortune as well.

Hannah was an only child of privilege when she fell in love with George Thornton whose family owned an importing and exporting business outside of London in the port town of Southampton.

He was the only son of a respected and well-known family. After the death of his father, George was ill prepared to take over the business. It was not long before he was selling assets to stay above water, and not long after, the family business folded.

Shrinking into humiliation and disgrace, he left his hometown to forge a partnership in the trade industry, relocating to Milton. There Hannah became the advantageous solution to his bleak financial situation.

Recently orphaned, the spinster daughter of a wealthy

merchant wed George Thornton. She knew that he married her for her money but she felt certain he would come to love her.

She had been wrong.

From the start, he abused her love, and then as times became progressively more desperate, he became abusive in other ways. By the time Fanny was born, hate replaced all regard for him and she turned her loyalty and devotion to her children, particularly her son.

Her husband's careless speculations and questionable dealings led to the depletion of Hannah's inheritance and eventual financial ruin. Rumors of drinking, gambling, and unchaste women soon followed causing any remaining relations to disengage themselves from the family.

Fearing for her children, Hannah appealed to her remaining relative, an aging uncle, who agreed to take in Fanny, and pay for John's education at a prominent boarding school.

Knowing of his father's abuse, John fought to stay with his mother; he did not want to abandon her. She would not hear of it and was forcibly insistent, saying she would be better off without having to worry about him. At only nine years of age and powerless in his mother's determination, he reluctantly was sent away.

John found stability and thrived in the dormitory in every way but it did not to last. At the end of the fifth year, the uncle died, leaving little left in his wake. The funding for his education ceased, and both children returned to their mother's care.

The weeks after were riddled with conflict and strife. More of a man than a boy, John now defended his mother and although he fought a good fight, his father always overpowered him, leaving him bloodied and bruised. The abused continued until the day of his death, bled out with a slit wrist.

Through the tribulation, his mother remained emotionless and unaffected by the final act but from that day forward, she only wore the grey and black colors of mourning. Fanny's astute ability to be uncouth, ask her mother why she insisted to wear such hideous frocks. Hannah's one-word reply left Fanny rolling her eyes, not understanding—that word was atonement. However, John, he understood.

It was because of that understanding that John aggressively took on the role his father miserably failed. He did not allow himself to think any further of George Thornton beyond his gravesite, and vowed that he would never become like him. That vow meticulously drove him to pursue success on his own merits and hard work. This included not marrying a woman for her money.

The first four years after his father's death was the hardest. Returning to his father's birthplace, he took work on the docks. The grueling labor of shipbuilding benefited him in strength and stature. Living in poverty made him tenaciously resilient and hungry for more than bread on the table and a satisfied stomach.

That was when his sharp mind and education came into play. Master's took notice and quickly he moved up from the docks to the procurement offices where the ordering and inventory of building materials for the ships occurred.

Then an opportunity to leave behind the dark shadow of his father presented itself, and he moved his family to Leicester, north of Milton. For the six years thereafter, he worked at a draper's shop. There he benefited by gaining experience on the goods and trades industry.

Every week, the family did without for the sole purpose of putting aside a handful of coins into savings. By the end of the ten years, John made good on all his father's remaining debts and had a fair amount put aside.

Impressed by the young man's principles and accumulated business sense, one of his father's debtors—a successful industrialist—took John on, first as an apprentice and then as a partner. From there, in less than three years, he rose up to become sole owner and master of Marlborough Mill. The accomplishment heralded a new era for the Thornton's, one of well-regarded prosperity and stability.

The strike brought that era to a close.

The station approached and reluctantly John straightened to stir her from her rest. As she slowly came awake, he studied her with renewed fascination.

Margaret, inhaling deeply while her body stretched, emitted petite sounds of disturbance from being aroused out of sleep. Semi-consciously, she drew her lips into her mouth to moisten the dryness as her eyes fluttered to open. He wished he could rock her back to sleep so that he could witness her waking again.

She suddenly sprung up, turning quickly, looking at him with wide eyes. "I fell asleep," she said breathlessly, "How long?"

He grinned. "Yes you did, and about an hour."

She was still in a state of disbelief when he took the opportunity to place his hand behind her neck and pull her forward to kiss her open mouth. She responded but the slumping of her shoulders made him pull back to see a pout form on her lips.

"An hour. John, why didn't you wake me?"

"Purely for selfish reasons," he said, "and don't try to get me to be sorry for it."

Defiantly she crossed her arms. "If you were, I'd find it hard to forgive you."

"I'll make up for it, besides, I needed to think, and you needed the rest for what is ahead."

"Your mother?"

"Partly, yes."

"When I left her this morning she was greatly concerned."

John's expression became one of surprised. "You saw her?"

"Yes, she came upon me as I walked the floor. She told me she didn't know where you had gone."

"My mother's life revolves around her children after the miserable circumstances of her husband death. The closing of the mill has been a major blow to me, and I believe that she may have been thinking that perhaps, history may repeat itself. I am sure by now you know what I speak of?"

She raised her eyes up to his and the depth of sadness told

him without her speaking that she did.

"For once in my life I acted impetuously. Remarkably enough, the end result of my impulsiveness has reshaped and brightened my entire future." John's hand smooth down the side of her face and cupping under her chin. "I am sorry for her anxiety, but that is all that can be offered."

After his words, his descent found her lips, moving slowly, breaking only when the train jolted to a complete stop. Her bag in one hand and the other on the small of her back, he guided her out of the passenger car into the chilled night air.

John looked up and down the boardwalk and frowned. The handful of late travelers' made their quick exits leaving the station deserted. Did anyone notice Margaret Hale's return? His mind flashed back to that agonizing night he witnessed her in the arms of another man. Knowing how he misinterpreted that situation, anyone seeing him with her this late at night could compromise her reputation. He must hurry.

Glancing at her, his concern etched deeper. Even with the sleep on the train, he could see she was done in and he wanted to get her back to the house immediately. Looking around he could see that no porter was available. Taking her elbow in his hand, he guided her to a bench and sat her down.

He whispered into her ear, "Another bench."

She looked up at him at smiled. "You're not going to sit down by me this time, are you?"

"Not this time," he answered, "but I daresay, I will always have a great fondness for benches from this day forward."

She could not help but agree with him and meeting his eyes she brought her mouth up for him to take, which he did not have the will power to decline. After they parted, he chided her lightheartedly.

"That, Miss Hale, is something you must stop doing."

"What have I done?"

"Offering your mouth, I am finding it hard to resist."

Her smile prettied and the palm of her hand reached up to run over his rough cheek attentively, then she drew her fingers delicately across his lips. Her touch had him wanting to pull her up from where she sat and crush her to him, but he lamented to let out a groan of frustration in its stead.

"You'll not make this easy for me," he told her.

"I do not care who sees."

Her exhaustion was talking. Taking her hand into his he returned it to her lap while muttering under his breath, "Then I will have to care for the both of us."

"John, this day is soon to be over, can we not wait until after it ends to begin our apprehension?"

He was feeling the day's loss as much as she, but he would not risk any harm on her of any sort. He bent down, kissed her forehead, and looked into her tired eyes with seriousness.

"A good tradesman always plans his day the night before," he said, "but I promise you, Maggie, there'll be more days like this for us."

Seeing her shiver from the cool night air, he pulled his black suit coat off and draped it over her shoulders, telling her that he would be back.

Margaret was not cold. She had thrilled from a combination of John's touch, manly concern, and words of promise. He took charge, not control, and did it with gentled regard for her. Pulling his coat more tightly around her, she luxuriated in its comforting warmth left over from his body.

This was the man she needed.

Submission was Henry Lennox's failing. Her father had a flaw in his character of indecisiveness. John fought for what he believed was right, and was strong whereas her father had been weak, two qualities never hidden from her view, even when they were at odds.

It was strange that now she was much more sensitive to everything about him—his looks, his masculine voice and scent, newly discovered mannerism and expressions, and most of all, the feel of him holding her in his arms and his tenderness.

Noticing a slight rip in the seam of the coat, she ran a finger over it wondering how it happened. She allowed her lip to curl up thinking about his reaction if he returned to find her mending it with her little sewing kit that she always carried with her. He would probably scold her for picking such a time to perform such a minor restoration. She would reply in defense that she was practicing for wifely duties. He would counter with some debatable statement thus starting one of many to come, to be sure, playful sparring matches.

Hugging his coat, she thought about his teasing and playfully goading her. Again, a side of him she was delighted to have witnessed for the first time that day, as well as, his face-changing smiles and laughter.

She never imagined herself as overly playful and animated with others and assumed that the same applied about John. Had these rarely seen characteristics always been a part of their natures, but needed that right inducement to be released? Perhaps, they both mundanely existed up until the point where love and happiness entered causing a remarkable conversion. She believed it to be so.

He was probably discovering many firsts with her as well. For the life of her, she could not remember a time she actually laughed aloud in front of him. She simply had no occasion for it until this day. She disliked her laugh and was surprised that she had not felt embarrassed when she lost her composure.

In retrospect, it was liberating to be able to express every emotion freely that she had inside for him. She wondered how they even came to feel such affection for each other. Such as they were merely acquaintances but somehow they must have known enough about each other to fall into that elusive life-changing condition.

Sighing wearily, she smoothed out a wrinkle on the coat. She was excessively tired. Much too tired to do any sewing or sparring. As much as she did not want to fall asleep on the train, she could not help feeling the security of waking up in his arms and seeing his handsome face before her. She felt pleasure in the prospect of the same thing happening each morning.

Margaret felt her face go hot again. It was not a blush of an unwed maiden thinking of such things. No, she had flushed with enthusiasm of becoming a wife to the man she loved.

A figure in the shadows observed the tall man walk away from the young woman sitting on the bench and contemplated the satchel on the ground by her side. It had been a slow week at the graveyard and he was becoming desperate. He had to have a drink!

He squinted in the dim light to make way for his escape once he grabbed the bag. His eyes then turned back to the woman in time to see her lift her head enough for the flickering light from the hanging oil lamps expose her face.

Margaret Hale! The man's heart began to pound like a huge drum. She was back in Milton! Who was that man with her? He ogled her lecherously. He thought that he would never see that face again.

His stare was broken when her companion returned and his identity revealed. A bitter scowl formed on his dirtied face. He knew the man all too well and watched as he helped her up from the bench.

Thornton took her arm into his and bent down to hear her speak and when she finished he threw his head back in rich laughter. Turning her to face him, he found the edges of his coat and drew them in to cocoon her further in the dark folds, then whispered something back into her ear. The hidden man's eyes narrowed as Miss Hale dropped at light kiss on his cheek in response.

Bile churned in the man's stomach and he fought not to retch. Even in Thornton's failures, he comes out on top. He had her! Seeing the obvious close attachment with Miss Hale made the sudden pleasure he felt in seeing her again turn into an all-consuming bitterness.

The disdain Billy Stephens had for Thornton was indisputable as a master, but since he drubbed him out of the factory, that disdain festered to a level of pure hate.

He became a wretched destitute because of him. Despised by his wife, she left him after his ousting taking with her anything left of value. Because of what happened that day, he could not get solid work at any mill. His home became the taverns by day and any place he fell at night.

Digging holes for the dead for a few shillings was all he could muster in way of honest work. That lasted for about a fortnight when he discovered that stealing from the dead was more profitable.

The dead knew nothing so he paid them no respect, and the grieving families were sentimental fools for placing valuables in the coffins to be buried like a treasure and then forgotten. He made one exception, the mother of Miss Hale. She, he allowed, to rest in peace. He did that for her daughter; the woman he came to worship.

She stood up to Thornton when he was knocking him about for smoking his pipe. This was as fine a lady as he had ever seen. Since that day, she became his obsession. The only pleasure he got out of life was his drink and when he could see her. He followed her every chance he could. That is how he ended up at the train station so many months ago, watching her as he was now.

Miss Hale was with a man who was boarding the late train out of Milton. When they embraced his gut spasm with jealousy and then he caught a movement up the way from the corner of his eye. Thornton! Seeing him fueled his jealousy with contempt, but Thornton left and his attention turned back to her.

A drunkard approach and confronted the couple, calling out the name Hale. There was a scuffle, the drunk stumbled away down the stone stairwell, and the man with Miss Hale hastily departed on the train leaving her alone.

Feeling a surge of adrenaline, Stephens licked his lips in anticipation; here was the chance he had been waiting for. Reaching down he made ready by pulling a blade out of its sheath, stepping forward out of the shadows he moved to follow her.

A sound of something dropping stopped him cold. A young man, laden with packages, was by the gate. There was no way he could get to her now. He watched as Miss Hale exited the boardwalk. His disappointment of this lost opportunity grew into rage and it consumed him.

He needed to vent his frustration and found the way in the form of the drunken man who had troubled Miss Hale. In his madness, he saw Thornton's face and channeled his pent-up lusts and hate by gripping the man by the head and viciously slamming it into the wall. He then flung him down the stairway to the bottom where he lay dead in a twisted heap.

The next day, for her, he killed again.

During the uprising at Marlborough Mill, he was in the crowd, standing next to Boucher, when he threw the stone that struck Miss Hale. Biding his time, he avenged her the day before the mother's funeral. The man had little strength to struggle when his head was being forced under the stained waters. As Boucher's lifeless eyes stared up at him, it gave him great satisfaction to take vengeance on those who would hurt Miss Hale.

Less than a year later, she was gone, back to London. When he could not see her face anymore, life became misery, which gave way to the need to settle scores, starting with Thornton.

Killing Thornton was always on his mind to do, but he wanted to bring him to his knees. Stephens planned to set the mill on fire but it closed beforehand, causing his attention to switch to others in Thornton's life—his mother, sister and the Latimer girl—and wait for the opportunity to strike.

He wished he had not.

Stephens seethed causing his lip to quiver. His hate-filled eyes focused on the woman he had killed for, then shifted over to the man who had her. He should have killed Thornton early on! Then she would not be with him now.

Was she Thornton's wife, warming his bed and entitled to take his pleasure from her anytime he wanted? If married, it would not be for long; if not, he would make sure they never do. This he bitterly vowed!

One way or another, Thornton would suffer. Squinting eyes followed the departing carriage. They both would!

Slinking into the shadows, his features took on a sinister appearance thinking that he got away with murder twice before. He could get away with it again. ଔ

Chapter Five
Expressed But Not Said

Descending the staircase, John could see his mother sitting in the drawing-room waiting. Walking in, he took both handles of the French doors and pulled them closed and walked the few steps to the liquor table. Picking up the decanter, he poured himself a drink and drank of the amber liquid before turning towards her.

Hannah sat patiently silent, but he could tell she was using considerable restraint. Moments before when he arrived, she had been considerably alarmed. At first, her concern for the woman who he carried in his arms touched him, but then he quickly recognized that her concern was not for Margaret but for the circumstances of *how* and *why* she came to be with him. Disappointed, he stopped her quick saying that he would be down to explain after he saw to Miss Hale's care.

Setting the glass on the table he began with what he thought should be obvious.

"She has accepted me, Mother. I will go first thing tomorrow to have our engagement posted."

Hannah released a deep breath of relief. "Then you are safe. You're not wed."

"Safe! Exactly what are you accusing her of?" he said defensively.

Hannah stood up. "Son, she was here this morning. What other reason would she have in coming all this way but to make a claim on you? And what was I to think, you coming in so late and carrying her?"

"Claim on me! Is that what you think? That she would—"

"She saw that you were the best man to manage her fortune so she changed her mind. What other reason would she come?"

"She loves me!" he stormed out loud.

Doubt registered on the woman's face. "All sudden like, she loves you! Have you forgotten about the man at the station? What happened to him? Don't be a blind fool, John. She is taking advantage of your—"

"It was her brother!"

Hannah blinked. "Her brother?"

"Yes, and nothing more needs to be said on that," John said angrily. "She was here with her barrister to speak to me about investing in the mill and had no reason to believe I still had any affection for her."

Hannah slumped back down into the nearest chair without a word. Trying to manage his surmounting frustration, he picked up the glass and finished the contents in one gulp. Why was she so against Margaret? Turning towards her, he saw that she became somewhat subdued.

"Do you want to assume any more about her, Mother," he said in a more controlled voice, "because I guarantee you, she is the better person here than both of us put together."

When she remained silent he continued, "We met by chance when our trains were delayed at the same time. We talked and found that we both made mistakes, which led me to ask again. There is no doubt in my mind that she accepted because she loves me."

Hannah found her voice and spoke rapidly, "How did she come to be alone with you? She must have known how it would look!"

Still! His mother was trying to find an impediment in Margaret. He let out an impatient sound and crossed his arms over his chest.

"Mother, she is not a child but an adult woman of means. I know it was out of place to allow her to get on that train with me alone but I daresay, I'll deal with the consequences. The rest is none of your concern and is between Miss Hale and myself."

"John, you'll not speak to me in that way," she said angrily.

"You haven't scolded me in years and I have used much worse language in disputing business matters. Why do I feel I have to defend her with you at every turn?"

"She is not of the same—"

"Enough," he spoke with an icy calm. "You'll not say any more. She will be staying here until we are wed. Until then, I expect you to get along and treat her with respect. Do you understand?"

"I only want your happiness."

"In my thirty-one years when have you seen me truly happy? I can tell you…the day I became my own master. One day and yet, you put off the woman I say will give me a lifetime of those days."

Hannah's head bowed and the room went silent. John fingered his glass, contemplating another drink but his mother's voice brought his attention back to her.

"Forgive me, John. A mother's love knows no boundaries and I have crossed one. My prejudices against Miss Hale will pass."

He knew that she was overly protective of him but it seemed to be extreme when it came to Margaret. His mother only saw the hurt and loss from his side. What she did not understand was that Margaret suffered because of him as well, even before her affections came to mirror his own.

He strolled over and planted a kiss on the top of her head. "I never imagined I'd end up with such a woman," he said with humility. "My life was nothing before her."

Hannah choked out a sob and her palms flew up to cover her face. Softening, he bent down to one knee to bring himself to her level. He rarely witnessed his mother so crestfallen.

She looked up with tears welling heavily in her eyes, and with both hands took possession of her son's face. "She has taken you from me. Promise, John, to never forget my love for ye."

"Nothing has been taken from you, Mother," he said, placing his hand over hers. "You'll always have me and I'll not soon forget all that you've done." He stood up and touched her shoulder, "I know you'll come to love her. Now, I must go. I will be by early but allow her to sleep as long as she wants."

He made his way to the closed doors, stopping right before, turning he added, "Can you see to getting the dressmaker here?" Hannah nodded.

"John?"

"Yes."

"Where did ye go?"

"South. I am sorry for not informing you," he answered, "but I will never be sorry for going."

"Why South?"

"I did not know myself. To find some light in the dark, I suppose."

He bowed his head as he reflected on how stunned he was when he glanced up to see Miss Hale standing in the middle of the boardwalk looking directly at him with such an air of calm. It was as if she planned their meeting all along.

A crooked smile formed as he raised his head and focused on his mother's face.

"However, it seems that the light found me."

Hannah sat for a long time after John left the room. His words kept repeating in her head. *My life was nothing before her.* That had her burying her face in her hands in dejection. Acute pains jabbed in her head, while her heart remained cold in her chest. Was she nothing to him as well?

He said that she would come to love her. How could she? What love could she have for the person who was stealing her treasure? There would be no sharing in that treasure, she was sure of it. The moment Miss Hale became Mrs. Thornton, she would become the unwanted mother-in-law and cast aside.

Impassioned tears filled her eyes, thinking angrily that John would never know to what extremes she underwent to better their lives. It was that intense love for her children, and a mother's willingness to purchase from the devil, that brought their salvation.

Where would her children be if their father lived? Hannah felt she had no choice and the opportunity was there. Slumped unconscious from too much drink, all it took was running the blade over his wrist that dangled down from the chair's arm.

He stirred, muttering a sluggish groan. Startled at the movement, she dropped the blade and staggered backwards, freezing a few steps away as the stark reality of what she did hit her.

Focusing solidly on his face, she expected his eyes to fly open and his rage to ensue. He would kill her for sure, and she would welcome it this time. It would be either him or her. As she waited for that divine decision, blood drained from his veins.

Hannah did not know how much time elapsed but the fast expansion of the crimson pool on the ground and his chalk white complexion told her that George Thornton's life would shortly be over. Fear subsiding, face void of all emotion, she straightened, turned and exited the room.

Hours later, she reentered the room and enacted the tragic character she needed to play and consoled her children. A ruling followed two days later. Holding the death certificate in her hand, Hannah read one section repeatedly—cause of death, suicide. Blamed was henceforth attributed to the dissolved partnership, failed speculations and financial ruin.

In the aftermath, even in their disgraced and impoverished state, she became content with her decision. What she had done was the necessary first step in their overall survival. Her declared penitence—the continual state of mourning—would be adequate as a reminder of her sinful act. Dropping the handful of dirt on her husband's remains ended that long unfortunate phase of her life.

The struggle after was profound, but she did not hesitate to believe that it was nothing compared to if her abusive husband lived. Hannah faced the future with steely determination and resolve, focusing on the molding of her son into becoming the opposite of his father. John would become a respected man, honorable and completely devoted to her.

She had been successful, until that is, Miss Hale entered their lives.

Margaret woke to find herself disoriented in a strange bedroom setting. Then pieces of the day before started to come together stirring up remembrances.

In the carriage, going to the Thornton house, John sat by her side but any indication of his feelings for her he kept at bay. Only his tender gazes upon her spoke of the past hours spent together.

Whereas he had strength officially to put the day to rest, she could not and found herself resting her head on his shoulder and entwining her arms around his.

Hoarsely he whispered, "You are testing me, Miss Hale."

"If it is improper for a tired woman to rest her head on a gentleman's shoulder then I will rest my head elsewhere."

She went to lean over to the other side and his voice warned, "Don't move. I'll risk ya." There was a brief pause before he added, "And gentleman, what did I do to deserve that title from you? I have been teetering on the side of ungentlemanly with you all day."

"I haven't been the model of a virtuous woman."

"You're perfectly acceptable in my eyes."

She let out a sigh and asked, "Was our conduct that shocking?"

"Not to us but others may not understand the rough road we traveled to bring us to this point. The bench and you getting on the train alone with me—it is more interesting to believe there is a love affair where forbidden desires overrule the head." John, suddenly uncomfortable, adjusted before he continued. "Remember when you ran out during the riot? It got misinterpreted and all who witnessed assumed you were announcing to the world that you had an affection for me. That night, every scenario I rehearsed in asking you was answered with you accepting me."

"John, I am regretful of—"

"No more apologies, Maggie," he said covering her hand on his arm. Desiring a change of subject, he asked, "Tell me about this new Margaret Hale that I am witnessing. Was she always there before?"

"She may have come out of her cocoon finally."

His laughter sounded, making her brows to draw in. It was a long moment before she was able to ask the reason.

Lowering his laugher to a muted chuckle, he was able to respond.

"Theorizing that the prelude to the cocoon was the larvae, and with that understanding, wouldn't that make you the ideal…bait?"

Her mouth dropped then formed into a full smile. "That, sir, is a brilliant deduction deserving of a kiss," she amused, "but since we are being more cautious, I understand if you should decline."

Taking her chin into his hand, he lifted her face to his. "I'll take my reward."

She proceeded to give it, thoroughly enjoying the practice. After, he kept his face close as he lowly droned his gratitude for her tender acknowledgement, then returned to his upright position.

Sleep threatened and she struggled against it. She wanted to be awake when they arrived at the house. Conversation seemed the way to alleviate the symptoms.

"John?"

"Yes."

"I feel as if we will never have cross words again. Can that be possible?"

"You are tired," he said with emphasis on the *are*, "but to answer, no, it isn't possible and I am thankful to say so."

She propped up, surprised. "You are? Why would you say such a thing?"

"I know Margaret Hale and her courageous spirit. It is a large part of the reason I fell hard for her. But—"

"There is a but?"

Ignoring her, he continued, "But, she has this insistent need to save the world and trust everyone in it. I have my job cut out for me of keeping her safe. I daresay shouting and threats will be involved in getting her to comply." A mischievous grin formed. "Even in saying that, I believe that I look forward to our next row."

Her eyes went wide. "What on earth could you possibly mean by that?" she exclaimed. "You better explain yourself, John Thornton."

"Our next heated discussion will be different. Before when I roared at you and you bravely stood your ground and put me back into my cage but we never had closure."

"Closure?"

"Me, asking for forgiveness, you giving it, and the gainful actions that come thereafter."

Her brow furrowed as she tried to decipher his meaning. It only took a moment before she went flush and released a breathless, "Oh."

"Did I shock you?"

"Why yes…you want us to have arguments so we can, if I understand you, make amends by other means without speaking words."

John lean down to whisper, "You understood me perfectly." Her blush darkened. Seeing her unease he added, "I do not want to have arguments but knowing our general dispositions do you think it can be avoided?"

"I suppose not and I understand having closure. I remember being angry with you for days…or distressed. I did not like that feeling."

"Now the difference is that I'll make it a point to not allow the sun go down until I beg for your forgiveness for whatever way I offended you during the day. That should give me a fresh start for the morrow."

Margaret raised her eyes up and squeezed his arm tighter. "You may be surprised, John, that some days I may have to ask for your forgiveness."

He grinned down at her. "Perhaps, but unlikely. I am of the opinion that you, dear lady, can do no wrong."

She was about to mention her refusal but she opted to calmly agree with him.

"Yes, you are probably right. Initiating this closure on these occasions will most likely be your responsibility."

His deep laughter echoed in the carriage again. He took up her hand and squeezed it affectionately.

"Do you realize that I have laughed more in these past hours than I have in years?"

"I find that very believable. Perhaps Mr. Thornton has come out of his cocoon as well. I will make it my mission,"—stifling another yawn—"to work hard to make you laugh or smile each day."

"Not much effort will be needed with you in my life." John rested his jaw on top of her head. "Now, close your eyes. As soon as we reach the house it is off to bed with you."

"What about your mother? I am anxious about her reaction."

"Leave her to me to explain."

She gladly accepted his want of handling his mother, and closed her eyes.

The rest of the night blurred in her semi-sleep. She remembered vaguely the carriage coming to a stop and John lifting her from the seat and carrying her into the house. Instinctively, her arms went around his neck and her head snuggled under his jaw, coming to rest on his shoulder.

Cradled in his arms, she did not feel courageous as he described her. She could have forced herself to become fully awake but she played the coward, feeling that she did not have the usual fortitude to face Mrs. Thornton. She stayed blissfully idle in his sheltering embrace.

In the house, she heard him order a room prepared for her and then the unmistakable female voice of John's mother. In her sleepy fog her mind did not registered any of the words spoken.

The conversation was brief, then she felt herself going up; John was climbing up the long, wide stairway. Stirring in his arms, she willed herself to open her eyes, but his low soothing voice commanded her to be still and that he had her.

Softness underneath engulfed her exhausted body as he laid her down, a whispered goodnight and he was gone. She wanted badly to have a kiss to go with that good night but with Jane, the chambermaid, hovering, she understood the reason for its absence.

Jane took over care of her. She hazily recalled the maid brushing out her hair and her groggily fumbling out of her clothes into a nightdress.

The welcoming warmth of Jane pulling the coverlet over her closed the miraculous day forever.

Rising from the bed, she found her bag and pulled out a clean lace-fringed blouse. Spotting her skirt, she undressed while mentally preparing herself for her reunion with John and his mother. She would be calm and remain controlled, yesterday was gone, and she must remember her place.

In thinking of him, and what transpired the day before, Margaret had a feeling that will be easier said than done.

The way his striking blue eyes looked intently into hers, his voice, strength, and touch—the idea to revert to her reserved self, she feared would go flying out the window. She could not wait to be in his arms again and learn all she could about the man who was to be her husband.

She had been right. Emerged from the shell of the cocoon, she was a newborn. Mr. Thornton, of all people, allowed her folded wings to expand out and take flight.

As for the mother, she refused to contemplate that meeting. She would leave it up to providence to direct her course where Mrs. Thornton was concern. In truth, she was becoming increasingly frightened to see her. She cannot possibly be happy to know she would be her future daughter-in-law, but if what John said was true, that she wanted only his happiness, perhaps all will be well.

Putting his mother towards the back of her mind, she allowed her memory to drift pleasantly back to the previous day's events. She never believed herself a romantic but she could not help the sigh of awe to escape.

Her own mother spoken often of her romance with her father. While she never disputed the deep love they had for each other, she could not bring herself into believing in happily ever after. With Frederick's court martial, her father's "matter of conscience", and the wild and bleak town of Milton, her predisposition seemed justifiable.

Such as they were before, gave evidence that the absence of these happenings, could entitle her parents lives as ideal. Yesterday had the feel of a fairy tale beginning, but will it have its happy ending? Still too much the skeptic to say yes, to Margaret, it remained to be seen.

Oh, but what a day!

It had been invigorating and liberating! She did what she did and never be sorry for it, and she suspected that she would not be the first woman to act impetuously for a man.

She wondered what would have happened if she had not boarded the northbound train with John and stayed within the confines of socially acceptable conduct. Poor Henry, she could not imagine what it would have been like returning to London with him. A shiver ran through her at the awkwardness; he obviously witnessed John and her on the bench.

Margaret's hand flew up to her mouth at her sudden realization of what her actions may have cost him. What did he say to her Aunt Shaw? How it must have looked. She put him in a terribly uncomfortable position of trying to explain. Her aunt surely would be beside herself with apprehension. Why was she only thinking of this now? Yesterday's folly was registering and her normal calm heightened. She must speak to John.

A faint knock on the door had her hastily finishing buttoning her blouse while asking whomever to come in. The door opened and a maid came fluttering in with a rattling breakfast tray. Margaret gave her a welcoming smile that hid her disappointment that it was not John.

The girl spoke animatedly fast, that Margaret had a difficult time keeping up with her.

"Oh, miss, you are awake and up. The master has come and gone, asking after you. You showing up last night was such a surprise and we thought that he would have stayed—"

"What time is…begging your pardon, your name?"

"Sarah, miss."

"Sarah, what time is it?"

"Nigh noon, miss. We thought you sleep forever but master made it clear that you are not to be disturbed and for me to check on you from time to time in case you needed anything."

This certainly was not what she wanted to hear. What would John's mother think?

"Thank you, Sarah. Please leave the tray and go tell Mrs. Thornton I will be down directly."

Setting the tray down on a nearby table the maid replied, "Oh she isn't here, miss. She left after the master saying she was going to town for some errands. She said she would stop by the dressmaker and have her come by for you."

"That is kind of her."

"Yes, miss, she couldn't help but notice you was traveling light."

Light indeed, and showing up so late at night alone with their master. Oh, and him carrying her in and to this room must have started the tittle-tattle and tongues wagging. There would be no question that the gossipmongers will spread the word like an infectious disease around the town within hours adding their own yarn to the story. She would not be surprised that by the time John was able to squash any such narratives, that she will find that she escaped London to elope secretly with Mr. Thornton or worse, be in a delicate condition.

Margaret felt her face warming profusely. It wasn't the thought of being the mother of John's child; it pleased her profoundly to think of it. It was the creation of that child and her naivety of the actual process that had her cheeks flaming.

Glancing quickly at the maid, she was relieved to see her scurrying about the room unaware of the guest's sudden discomfiture. Certainly, she was making up for the lack of color the day before.

While the act of kissing was the true mystery of courtship that she found to be quite intoxicating, the procreation of children remained the mystery of marriage. Even at her age, she remained quite ignorant.

Having been around babies and noting the difference between male and female, she had some sort of idea but still, of course, she never seen a grown man completely unclothed. Knowing the many changes that occur with a female growing into an adult, she assumed there were many changes for a male as well. In truth, she never really pondered seriously on how a man came to "know" his wife as it states in the Bible.

Her mother was too modestly sensitive for Margaret to consider broaching the question. Maria tried to initiate a discussion, but it ended abruptly with Dixon interrupting. Maria never attempted the education after that. Asking Edith to take her into her confidence crossed her mind, but to ask for the sake of easing her curiosity, why put Edith through such awkwardness?

The acceptance of becoming a spinster of means had been tossed out the window when Mr. Thornton, enthusiastically, opened the door. She will marry and have his children, and the mystery of procreation loomed before her.

Whatever was to happen on their wedding night she imagined it not to be all unpleasant with the ardent attentions he bestowed upon her the day before. His command over her senses and his passion, melting her at the slightest touch, wanting more, and seeking it every time his eyes and hands beckoned. Was it all to be that pleasurable?

She knew that childbirth was painful and something that woman endured. Was it the same in the creation of? Margaret chided, telling herself to stop. Whatever was she thinking to make her mind turn to such things?

A growling stomach helped her to put it out of her mind. Walking over to the tray, she noticed the sealed note with her formal name written on the front. John was clever in foreshadowing prying eyes viewing the addressee; it was simply addressed to Miss Margaret Hale.

Breaking the seal, she opened it to see the bold strokes of his hand.

Dearest Maggie

I have gone to post our engagement in the papers. I did not sleep thinking I would wake to find that our miraculous encounter had not occurred. Realizing the reality of you in my life, I am renewed and reborn. Yesterday, although expressed, I did not say what I should have repeatedly.

I love you.

- Always, John

Margaret read the note twice again before closing her eyes, clutching his message to her chest, and letting his written words run through her like a benevolent spirit.

Then her eyes flew open wide. She neglected to tell him that she loved him as well! Expressed but not said. She wanted to rush out of the room and find him. Peeking at Sarah, tidying up the bed, she let out an impatient sigh. Her momentous response would have to wait. Sitting, she concentrated on filling her angry stomach.

"Miss, I mean to ask if you know if the master will be returning," Sarah said nervously. "He wasn't here last night and us girls were wondering if he won't be staying here no longer?"

Margaret's mouth formed into a feminine grin; the maid was fishing.

"Sarah, I know how my sudden appearance here may have looked but I will offer to you that it is not as it seems. Until Mr. Thornton is ready to reveal the circumstances of me being here, I'll ask you, as well as the staff, to not assume anything until verified by him."

"Yes, miss."

Thanking her, Margaret gave the maid a grateful smile knowing that her request most likely fell on deaf ears. 03

Chapter Six
Afternoon Reunions

John entered the drawing-room, halting a few steps in as his eyes settled on the woman sitting at the writing desk. Her back was nearly to him but a slight angle allowed him to view her profile. Fully engrossed in her depictions on paper, Margaret remained ignorant of his entrance. Standing in place, he took on his normal stance with arms crossed, welcoming the chance to observe her unnoticed.

Many times before he imagined her sitting at that same desk as he walked in at the end of the day. Whether by her rising or him going to her, they rejoiced in the daily reunion. Little reveries, such as these, had her near to him in every room of the spacious house at one time or another.

These imaginations varied in size and scope. One would have her sitting across from him at the morning table as he shared news from the posts. Another had her standing by his side, breathtaking in a beautiful ball gown, as they greeted guests in their home.

At his own desk, whether in his study or office, lack of sleep had him staring wearily at the open doorway where a mirage of her would appear, gracefully entering his domain. She would place her hand on his shoulder to persuade him to come away from his work and join her for the rest of the evening. Together they would find themselves relaxing by the warmth of a fire, reliving the day's events and planning for the morrow, then retiring to the bedroom where he would reach for her intimately and hold her close.

Unfolding his arms, he inhaled deeply then exhaled the reality of her in his life. The dream-like visions were prophecies coming true and the angelic figure had materialized before him in the flesh.

Margaret's pen stopped on its way to the inkwell as she stilled, turning in her seat, her eyes found him. Her face lighted but she did not rush to be in his arms again. He was disappointed at first but then that dissolved as her alternate actions played out.

She rose from the chair and came towards him, meeting him halfway in the center of the room.

Doe-like eyes blinked in a slowed motion as she regarded him. A faint, amused smile formed as fingers reached up to comb some hair back in place that had fallen on his forehead. Then she deliberately moved to adjust his collar that had gone distractingly out of place.

"There…that's better," she said with quiet emphasis, "it must be blustery out for you to come in looking this way."

Her feminine attention had him completely mesmerized that he found he could not speak or move.

Moving her hand over his shoulder to the back of his neck and bracing her palm on the front of his black vest, Margaret brought his head down as she lifted hers up.

He took what she offered, tenderly at first, but then his increasing need for her demanded him to strengthening the intensity. She allowed his eagerness to take full control, causing his heart to thunder in his chest. No change of mind, no regrets, she still accepted him, and his joy reached new heights. Unable to contain himself, he captured her waist with both hands and lifted her effortlessly up high.

"Now that was a kiss!" he richly proclaimed.

His jubilant actions had her laughing in delight and throwing her arms around his neck to draw him closer in her flight. Together their reunion rang throughout the room.

Bringing her down into his arms, he swung her around to continue his show of happiness. Her feet found solid ground but he did not break his embrace. His arms were secure around her midsection as he scanned her upper section. Her breathing was quick and face flushed with a full decorative smile. He received as much pleasure in witnessing her joy as he did in feeling his.

He spoke her name as he brought his hand up to gently stroke her cheek. Margaret's eyes closed and tilted her head into his warm palm. After a moment, her lids lifted.

"I love you, John Thornton," she whispered softly.

"How could that have possibly happened?" he asked, grinning.

"Seems quite impossible but it is truthfully said."

"Say it again. My hearing may have been impaired."

The corner of her lip drew up. "Sir, I have yet to hear it from your lips. I reserve the right not to repeat myself until—"

His hand moved swiftly up her neck to tilt her chin up, kissing her squarely on the mouth, and cutting off her words. Parting, he moved his mouth to her ear and spoke the words she requested to hear. He followed by asking if she was satisfied.

She nodded like a schoolgirl, wrapped her arms around his waist, and rested her head on his chest. His hand found the back of her head and he held it in place while his other arm possessed the small of her back. He then buried his face in her neck.

Her fresh floral scent had him walking the countryside in Helstone again, only difference being that this time he was not alone.

Margaret felt his breathing on her skin from his face intimately implanted. In every manner, by his touch, his actions, she knew that he was saying he loved and needed her.

She determined that she rather liked the expression of love standing in his embrace and feeling him holding her against his tall frame. Before his embraces were while they were sitting—on a bench, in a train car, in the carriage. She felt the difference profoundly.

Standing, she felt his dominance over her that was reassuring and afforded much comfort rather than apprehension; a sense of security she never would have imagined in their togetherness. She now understood the reason why God created man first.

John moved his head and came to rest it on her shoulder; she could feel pent up tension escape from his body. She brought him comfort and it pleased her. God may have made woman for man but it did not lessen man's need for the soft touch, love, and care that only a woman could provide.

She wanted to do whatever she could to bring that long deserved happiness to his burdened life and if that meant evolving more as a woman, then so be it. Always the struggle from what is proper to do and going against what one would like to do. If she were a young girl, only a day into their engagement, her acceptance of his heightened passion would have been taboo.

Wrapped prettily and stored in a box, she did not comprehend what it would mean to be free from the box's confines until Mr. Thornton pulled open the lid. What he lifted out was no longer a girl but a woman. That woman will do what *she* thought proper and acceptable, and not conform to those around her with their sour looks and disapproving voices. This time, she determined that the struggle would stop and in its place, she would please the man before pleasing the ingrained social protocols.

Remembering his sudden reversion to proper decorum in the hired cab and his rather over enthusiastic attention now, Margaret got the distinct feeling that John—a hot blooded, viral man—knew what he desired but was finding it hard to restrain from what was right in front of him to take.

There was a clear boundary to his attentions, which she found herself ignorant of, but she trusted that he would not go beyond it. In saying that, she wanted to let him know that he could be as free to take her as close to that line without crossing. That, of course, excluded any demonstrations with others in their presence, which reminded her that until they were husband and wife, time alone together would most likely be restricted. She let out a disappointed sigh at the thought, which grabbed his attention. Pulling her back out of his embrace, he asked her what was the matter.

A dramatic pout cross her face. "Now that I have practiced, I suppose we must start being better behaved."

"Practice! Was that what that was?"

"I thought I did well. Do you not think so?"

"Too well I am thinking which leads me to say that I am in agreement with you, Miss Hale. I expect to be put in my place from now on if my attentions become overzealous," bending his head closer he added, "in public."

She tilted her head to regard him with a serious look. "I am unfamiliar with this putting you in your place. What exactly does that mean?"

"Depending on the offense, I recommend either a disapproving glare or a sound slap."

Margaret parted from him suddenly. Settled her hands on her hips she gave him a contrived frown.

"If it was in my nature to strike a man for an offense, John Thornton, do you not think it would have happened long before now?"

He got her meaning and chuckled. "Undoubtedly. I thank you for your restraint but perhaps you should get into the habit."

"I could never do such a thing to you."

"Then you must reframe from advancing your knowledge until we are wed." Her face took on a confused look and he moved closer to clarify, "No more serious practicing. Could lead to a loss of control on my part."

Understanding registered. Shaking her head, she pretended she did not hear him.

"Then it has been decided that I will agree on the disapproving glares," she said, putting her hand on his arm, "and John, I expect to find *you* giving me these looks as well when justifiable, for I fully intend to keep up on my training."

It was his turn to look confused but his eyebrow rose with comprehension. Before he could reply, she raised herself up on her toes and found his mouth with hers.

His arms took tight ownership of her. Margaret did not mind the role reversal. Her senses took in his male scent as his hands took command by spanning her back and roaming up to her neck to cup her head to bring her deeper into the kiss. She could have stood there all day with him but the fear of his mother or servants caused her to pan her head anxiously towards the entryway.

"Seems that you are concerned about receiving other disapproving looks other than my own," he mused. "I briefly explained last night and believe my mother is accepting of the sudden turn of events."

Margaret, nodding acceptance, wanted to believe but for some inexplicable reason, she could not.

She nodded but John sensed she remained unconvinced. Picking up her hand, he stroked its softness in reinforcement of his claims.

"I had to tell her that it was your brother that night and the reason for your trip to Milton. That seemed to redeem you in her eyes," he said. "She got it into her head that we must have eloped."

Margaret looked up at him in surprise as he nodded his confirmation. "She was certain that you wanted to use me to grow your fortune," he laughed thinking how ridiculous that sounded.

"Papa and Mamma married for love and I will as well," she replied, "and as much as I am sure you'll grow my fortune, I would burn it if it was the only way I could be with you."

He rewarded her for her endearment by leaning in and giving her a slow, lingering kiss.

Deciding there was a need to change the subject, he wrapped her arm around his, asking if she had eaten while steering her to a settee and sitting her down, he taking the space next to her.

"You mean this afternoon," she said guiltily. "Yes, I did. I was famished. I had not eaten since early afternoon."

"Forgive me for not thinking of you. I have adapted to missing meals and going without but I agree, I was hungry," he said, "but it was a different kind of hunger and although I didn't get filled, I found myself pleasingly satisfied."

Margaret's cheeks pinked but a hint of a smile reveal that she had not been embarrassed. By her display, he had surmounted that hiding his desire for her was no longer necessary.

"I am grateful you know your manners, John," she spoke sweetly with no reservations, "and allowed me to partake of that meal with you."

It was his turn to drop his jaw and then throw his head back in laughter. Apparently, she felt the same about holding back as well. He was in awe of this woman, and it was certain that his life would never be the same again.

Finding a semblance of control in his amusement, he threw out another question, anticipating another delightful answer.

"Yes, I am fully recovered from my sleepless night, thank you," she said, smiling with pleasure.

"No more working on future speeches or beating the pillow?" She shook her head. He then added, "That is unfortunate for me. I rather liked *showing* you how I would have replied."

Delicate brows lifted. "Would this be an ideal time for one of those disapproving glares?"

"Not at all. We are alone."

"Oh, I had forgotten," she said, "I am not sure if I am able to deliver these expressions when needed."

"I recollect that you are quite good at giving disapproving looks."

"I didn't know I had such talents," Margaret countered.

"You do. Talents that need very little of this practice."

This stirred up her laughter and coming back at him saying that she intended to perfect these talents for any of their future public or private outings together from which he replied he would rehearse, what was sure to be, his daily begging for her forgiveness.

The lighthearted debate and humored conversation had them both feeling the newness of feeling reborn. Both cherished the significance of what was happening—now together, they were becoming one.

John's mirth began to dissipate as the playful back and forth evoked his thoughts to recall their lack of discretion the previous day.

His expression turned serious.

"John?"

"Maggie, I need not tell you that our combined actions yesterday may come back to haunt us."

She nodded her head in agreement asking about Henry returning to London without her.

"I took the liberty to send an express to your aunt telling of my commitment in regards to you. I assumed that you wouldn't want her to find out in the posts. Then I sent a note of apology to Lennox for putting him in such an awkward position and assured him of my honorable intentions. Although it was not required of me, I felt it was warranted." He paused for a moment then added, "I daresay, I wouldn't want to be in his place facing your relations."

"Thank you. I wouldn't have known what to say."

She paused then inquired further about him speaking to his mother about Frederick.

"I'm sorry for disclosing that when you have not authorized it. All that my mother knows is that the man was your brother."

"No, I am glad that you did. Should I tell her…well, do you think she should know everything?"

He thought about his mother's accusatory tone and general prejudice towards her the night before.

"No, I think not. I will explain that it could put him in danger and that she must remain silent on the subject."

Margaret's sudden withdrawal had him bending his head to get a better glimpse of her face. "If you rather I tell her, I will do so."

"No, not at all. That is agreeable."

"Then what were you thinking just now?"

Her eyes lifted to his. "I was thinking how comforting it is to have you make these decisions for me. Even papa was in a constant state of deciding what to do," she said, "I imagine he got tired of seeing mamma and I with wrinkled foreheads."

Queued, he kissed that area of her face and then leaned back to speak. "I am sure that you'll not always favour my decisions," he said, "and you a picture, hypnotizing me with you charms, could sway me easily in either direction."

"Hypnotizing…it is good to know I have such power."

John brushed back a lock of hair behind her ear that fell loose from his previous attentions. "I need to check myself where you are concern. I seem to disclose my weaknesses too readily. Soon, it will be you who is master over me."

"That is not likely to ever happen. Nicholas would find that laughable to say the least." Suddenly she turned animated, "Oh Nicholas, Mary and the children! I must go to them. It will be such a surprise."

Grinning at her he confirmed, "Yes, we will go to see them later. And I can say with all sincerity that you would make a tolerable if not interesting master."

His statement went unacknowledged as she put her hand on his arm, "I cannot believe I haven't asked after Nicholas. How is he?"

"He is settled back at Hamper's after a glowing recommendation. Unfortunately, Hamper's might go under as another casualty of the strike. I am sure he wouldn't mind me being master again."

"Then you both have gotten along well after you took him on."

"Yes, he became one of my best workers and I quickly recognized him as an intelligent and honorable man."

He told Margaret of the little reading Thomas, the dining hall with Mary cooking, and Higgins getting a petition together.

"If the mill would have continued, I would have promoted him as overseer. I even find myself taking in a pint with him from time to time," said he with fondness.

"How is it that I cannot see you taking in a pint of ale with anyone let alone a past committee man?"

"You still see me as the overbearing master then?"

"Yes it's true," she responded, "but I think that you're improving on better acquaintance."

"Well, I hope for your sake that is true because we are going to be acquainted for a long time."

She blushed shyly and offered her mouth to him and he moved in close to accept but he stopped to finish his thought.

"Because of you, I am sure that I will improve upon acquaintance to a good many people other than yourself. You being in my life will make me a better man."

His palms reached up, took her face into his hands, and closed the gap between their mouths. Tenderly he probed her lips; her mouth yielded completely causing him to move to take custody of the inside of her mouth.

He could not get enough of her. The deepened kiss was involuntarily given and he felt her tense at the first entrance. He was about to pull away but she relaxed and took him in without any further hint of displeasure or aversion. It was a whole new level of intimacy that he had not expected to introduce; it was out of his control. He became pleasantly surprised to find her consenting.

Margaret invited him to continue, but he needed to subdue his want for her, so he broke the contact to look upon her face. He had to drop a quick kiss on her again after seeing her breathless disappointment of being released from this new form of physical affection.

Clearing his throat, he thought it wise to go back to safe conversation.

"Higgins has become the first true friend and confidant of my life. You benefited me a great deal sending him my way."

Still distracted by his enhanced kiss she smiled and answered sweetly, "I am glad of it."

Her beautiful smile, how he loved seeing it. Not that it was rare. He recognized that she was now smiling for or because of him.

From there, Margaret's excitement grew, causing her to speak animatedly about seeing her friends once again and how glad she would be able to help him get Marlborough Mill up and running.

John flinched. He knew it was coming. Her voice was musical as he listened, waiting for the opportune time to interject.

"Oh, John, Henry had me write letters for the banks. He said you need to sign them then they can transfer—"

"No, Maggie," he interrupted with sedate calmness, "the letters will have to wait. Until we are married, I'll not be using your money."

"I do not understand, the sooner you get the mill back in production the better for the workers."

His eyes took on a mischievous glint. "Why, Miss Hale, you sound like a woman of business and trade."

"Father would have been shocked," she mused. "But, John, you cannot be serious."

"I am serious. I would like to see those who have no income back to work, but sooner isn't always better or, in my case, possible. I left the business in good standing with the buyers, but there are loans that have to be paid off before I invest."

"It is possible! There is more than enough to cover what is owed."

She was getting alarmed, sighing he took her hand to issue calm. "How can I explain this?"

"There is nothing to explain. Can you not think of the investment money as Mr. Bell's?"

"No, I can not. Paying debts is not investing. Having responsibilities and investing in a volatile market at the same time is not using good business sense."

Frustration registered on her face and she pulled her hand from his. "If I was a wealthy stranger would you have taken what was offered?"

"Yes, I would have but not to satisfy my creditors."

"And a woman?"

He wanted to answer falsely but he found he could not and replied with a yes again.

"Then I do not see the difference. I came yesterday as a wealthy woman wanting to invest and moreover, to aid downtrodden families. The only change is that I am to be your wife. Can you accept that the moment I said yes, what is mine became yours?"

John looked at her tenderly but shook his head. "Maggie, you aren't hearing what I am saying to you. I'll invest eventually but it is important to me to clear my loans on my own," he said in a tone that was respectfully patient. "Unfortunately, I find myself in that position of reduced circumstances."

It offends me that you should speak to me as if it were your duty to rescue my reputation…you think because you are rich and my father is in reduced circumstances that your can have me…

Her eyes widened with recollection. "John, I was not myself when I said that. Please do not use that as a reason."

"Even if it wasn't said at the time, my mind would still be made up. My debts will not be a burden to you as my father's were to my mother and me." Lifting her chin to look directly into her distressed eyes, he added, "And not until you are Mrs. John Thornton will yours become mine. Not before."

"Then marry me this day."

Her calm confident reply stunned him and his love for her went beyond what his heart could possibly contain. For a moment, he was ready to dismiss every logical thought and make her his wife within the hour. Shaking his head clear, he let his resolution take its rightful place.

"As enticing as that proposition is, our actions of yesterday make that quite impossible. I'll not marry you until everything has been properly done and I can bring my wife into a clean slate from all my past failures."

"The doors of a mill were closed—hardly failures. You are being unreasonable and stubborn, John Thornton. I won't allow your pride and arrogance keep those doors closed."

His eyes darkened. "Arrogance destroyed my father, Margaret, and his legacy was that of debt and years of struggle for his family. I will not risk passing that to you or our children," he said sharply, "and pride is not a word to be used lightly around me. It has proved to be more an asset than a hindrance to the Thornton name."

Her face looked impassive by his heated assertion and it was difficult to tell what she was thinking. He knew that she always spoke her mind and prepared for a fiery rebuttal.

In its stead, she pushed herself up from the seat and stood

before him. Calmly she spoke, steadily, without any emotion.

"Unreasonable and stubborn you'll allow. Very well, John, I will respect your wishes."

His temper abating, he let out a sigh of relief, readying himself to seek forgiveness from her for his harsh tone but her calm, determined voice stopped him quick.

"In the meantime, I will be making inquiries about the start up of Marlborough Mill myself."

Before he could even blink, she bent down and kissed his clean-shaven cheek saying, "If you'll please excuse me, I must finish my letters."

With a rustled swirl of her skirt, she walked purposefully back to the desk, sat down and continued with her correspondences. ೞ

Chapter Seven
Man or Machine

Trying to concentrate on the letter to Edith, she heard John rise and walk over to the desk. He stood watching, with hands locked behind his back, presumably contemplating his next words to sway her from taking matters into her own hands.

"If you mean to be intimidating by standing over me, John, it will not work. I cannot ignore the suffering of those around me when I have the means to end it," she said, not taking her eyes off the paper. "I will reestablish Marlborough Mill with or without you."

"I cannot tell you what to do with your fortune, but I will ask you to wait until I can make use of it."

"Why?"

"To be a part of this industry, it is harsh—too harsh for a gentle woman. I cannot allow you to be involved."

Placing the pen down, she angrily looked at him. "How could I possibly avoid not being involved? And why, might I ask, is your mother excluded?"

"Her involvement had been necessary for the survival of her family."

"Then the survival of many families will be my motivation."

He bristled. "Circumstances were different back then!"

Noticing his darkening storm, Margaret made a calming gesture by reaching out for his nearest hand and entwining her fingers with his.

"Please, let us not argue about this. I do not know in what manner I will be involved. Perhaps providing capital will be all that is needed."

"A lamb amongst wolves. They will take advantage of you, Margaret."

"Not all, certainly, but of course, I prefer a person I can trust over a stranger. John, that can only be you," she said earnestly, "I would be grateful to stand aside and be ignorant of all things pertaining to your industrial world."

His brow rose. "Ignorant you say. No one would accuse you of that," he said. "No, there is a sharp mind in that beautiful head of yours and the ability to cast spells and charms on unsuspecting men."

"You are mistaken. If I had such powers, there would be nothing to settle, and you would be walking me to the church."

He let out a short grunt as a wide grin appeared. "Maggie, your logic always seems to get the better of mine."

"Then why not go with it? Allow me to help, John. Use the money, pay your loans, and bring the mill back."

He did not answer, but he squeezed her hand, letting it go to walk over to the window. Hands clasped behind his back, he silently looked out over the quieted yard below. To see no activity must be a painful reminder of the gravity of their discussion. She waited patiently knowing that, when ready, his complexity would demand a reply to her question.

At length, he turned to face her. "Margaret, the debts must be mine and mine alone. I must work to pay them off so I can get back to the beginning where I was a feeling man and not a machine," he said firmly.

"A machine?"

He walked back over to her side and placed his hand on her shoulder, "Yes, methodical and unrelenting with oil in his veins. I wasn't always that way. You brought me back."

Her eyes questioned and he offered his hand to escort her back to the cushioned settee. Pulling up a chair in front of her, he sat to talk face to face.

"Each time I saw you, no matter if civil or not, warm blood began flowing and I found that human side of me that could feel." His face took on a pained expression. "When you were gone, I feared the return of that heartless man made of steel."

"I know that is not who you are."

"Deep down was the man you come to have a deep affection for. You are a large part of his restoration, but there is still work to be done and that must remain separate for me to repair on my own."

"Please, I want to understand."

He took her hand into his. "My father's shame did not end at his death. He left debts in his wake and a deep stain upon the Thornton family's name. It had been expected that those debts would go unpaid because of our impoverished circumstances. It took years and doing without, but I fulfilled my father's obligations."

John sat back as he remembered the impoverished lot that he ran with in those years. He had friends, like Higgins, and learned most of his harder life lessons, and the physical solace found in the arms of a woman. He was a hot-blooded man, taking on the world and finding his way, fighting and scraping by as his peers.

"During those years of struggle, I had empathy for others around me because we were equal in circumstance. We all pulled together and supported each other. I was the furthest from being like my father," he said in a low, composed voice. "But the more I succeeded the more I became disconnected and hardened. I forgotten what it was like."

"You made me take a hard look at my treatment of others. And Higgins, he took over those orphans. I daresay, I would not have done the same and I became ashamed. Higgins is the measure of a man I want to be." He got a far away look on his face as he finished, "You would've accepted me."

Margaret touched his knee to bring his attention back. "John, do not look back, look to the future."

He let out a deep sigh. "I have to deal with the past before I can move forward," he said. "Do you know when I began to love you?" She shook her head, curious for his answer. "During my first lesson with your father."

A look of astonishment registered on her face.

"That is not possible. I had been rude and accused you of beating that worker."

"Yes, but if you remember, I was unkind as well. I walked out thinking that you were the most disagreeable young woman but you kept on rattling around in my head. No amount of shaking could get you out."

"How could this be the beginnings of love?" she asked.

Leaning his face forward, he spoke, "Because disagreeable as I found you, I would have fought the devil himself to see you again. You stirred up something in me that day and it wasn't only my ire."

Straightening his frame, he continued, "During that first meeting, your lecture on the worker had its effect. I should not have acted as I did. The beating I gave him…"

"John—"

"Please allow me to finish…it is hard for me to say," he said with building emotion. "My father, he was a violent man, and I got in his way and he reacted. Do you understand?"

She gasped as her hand flew up to her mouth.

"You were never to know but I felt obliged to talk of it to better help you to understand." He picked up her hand, his eyes searching her sympathy riddled features. "None of that, Maggie. The time for pity is long gone."

"John, your mother…Fanny?"

"Fanny was safe."

Her eyes moistened as she nodded in understanding. Her compassion ran deep and he adored her for it.

Patting her hand reassuringly, John continued, "The strike…I didn't want to give in. I didn't think nor care for the workers and their families. It all would've been avoided, the riot, Boucher, and you being hurt." He reached out to touch the area where the rock struck her. "If I did, the mill would be in production this day."

"I am beginning to understand. You feel responsible."

"Yes, but not in the way that you may think. I slowly became the unfeeling, brutal master, reduced to violence and callousness," he leaned forward to bring emphasis to his next words, "like my father."

John watched as his words penetrated Margaret's mind. Her reaction was what he expected.

"You are not and never will be, John Thornton," she exclaimed heatedly. "I am sorry for what you went through but to infer that you inherited your father's madness is incomprehensible. I insist you never speak of it again."

"Now I have the proof, only a woman in love would have responded in that way," he mused affectionately.

Crossing her arms, she turned her head aside, letting out a long exasperated breath. Seeing her mulling over what he said, he remained silent.

Rising from the chair, he went to the liquor table to pour each a drink. Returning he offered it to her and sat back down. The needed break continued until both emptied glasses sat on the side table.

"I understand, John, why you must take these financial burdens upon yourself. It is a fine thing and I believe I love you more because of it," she said, "but how will you accomplish this given your—"

"Reduced circumstances?" She nodded. "Finding work and earning a salary," he replied simply.

Her eyes widened in disbelief and stammered, "It…it will take months…years!"

"I've come a long way from working on the docks. It won't take as long."

"As long!" she said, alarmed. "You not being master, how can you possibly recover quickly?"

"Everything will work itself out. Do not worry."

John knew he was placating her but he wanted to move on to a more pleasant noonday and avoid distressing her further. However, it was not to be.

"What does that mean for our marriage? Will you wait?"

Unwilling to tell her what she did not want to hear, he stayed silent and sat back in his chair with a grim expression; he answered without saying a word. Margaret turned her head away as disappointment registered across her face.

John waited for the moment he would have to bring reassurances and promises, but she surprised him by standing up to speak.

"Mr. Thornton, will you take work with me?"

"What!"

"I want to hire you as master of Marlborough Mill," she rephrased confidently.

"Margaret, don't be ridiculous," he scoffed, "I'd have all the North laughing at my expense."

He knew immediately he spoke hastily. Her face went red and her expression dropped from certainty to one of hurt. Standing up he went to reach for her but she backed away which stopped him in his place.

"You are mistaken in thinking warm blood is flowing in your veins," she said, visibly shaken, "you still are very much a machine."

John flinched, setting him in motion to reach for her with good intentions only to have her stop him again with a look of stricken crossness. Walking stiffly over to the desk, she sat down, pulled out a blank piece of paper, and started writing.

"Maggie, what I said is unforgivable. What I meant was—"

"Stop…please stop, you have made yourself perfectly clear. First the money and now you and your abilities," she said with rising anger, "if I cannot invest in these, I won't invest at all."

"Who are you writing too?"

"If you must know, Henry Lennox."

His brows drew in. "Why?"

"I wish him to start a charity fund for families that are without income or education. I will instruct him to transfer the entire amount of Mr. Bell's gain. I want none of it."

He placed himself by her side with legs spread and arms

crossed. "This little ploy won't work, Margaret. You're not being sensible."

The interest alone could feed the whole of Milton's deprived but she continued her resolve without faltering in her speech.

"Is it sensible to tell the woman you profess to love that because she has too much wealth that you'll not marry her? Usually it is the other way around. Therefore, I am giving away the majority of my wealth or should I say, symbolically burning it as I said I would." She glared at him and added, "Perhaps then there will be no hesitation when we speak of marriage."

John did not miss the moisture pooling in her eyes as she dropped her head to focus back on the paper. He laid his hand on her shoulder.

"Maggie, Love—"

"Please, John, I must ask you to leave me to my letters."

His hand dropped. "You do not want to talk about this?"

A faint sob sounded as she shook her head. He saw a tear fall on the paper, but she continued to write.

John's gut wrenched at the hurt he caused her. His hand flew up to rub his forehead of the dull ache that had been building. Strange and disquieting thoughts began to race through his mind.

A cold knot form in the pit of his stomach as he realized what he was doing; he was negotiating their future life together. It was an awaking experience that left him reeling. She was not a business acquaintance to make bargains with and draw up contracts to sign.

Was he punishing her for being wealthy; thereby, keeping both from happiness? Again, he could answer this question with a disconcerting 'yes'. The worse of it, he allowed the tainted memory of his dead father give reason to keep them apart. The admission was dredged from a place beyond logic and reason.

Margaret was right. He was still being that machine. What a hypocrite! It was pride. The same pride that he warned her not to accuse him of less than an hour ago.

Margaret heard his deep laughter sounding behind where he stood. A bevy of emotions, mostly hurt, expelled causing more tears to spill on the paper. Finding that her humiliation could not be alleviated, she rose from the chair and rushed towards the door to escape while choking back sobs.

A gasp of air released from her as John grabbed her around her stomach, forcing her back into his arms. Her hurt feelings turned to anger. Placing her hands on his chest, she tried to resist by pushing herself out of his hold.

"Stop struggling, Margaret, listen to me."

"No, I won't listen," she sobbed as she turned her head away.

"Ask me again, Miss Hale. I promise you, I'll answer as I should have the first time." He moved his hands to brace her arms to better control her attention. "Did you hear—hire me!"

At his loud exclaim she stilled, turning her head back to look at him while wiping her wet eyes clear with the sleeve of her blouse.

"John, do you mean it?" she breathlessly asked.

He nodded, pulling out his handkerchief out for her. "Give me a salary, Miss Hale. Be Milton's first female master. I will be your most devoted laborer." Lowering his head close, he added, "And I promise you that you do not need to fear a strike from me."

Margaret shook her head. "You were laughing at me."

"Is that what you thought I was doing?" When she did not answer he continued, "I wasn't laughing at you. I was laughing at what a fool I have been."

"Are you in earnest?"

Wiping a remnant of a tear from her cheek, he nodded. "You are the master of my heart. It is fitting that my mind and body should follow."

"And the letters to the bankers?"

"Where do I sign," he said smiling. Holding up one finger he added, "Only the amount that you initially wanted to invest. Pile it all into my lap. It will go to our future and that of others. In the meantime, my salary will satisfy any outstanding loans and perhaps, leave me enough to purchase my lass some pretty bouquets."

Relief washed over her face and a beautiful smile bloom. He press her back to his breast and felt her arms wrap around his waist.

"I didn't expect to start the pleading for forgiveness this early." He kissed the top of her head. "Forgive me, Maggie?"

"Yes, I forgive you, but you did say daily begging's," she mused.

"That I did," he said chuckling. "Does this mean that I am done for the day?"

"That has yet to be determined but be assured that the result will be the same. I will forgive you every time," she whispered, hugging her face to his vest, "except for the day you draw your last breath. I'll not forgive you for leaving me."

John thought the same about losing her. It tore at his insides thinking about it, causing his voice to break with huskiness, "Prepare yourself for that day, Love, for it is my intent to leave this earth before you."

He felt a disturbing quake in her serenity, which he soothed with reassurances that it was in his plan to live a full and long life complete with grey hair, rocking chair, and great grandchildren. Margaret's response was to tell him that she was in support of that plan wholeheartedly and would make sure he kept to it.

He pressed his lips to the top of her head, and tightened his hold on her. Contentment engulfed them both as they held each other, glad for the peaceful resolution of their conflict.

Not a day in, and their personalities were clashing, but he knew he would have it no other way. Margaret Hale was his Eve as sure as the Lord took one of his ribs and made her for him.

She moved her arms from around his waist to rest on his shoulders, her fingertips finding shelter in the tapering hair at the back of his head.

He was pleasantly conscious of where her flesh touched his no matter how slight. The day before, right about this time, he was traveling back to Milton, alone and dispirited, never imagining he would experience her in the manner as he was at that precise moment.

John looked down to see her lift her chin in readiness for a kiss. Feeling roguish, he did not take the bait.

"Now about that job, Miss Hale."

Feigning disappointment, she raised her eyes to his with a slight pout on her lips.

"Mr. Thornton, what of these gainful actions that you spoke of?"

It was in him to lift her up into the air and twirl her around for her answer, but he knew his mother would be returning so decorum had him cocking his head and regarding her with an amused grin.

"How could I've forgotten?"

Margaret raised herself higher and his grin turned into a broad smile as he descended to trail his mouth over her tear stained face eventually moving to her wanting lips. He kissed her until he sensed her false upset was gone.

"Satisfied?" She nodded her confirmation. "Now can we discuss getting the factory up and running again?"

Margaret rewarded him with an approving smile as she dropped one of her hands from around his neck to finger his coat's lapel.

"It is good that you are finally being reasonable, Mr. Thornton."

"Yes I agree, Miss Hale," he said dropping a peck on her forehead, "and I promise you that I will have you Mrs. Thornton within six months even if to keep me warm in my failures."

"I am sure that your mother was right, you'll grow my fortune," she said softly, "but part of re-humanizing you is to help you see that I do not need a fortune to be your wife and keep you warm at night."

John's eyes smoldered as he let out a big breath of air from his lungs at her reply. As if to prove her point, she pulled herself up and planted a soft, warm kiss on each of his eyelids.

He could not help the groan that rumbled in his throat, thinking how difficult it was going to be to survive on months of courtship and gentlemanly behavior. Thankfully, he would have plenty of work to keep his thoughts preoccupied. Clearing his throat, he focused on that subject.

"I will forever be grateful for second chances. So I'll ask again, for verification, if you'll take me on?"

She backed out of his embrace and crossed her arms before her displaying her best female version of authority.

"Although I have not had opportunity to interview you for your qualifications, I am confident that you are the man for the position." Dropping her arms and holding out her hand, she asked when he could start.

John grinned at the remembrance of the first time he took her hand at the annual dinner-party. That delicate first touch had delightfully haunted him for days.

He took her hand into his. "Immediately after you rip up that letter to Lennox."

"I can not."

"What!"

Walking over to the desk, she picked up the letter. "I wasn't going to send it but now that I am thinking about it, I want to help the families that may need it until the mill is up and running. I will still need Henry to see to it." He was about to say something when she piped in, "Oh not the whole amount of course. That would have been ridiculous."

John let out a masculine sigh of relief. He would never deny her need to be charitable. It would be like changing the current of a river.

"Margaret, trust me to get it done for you. Call it jealousy, but I don't want you writing to him."

"I understand."

As she tore up the letter, he saw an opening. "Lennox wanted to marry you."

"Right before we moved to Milton, he asked."

"In London?"

Limpid eyes lifted up. "I would have refused him," she

replied, "my heart was here with you."

He pulled her back into his arms unable to speak. After a moment, she lifted her head to address him.

"John, now that I know you have jealousies I will use it to my advantage in informing you that your salary will be offensively handsome."

Brow rising, he questioned, "And how is this going to provoke my jealousy?"

"If you dare refuse, I will drop you in an instant and find the most attractive overseer to take your place."

His deep laughter echoed in the room. Gently grasping her upper arms, he looked in her glowing face.

"Definitely using your womanly wiles on me."

"Now that I know I have them. Yes. Guilty as charged."

His eyes softened and drew her face within a breath of his. "What sort of punishment should I hand down for this guilty plea?"

"Once again, I am at the mercy of Milton's magistrate."

His hand reached up behind her head as he whispered on her lips, "Mercy? Not this time."

He took her mouth eagerly.

Hannah Thornton walked into the room; her eyes focused on the removal of her gloves. Sensing others present, she looked up to see her son and Miss Hale in a passionate embrace. Her audible sound of surprise broke the couple apart.

Miss Hale took shelter behind John's tall frame as he turned towards his mother. He must have seen displeasure etched in her expression because he countered with a severe look of caution.

She never received such a glare from him; he was always dotingly affectionate. She no longer had her son's devotion. The realization caused her gut to knot and stomach to sour.

"Afternoon, Mother."

Hannah knew that he would not tolerate incivility that she wanted to release. Nicety was the course she reluctantly had to take.

Moving closer to the pair, she returned his greeting as she casually finished removing her gloves.

"Hiding behind my son is not necessary, Miss Hale. Believe it or not, I experienced young love and know what goes on when lovers think they are alone." Seeing his approval she added, "The dressmaker will be here after hours."

Miss Hale stepped forward only to have John's nearest arm snake around her waist to draw her protectively to his side and guide her forward.

"I apologize for any inconvenience, Mrs. Thornton," she politely said.

Hannah waved her off nonchalantly. "No apologies needed. My son is clearly happy and that is all that matters. And you can dispense with the formal addresses. We cannot have that if you are living in this house."

"Oh, but I am not," she said while glancing up at him. "I know you meant for me to stay here but I will not put you out of your home. I wrote to Dixon to come and we'll stay in the house on Crampton."

John crossed his arms before him. "If you think that this is even an option, you would be wrong. I'll not have you stay there again."

She ignored his stern tone, stepped forward, and embraced her future mother-in-law warmly.

"Thank you for going to the dressmaker for me, Hannah. My late night return to Milton will have many asking questions that I am not yet prepared to answer."

"To be sure," she replied stiffly.

"I hope that you are not offended that I choose to not stay in your home until after we are married."

"Not at all."

Hannah meant what she said because that left John all to herself. Seeing his disappointed frown, she continued. "But do you see any wisdom of living on your own."

John quickly added, "This is not the South."

"I am aware of that but my mind is made up."

"So is mine," he asserted with governance.

This was further proof to her that Miss Hale was not for John. How dare she challenge him and go against his wishes!

Miss Hale turned to her. "If I could trespass on your hospitality until Dixon arrives and the house is made ready, I would be grateful."

"Of course you may."

His serious expression had Miss Hale putting her hand on his arm. "I'll be fine, John. Dixon is fiercely protective. A whole regiment could do no better."

"You'll not win this one, Margaret."

"The only way you'll have me staying in this house is by marrying me this day," she boldly proclaimed.

This day! Hannah paled as her mouth dropped open to protest but no words came out. She could only look to her son for his answer and rigidly prepare herself when he eagerly accepted her improper ultimatum.

"No, my unrelenting temptress, our vows will have to wait."

Hannah felt a flood of relief go throughout her system, but quickly resentment replaced the relief.

Stepping backwards, she felt invisible as the lovers became engrossed with each other. Her face withered with melancholy; it was thus happening. She could do nothing but fade into the background while her heart turned to ice, glaring contemptuously at the woman who monopolized her son's attentions.

Margaret's eyes sparkled with challenge. "Well then, shall I recruit Fanny to help with the new furniture I will need? Perhaps a piano that I may add to my short list of accomplishments," she said in amused defiance.

Leaning even closer John reemphasized, "You will be staying in this house."

"You forget yourself, Mr. Thornton, if not by your surname, it is to be Miss Hale as your employer. Do you not have a position to start?"

"Yes. Shall we take a walk to discuss my generous salary?"

"If that walk will lead us to Nicholas' door."

"It will. Furthermore, I'll persuade you that Fanny's old room has no need of new furniture."

"The Crampton's drawing-room will need repapering and the—"

John cut her off by taking her waist and drawing her nearer to him. "Fanny's taste in wall paper is impeccable; therefore, there is no need to replace it."

Exchanging a smile with him, she shook her head. "I cannot be swayed."

He moved in, teasing her mouth with his lips. "Let me show you that you can."

She released a soft sigh and he felt the tension in her body melt away. This persuaded him to take her lips fully.

Both were completely enraptured with each other causing everything surrounding them to disappear including the grave-looking Mrs. Thornton that stood steps away.

Hannah watched from the bedroom window as Miss Hale and her son walked down the street together with her arm hooked possessively around his. The happy couple was oblivious to the many turning heads, double takes, and curious stares from all sides.

John's face, animated with cheerful contentment, talked and pointed out things to her in the square. Respectfully, he tipped his hat to others and stopped acquaintances in greetings as they made their way to this Higgins' residence.

Her lips pursed in a tight frown. She never saw him this way before. Miss Hale was bewitching him into a total transformation, molding him to suit her idea of how a man should be—a weak minded, dutiful Southerner as her modest father was. She would make her son a shadow of his former self and take away the strong and steady man she raised.

Who was she to fight John on where she was to live and

undermine his authority? And what was this about her being his employer and giving him a salary? Ridiculous!

She no longer had reservations that Miss Hale was bending her son to her will with her prettied innocent act and converting him into a docile lap dog.

Earlier that morning, John informed her that he stopped to have notices posted of their engagement in the local and London newspapers. She hoped that she would have time to persuade him to delay the announcement.

Miss Hale's brazen attempt to get him to marry him this day spoke of her desire to get him for herself as soon as possible. She did not fool her. Once she had her son as her obedient husband, then she could weed the mother-in-law out and send her off to live with the daughter. The scheming woman was wasting no time and it struck her with anger and frustration that she could not stop her.

Hannah recoiled at John's subtle disregard and snubs. Her son would no longer be seeking his mother for attention and comfort. Miss Hale would get all of him while she would be left with loneliness and abandonment.

She did not deserve it! Not after all that she had done!

Her lip started to quiver and eyes squinted at the back of the woman who was taking her reason to live from her. A volcano of bitterness and resentment came boiling to the surface and she searched for a method for its release.

Picking up the first item within reach, she hurled the porcelain vase across the room shattering it against the wall with a deafening crash. ଓ

Chapter Eight
Dismantling the Machine

Bending down, Margaret placed the bouquet of wildflowers on Bessy's grave and stood in prayer for her lost friend. Struggling with the uncertainty and disquiet roused of late, she missed her trusted confidant more than ever.

In the thirteen weeks since her return to Milton, much had happened; the main activity focused on Marlborough Mill becoming productive once again.

Revitalized by the challenges, John seemed to work endlessly which caused her to fear for his health. She saw signs that the long hours were taking its toll. Speaking of her apprehension on one of their walks, he easily dismissed her concern saying it would be different after they became husband and wife.

His perfunctory work ethics and unbendable tenacity had the factory's recovery progressing at an astounding rate, but she did not see any indicators of him altering his routine. Her anxiety for his welfare soon turned into exasperation with his obvious lack of care for his own well-being.

Having no success influencing her son, Margaret appealed to Hannah to convince him to slow down and rest. Her reply was snappish, telling her she would most certainly not and that John thrived on the mental stimulation and a demanding schedule. She followed with the proud declaration that her son would never be a man of idleness and leisure.

Margaret expected this sort of response from her. This was not a one-time incident of Mrs. Thornton's unpleasantness. It was happening often and she soon became unhappy at the Thornton house because of it.

Each day brought regret in allowing John to "sway" her away from her resolve to stay in the Crampton house. Most days she would have gladly dealt with the haunting ghosts of her dearly departed than the flesh and blood that made up the indomitable Mrs. Thornton.

Margaret remained passive and courteous for John's sake but the woman tested her on many occasions. Not forgetting the abusive husband, compassion had her biting her tongue, turning on her heel and walking away. However, holding her temper was increasingly becoming a challenge as Mrs. Thornton's incivility grew. She knew it meant a great deal to John that they both get along. She was determined to preserve the peace and save him from any further apprehension.

To meet that end, for Margaret, the purposeful act of avoidance became necessary whenever possible but Hannah seemed to seek out and monitor her every move. It became suspicious that the majority of outings to see John been conveniently redirected under some pretext by his mother. She found it disconcerting that Hannah would purposefully find every opportunity to keep John out of reach from her, but the growing evidence was suggesting that was exactly what was happening.

And all the time there she is, looking down on us like a great black angry crow guarding the nest. As if I were to ever consider her son as a suitor.

Fathers and daughters. Mothers and sons. So may be we shouldn't be too hard on old battleaxe Thornton.

Bessy's words kept her from speaking her mind, but time spent alone with John was only a fraction of what it was in those first weeks back in Milton. He seemed too easily distracted lately to be mindful of her and she became increasingly resentful. This troubled her deeply.

The seeds of discord grew that his work became more

important than his future wife. Her confidence began to wane and it was that kind of thinking that alarmed her. She feared that his mother would win this duel for she had no one to act as her second, not even John.

The only redeeming grace was becoming his wife. Margaret believed that once they were married, Hannah would be resolved to accept her and John would rededicate himself to becoming husband and family man.

That belief shattered to pieces when Mrs. Thornton convinced her son to take on the failing Hamper's Mill.

It had been poor management and a crooked overseer that resulted in Hamper's lowly financial state. It had not been because of the strike as most assumed.

Once the news spread that, the distant owner, Mr. Hamper, was at the point of selling the mill; Mrs. Thornton took it upon herself to correspond directly to instigate a business proposal on taking on John as master and vested partner. Mrs. Thornton gave the owner every assurance that capital was available and that her son would restore his mill to profitability.

If he had been angry for his mother's unsolicited application, John gave no indication except to say that he was not interested in the opportunity even with its possibilities. With persistent doggedness, Hannah soon influenced him to accept saying that it would help him expedite his overall objectives and further secure the future of his children.

Only after the signing of the contracts and handshakes exchanged, was Margaret to learn what had transpired that noonday behind closed doors. At that night's dinner table, John requested the serving of champagne and when she asked what the occasion was, he proudly informed her of the sealed merger.

As mother and son drank in celebration, she felt the nauseating sinking of despair. She masked her hurt and inner turmoil with a deceptive calmness, while they talked casually about the new undertaking.

She quickly loss her appetite and toyed with the food on her plate. John took notice, placing his hand over hers, asked if she was unwell. Finding inner control, she calmly inquired why she had not been included in a decision that clearly involved her.

Hannah quickly piped in, taking on the false air of polite authority, saying that there will be little change. Her stare drilled into Margaret, testing her nerves, as the mother continued to patronize her by coolly stating that *they* did not want to trouble her with tiresome business dealings that she was not likely to understand.

Only her ears heard the defiance in Hannah's tone and the subtle challenge to dare speak against her. Margaret's annoyance increased when she found that her hands were shaking. Unwilling to expose herself further to Mrs. Thornton's well disguised condescension, she excused herself from the table professing a headache.

John caught her at the stairwell, leading her to the drawing-room, and sitting her down. He then pulled up a chair in front of her for him to sit. Taking both hands into his, he spoke of his sincere regrets of not informing her. He explained that he had to act quickly; a buyer from the Americas made an offer to purchase the mill outright and he could not allow such a lucrative opportunity to get away. Lifting her intertwined fingers to his lips, he promised that he would be sure to discuss any future decisions with her that would involve their future.

Margaret turned away to hide the tears that she felt were bordering her eyes. John turned her head back to face him, seeing the sadness he pulled her onto his lap and sheltered her in his arms. His soothing voice and probing stare had her speaking the other reason behind the tears, telling him how unhappy she was about the extra hours he will have to dedicate to the mill.

His answer was to pacify her as if she was a little girl, with sweetened assurances and coddling. Feeling defeated, she obediently accepted his justifications. The ink of the signatures had dried, rendering her helpless to alter history. Starting a quarrel with him was not going to change him being master over Hamper's.

A few days later, Margaret learned the details of Hannah's part in bringing the merger to fruition. Fanny was, if anything, highly informative. She relayed to her future sister-in-law how it was all her mother's doing and that she pressed John into taking the partnership when it was in his mind to reject the idea. Temper flared, she did not delay in locating the mother to voice her displeasure.

Hannah responded sharply, informing her that what she had done was for the good of the Thornton name. Margaret endeavored to try once more for peace between them, but she responded with tightly pursed lips, a severe glare and crossed arms, which silently accused her of being a pouting child that should be ignored.

Giving in to the tension and animosity, she rushed to the security of her room. Feeling like an outsider, she angrily cried out her frustration at the growing resentment towards Hannah. She wanted to seek comfort in John's arms but she feared all that she might say about his mother to whom he loved and trusted completely. Margaret fought an emotional battle not to allow the bitterness towards Hannah to overwhelm her.

After a few weeks, it became clear that she won that battle but was losing the war. Now that John was master of two factories, as anticipated, she found him missing walks, dinners, and time with her. She began to think that she was only an appointment on his work schedule.

Another disagreeable aspect of John's absence was that she could barely tolerate dining alone with Hannah. She tried to engage her in pleasant conversation but she received icy replies and obvious disinterest.

Hannah masterfully hid her dislike of her when John was present; she became a picture of a warm and attentive motherly figure. Her deceptive behavior wounded Margaret deeply. She thought to tell John but felt strongly that she could not burden him further, and sadly, his partiality would have it that he would most likely not believe his mother could be that way. Any words spoken would bring about conflict and she wanted to avoid it.

It would be different after John and she were married.

Margaret's only course of action was to pray that Hannah would open her heart to accept her. In the meantime, the opposition in the residence between the two women kept on growing thick and prickly.

John remained oblivious to it all.

Bending down she removed some twigs and leaves from her friend's grave. "Oh Bessy, what advice would you give to me?"

John was now ever mindful of the welfare of his laborers and softened a great deal in that regard. But when it came to remembering that he had an obligation to her, Margaret was at her wit's end.

Was she going to allow the mills became first priority in his life and put him into an early grave? He would be mistaken to believe she would allow it, but what power did she have to bring about a change?

Rising she turned to the sound of children's laughter. Young boys were playing near the canal that ran through the town. The smallest boy reminded her of Tommy, one of the Boucher orphans.

Thomas often was left with Mary in the re-established dining hall after his afternoon lessons. He would sit quietly in the corner, reading and practicing his letters on the chalk tablet.

John spoke often of the boy and admired how smart he was for such a young chap. Margaret thought that he appreciated that Tommy was not a bit frightened of him who dominated menacingly over his laborers.

The shy boy would often move to sit next to him when he came into the hall to sup. John's face always lighted with the boy's approach. It was certainly a huge contrast to see the tall, daunting man-figure grinning down at the scrawny boy, confidently by his side.

Witnessing him with Thomas was always heartening. Soon the lad would be old enough to go to work on the floor but she had a distinct feeling that John would derail that for a time if he could. He had taken a great interest in the boy, becoming a surrogate uncle of sorts.

It was one particular early afternoon, as she was sitting by the window sketching some of the activity out in the square, when she was surprise to see John enter the residence with Thomas in tow. He gave her a passing nod of greeting and led the boy to the direction of his sanctum. Curious, she could not help but rise and follow right behind.

Margaret understood the purpose when she heard the little boy let out a gasp at the number of books in the large room. The study could have easily been accepted as a formable library because of John's lifelong passion for the written word. True, the room had a looked of disorganization, but he seem to know exactly where each book rested.

The shelves were crammed with titles and piles were stacked all around covering any table space and cluttering up corners. She heard maids grumbling at the maze they had to meddle through to bring about a good dusting. John loved his literary corner of the world, and it looked like he now had a little friend to share it with.

She watched with pleasure at John's satisfaction in sharing his vast collection with the young reader. Little Thomas stood wide-eyed with mouth agape as the tall, dark-suited man reach up and pulled an array of novels. Soon the boy held a mountain as big as his obvious, surmounting delight.

Margaret went over to help with his load. Bending down to his level, she asked which book he was going to read first. Eyes sparkling with excitement, he breathlessly mouthed that he was going to read the one about the big white fish.

John's eyebrows drew in and he frowned at the boy saying that he was disappointed that he wasn't going to read Foster's excellent publication on the industrial revolution and the factory system.

Tommy's expression went from animated pleasure to one of shamed uneasiness for not choosing the title. Her eyes pleaded on behalf of the boy knowing that he would not understand his way of teasing. John's face relaxed into a grin and tousled Tommy's hair letting him know that book was for Higgins and that he did not have to read it, adding after a slight pause the word "yet".

Rewarding him with a light smile, she raised her hand to him, and he took hold, helping her up to stand by his side. John explained that he learned from Mary that the child was reading the same worn books for weeks, which were perceived by him to be mind-numbingly dull for a boy his age. He needed adventure and intrigue to promote his love of reading. Margaret rose up on her toes to place a light peck on his cheek. He given her a glimpse of the good father he would become to their children.

As they escorted the boy out of the room, Hannah was descending the stairway. Margaret did not miss her reaction to seeing the impoverish boy within the residence. It was unsympathetic to say the least. John briefly spoke to his mother and gave Margaret a fleeting kiss before taking his leave with the book-laden child.

Hannah spoke what was really on her mind saying under her breath that John should have noted the titles, because whether by ruin or trade, he would surely never see the books again. There could be no mistaken her views on the lower class.

Margaret thought this to be surprising because, as John had said before, they had lived in poverty for some years. Had Hannah forgotten what it was like as well?

Margaret quickly dismissed it because she found it was more disturbing that she had to fight feelings of envy for the little boy. It seemed that little Tommy had more of John's time than her.

Turning her attention back to the gravesite, Margaret found herself speaking her thoughts, "Bess, you would be proud of how well all six are doing under Nicholas' care. And Mary, such a young mother, she dotes on them all."

For all the Higgins' struggles and hard work, they managed to keep all the children healthy and educated. They had been able to move into a larger residence but they were still in the unsavory part of Princeton. Even with John making Higgins overseer of Hamper's, Nicholas still could not make enough to move his mob to a better location or buy the small indulgences, such as books.

She would love to see her dear friend's family settled in a larger home outside of that part of Milton. Nicholas would never accept any charity from her. Perhaps she could convince John to—

Her mouth dropped, as heavily lashed lids flew up.

"Bessy, what an idea I just had!"

She pondered the inspiration over in her head and within a few minutes she knew with pulse-pounding certainty, this was the answer.

"Not only is this going to help Nicholas, Bessy," she said, smiling ruefully, "it's going to stop the old battleaxe from turning her son back into a machine."

Bessy would have gotten a good laugh out of that ungenerous remark from her. Her friend would have further warned that her Mr. Thornton was not going to appreciate what she was about to do, but she was determined. Like it or not, Hannah's son would not be master this day. She would be taking on that role.

Reaching out she touched the grave marker. "Thank you Bessy." Hitching up her skirt, Margaret walked in the direction of Hamper's Mill.

The loud steady rhythm of machines and delicate rain of cottony snow engulfed John as he stepped out from his office. Turning his head purposefully, he surveyed the rows of working machines and the operators with a critical eye.

Motioning to Williams, he pointed to one of the laborers who seemed to be having trouble with his loom, directing him to see to it. Williams took to the stairs.

Satisfaction overruled his exhaustion as he gazed out over the vast space. His hard work was reaching reward, coming to that point in time where Marlborough Mill was fully functioning and soon to be profiting. The disastrous strike had been historically filed away and forgotten.

With his duel salary and resources aplenty, everything was

righting itself smoothly and quickly. Margaret had been right. He allowed his arrogance and pride make unreasonable decisions. Because of her, he was discovering the many flaws in his thinking and character.

Like her father, Margaret had lessons to give out. The subjects had changed from literary discussions to life alternating renovations. He was grateful that he received the rare opportunity to go through such a transformation.

The same premise could apply to the two mills. Under Thornton's management, with the more-than-fair wages, improved working conditions, and luncheon halls, both mills upheld the reputation throughout the industry as the prime places to work.

John knew that he reached a completely new level of success when Higgins told him that he overheard workers boast proudly about working at one of the mills. Men and women alike, often came in the defense of their master, showing respect and gratitude. He was stunned.

When he told Margaret, she said that he would find that happy workers were much easier to rule over than intimidated ones. It troubled him that he did not recognize that fact. For years, he believed the opposite; that fear of repercussions made better laborers.

It did not occur to him that earning his workers respect may amount to anything, but the proof was right before him—Nicholas and Mary Higgins. Respect built the foundation of solid friendships and unwavering loyalty, both of which, he now valued far beyond any monetary amount.

He asked Margaret how he could have been so sightless and unfeeling. She answered by kissing his lower jaw and allowing her soft lips to linger on his skin. Finishing, she broke into a wide, open smile, confirming simply that he was getting warmer.

Her perfect answer compelled him to nuzzle her own warm skin, huskily asking where he would be without her. Margaret's answer was plain but emphatically true—as unhappy as she would be without him.

As he was in the process of going through a renovation by

his Maggie, he was doing the same to Hamper's Mill. The factory's location would allow for expansion. Plans were all ready being made to make the mill bigger, better, and more productive. He wanted to ensure that its doors would remain open under his watch. His mother had been right; taking on another mill would allow him to reach his ultimate goal—Margaret and their life together.

Exactly as his thoughts turned to his future wife, he caught from the corner of his eye the woman herself walking his way with Higgins following right behind. As his eyes followed her approach, he could not help the feeling of humility well up inside. He still could not believe she was to be his.

Normally she would look up at him and give him one of her light, beautiful smiles but this time, he saw determination etched on her face. He chose to ignore it thinking there was another glitch in the wedding plans she wanted to discuss with him. But, if it was about the wedding, why was Higgins following behind?

Margaret reached the stairway, hitching up her skirt, she began to make her way up to where John was standing.

His eyes trailed off her and refocused on the man following behind. "Higgins, why aren't you back at the mill? Who is overseeing the place?"

Glancing up at his master, Higgins shrugged his shoulders. "She pulled me off not giving a reason. I left Johnston to look after things. He's capable enough."

Margaret pulled him off! His temper sparked but seeing her approach he found his curiosity was feeding the spark more, as well as, her beautiful face. Reaching his side, he gave her a questioning look.

"What is this all about?" he asked.

"Let us go and talk privately in your office, John. Nicholas, could you please wait here until we call you in."

"Yes, miss." Higgins looked at his master for further approval and John's nod gave it.

Putting his hand on the small of her back, he directed her into his office, shutting the door behind him.

He did not waste any time. "Now, Maggie, why did you pull Higgins off?"

"I am sure you are not aware of this, John, but you now call me Maggie when you feel you are speaking to a child. Please stop addressing me in that way," she said in a disapproving voice. "As for Nicholas, as the employer paying the wages, including yours, I didn't think I needed your permission to ask for a meeting."

John was momentarily speechless in his surprise. It was the first time she titled herself as the employer and set him apart as the hired help. As for the name, she never indicated she was displeased with it before. Was he being condescending?

"I didn't know you found the name offensive."

"It is not…what I mean is, not until recently. I disliked it when Frederick babied me with its use as a little girl. It pleased me to have you addressing me in such a way. But then," her eyes lifted to his, "you began to sound like Frederick."

He took the steps to her side and took up her hand into his. "I have not one trace of brotherly affection for you."

"I am glad to hear it."

"I will call you Maggie when I am confident you are not comparing me to your brother or as one of your workers," he said while brushing his lips lightly across hers, anticipating a return response, but she did the opposite and pulled away.

"John, I never thought of you as one of my workers until this day. Right now I need the respect as your employer and not the affection of a man."

It was true. Margaret never treated him as a subordinate. She had total and complete trust in him and never mentioned the use of her money even when the investment into Hamper's occurred. She voiced her displeasure in him taking on more work but not the spending part.

John found that over the course of the few months, her opinions and input on certain business matters brought up during conversations were intelligent and welcomed. It pleased him that she took an interest in the functioning of the factory.

When the problematic issue of production slowing during the later hours when the laborers were eager for the quitting horn, she suggested starting a monthly, motivational recompense for those who produce the highest yardage. Hannah argued that keeping track of such nonsense would cause more headaches than a solution, but John gave it a trial run and production went up significantly with little trouble.

With Margaret standing before him in all seriousness, asking for equal treatment, he decided she deserved that much from him. Crossing his arms before him, he nodded once in polite acknowledgement of her request.

"Miss Hale, you have the floor. Why, Higgins?"

"He is getting a promotion," she declared in an even voice.

"What sort of promotion?"

"Of becoming a master. John, I want you to apprentice Nicholas and after we are wed he can take over Hamper's."

"And, Miss Hale, what justifies Higgins getting this rather generous advancement?"

"Because it is good practical business sense and he is the best man for it. You cannot do it all alone John."

"Is that the only reason you want him to be master, because you don't think I can handle it?"

"No, you misunderstand me. To be sure, you can handle it but it is what you'll be sacrificing if you continue."

"I told you, Margaret, that things will change."

"When you told me that you had one mill. Now there are two," she said adamantly. "Nothing is going to change."

"You don't believe me?"

"No, I do not. You will enjoy the newness of having a wife for a period but our time will become less as the mills become more demanding."

"That is not possible."

"How can it possibly be avoided?"

"I have told you it would not be that way," he said slowly with angry undertones.

Not in the least intimidated, she crossed her arms to mirror his stance as invisible fiery sparks flew between them.

"I want this and will not bend. I am sorry for the ultimatum, but if you don't agree, your stake in Hamper's will be sold to the first reasonable offer," she spoke in an unfaltering voice. "I prefer that Nicholas get the living. You told me that he was the measure of a man you like to be, well, he deserves this and I hoped that you would agree."

"Are you sure this idea isn't in retaliation because I took my mother's advice?" he accused harshly.

John heard her quick intake of breath and her face turn pale.

"How could you suggest I could ever…"

Her voice trailed off as she bowed her head to hide the hurt that had been written on her face. He instantly regretted and grabbed her upper arms.

"Margaret, I was angry. Understand that I am not accustomed to a woman telling me what to do."

"Woman meaning me but not your mother. I naturally have no say."

"Of course you have a say!"

She twisted out of his grip and took a few steps back from him. "I tell you, I do not and that changes this day. I will not be dismissed so easily."

John rubbed his forehead to help ease the strain that was developing on top of his fatigue. He still was trying to ascertain the best method to manage his determined lady when her voice sounded. Her stringent tone immediately caused him to drop his arm to focus his attention back on her.

"If you are going to accuse me of anything let it be for the selfish want for you. Seeing you and being near you for a few moments in the day is not enough for me, John. Do you understand how difficult it is to battle for time with your two mistresses?"

Mistresses! He groaned at the comparison she made. Could she actually see him as being unfaithful? It had been his belief that he needed her more; life without her would be misery. It never occurred to him that she might feel the same about him.

"Margaret—"

"No. Stay back, John, until I finish."

John stilled. He had seen her like this the day she refused him when she called him "ungentlemanly" and turned away from him. The tempered plea, although barely controlled but contained, had more impact on him than an angry crowd.

"I have stood silent long enough. You not only address me like a child but you pacify me like one as well. If you will not listen to me on a personal level, I will have to address this on a business level. That seems to be the only way to get through to you," she said fervently. "I'll not have my husband and father of our children run himself into the ground!"

Embarrassed by the emotional outcry, Margaret turned her body away from him. John responded by taking her shoulders and turning her back to face him.

"How long have you felt this way?" he asked.

"A long time," she answered meekly. "I tried to tell you but you didn't listen, and often dismissed me and my concerns."

His eyebrows drew in, recounting events and thinking about those attempts. He found himself inexplicably dissatisfied with his own treatment of her, and recognized how time spent together had been shortened. Humbled, he could not find words to speak. He was too ashamed.

Margaret suddenly broke from him and went to the window to look out. He sensed that there was more that she wanted to say.

"John, I hope you'll allow me to speak on a more personal matter. It may be painful for you to hear."

"You have my full attention."

Turning her face towards him she spoke, "It is about your mother. She is coming between us. I can see that she well-nigh did with this conversation and your accusation."

"Margaret, I was wrong in saying that, my ego had been wounded, and I acted out."

"I know your temper. I thought I was prepared for it but you took me by surprise. I wasn't going to speak about your mother but now I see that I should," she said. "We can discuss your ego when you initiate your daily ritual of seeking forgiveness."

This brought a hint of a grin to his bleak expression. "Then perhaps, I should include a noonday begging session."

She walked over to stand in front of him. "Pen me in on your calendar, Mr. Thornton. I would gratefully agree to see you in whatever way that is made available to me."

"I didn't realize I was…"

The start of his apology trailed off. His hand went to the back of his neck to massage out the increasing annoyance he was feeling about himself. Margaret's reassuring grip on his arm prompted him to proceed with a better evaluation.

"What I mean is that I got caught up in things and never wanted you to feel like an appointment I have to keep. It is frightening to me that I was unknowingly the cause of us being apart."

"John—"

"More frightening is that I missed you as well, but continued on," he involuntarily interrupted with his rising ire.

"You have years of habits and ways of thinking to overcome, and still searching for that warm-blooded human-being," she said in a soothing voice. "You'll find him. I'll make sure of it."

He could only nod as she kissed his cheek. Her faith in him was what he needed to hear. As she trusted him completely with her finances, he completely trusted her in the healing of his mind and spirit. She had thus far renewed his heart and made his happiness.

Remembering her personal matter, he bent his head to level his eyes with hers.

"Now, what is this about my mother coming between us?"

"John, Dixon and I will be moving back to the Crampton house. I can no longer be in the same house with your mother." ଓ

Chapter Nine
True Vision & True Blindness

"What is this? I thought you two were getting along."

Margaret sadly shook her head. "I didn't want to trouble you and believed that with time things would improve but it has not. It is much worse."

"Worse!"

"John, this is going to come as a shock to you but she is barely civil towards me when we are in the same room." Margaret drew in and released a quick breath for courage, knowing that what she said next would be a severe accusation. "She treats me with blatant disregard, but when you are present it is an entirely different story."

Dumbstruck and confused, he wandered restlessly around the room stopping suddenly to ask her what she meant by her being treated differently.

Margaret proceeded to give him instances whereon his mother's countenance towards her would abruptly convert from politeness to incivility the moment he stepped out of the picture.

"I wouldn't blame you if you didn't believe me, but I have done nothing to provoke such conduct."

He blinked in disbelief. "And this has been happening all along?"

"Subtly at first but when she realized that I would not run off to you, she got emboldened. It was only within the last weeks, after the deal with Mr. Hamper, that it became unbearable."

"Weeks! You should have told me!"

"I am sorry, John. I thought I could…if Dixon and I were to live separate, I am sure all will be well until the wedding."

He could not wrap his mind around what she was telling him. He had to find further confirmation.

"So, this isn't only about Hamper's," he asked, "it was happening before?"

She nodded without speaking. He saw that she was ill at ease and hesitated to continue, not wanting to cause him further injury.

"Margaret, I need to hear it."

Tilting her head back, she peered in his face. "I am sure it is unconsciously done but she has come between us in other ways."

His mind worked, and it did not take long for it to dawn on him.

"The planning of the wedding."

"And the property outside of Milton."

"How did you know?" he exclaimed.

"Fanny."

John groaned and turned away from her. He had spoken to Fanny's husband, Watson, about the property in a private conversation and either he told his wife or she overheard. If he were gambling, his bet would have been on the latter.

"Fanny in her own unique way divulged that you were considering its purchase. She believed that since Hannah convinced you not to take it she could freely disclose your intentions."

"It was to be my wedding gift to you," he said dejectedly as he moved closer to her.

"It doesn't matter where the door is as long as it is you who steps through it back to me each day."

"That is not good enough for me to accept." John's finger moved a stray tendril behind her ear, resting his hand on her shoulder. "I'll see to your happiness on every level, and in this it seems I am failing."

"John, I am happy."

His eyes locked on hers. "Then we wouldn't be having this discussion now, would we?"

Margaret's head turned to the side with eyes lowering to the floor, acknowledging the truth in his statement.

"What did Fanny tell you?"

She must have sensed his building indignation and frustration. Quickly, she tried to defuse his coming storm by giving him a comical look and speaking in a lighthearted voice.

"That I should be glad for the escape. She believed it to be in the wilderness with uncultured heathens and the cottage, in all probability, will be dirty and uninhabitable. She assured me that she would have never stepped foot in it."

His humor did not improve.

"Did she tell you how my mother easily swayed me to give it up?" he asked sarcastically. Running his fingers in his hair, he turned and then slammed his fist on the desk in anger.

Margaret startled, gripped his arm to steady herself, and lifted her eyes to his imploringly.

"John, please stop, I'm sorry I spoke of it."

"No! I needed this slap in the face to wake me up."

"I wanted only to give a disapproving look," she said sullenly. "It will right itself once I move."

"And forget what she had done to you!" he rumbled, rejecting her want to be forgiving. "I cannot do that!"

A tense silence enveloped the room. Suddenly uncomfortable, John moved to the end of his desk. After a moment, he glanced over towards Margaret, and immediately rushed back to her side.

Clutching the back of a chair for support—she was swaying with hand to her brow—visibly unsteady on her feet. His arms caught her falling weight and helped her to sit down.

Concerned, he bent down on one knee to examine her more closely. Seeing the tragic expression on her face caused his warring emotions to evaporate. So disgusted with himself and his mother, he did not realize how his anger was affecting her.

He knew how his mother felt about her going in, and this only accounted further to Margaret's believability. Once again, she was showing him the light and this time what it revealed was painful and ugly. He wished only she had confided in him sooner.

He looked to sooth her and brought about a switch where he sat in the chair and she was secured on his lap. His palm smoothed over her face, trailing back over her hair to the back of her head, holding her until her episode had run its course. Kissing near her ear, he spoke.

"This time, Love, no look would have gotten through my thick wall. The bigger blow had been necessary." Thinking of her regret for telling him, he added in a lighter tone, "Coming from you it softened the impact considerably."

It did not lessen him feeling like a fool. In his heart, he knew that Margaret would have loved that property.

When John went out to view the land and cottage, the feel of the South and Helstone came to mind. He could see Margaret happily situated in every corner, and him standing right by her side in that happiness, complete with wild roses, a patch of woods and a tranquil stream running through it.

The cottage was not dirty as Fanny might have imagined it to be. It was well kept, perfectly furnished, large, and comfortable with much character inside and out. He had liked it instantly and certain she would have as well.

Not as spacious as the grand house in Milton, the cottage had the missing charm which compensated, and with Margaret mistress of it, he was certain that love, warmth, and eventually, laughing children would fill the rooms. He never believed he could be happy in the country but since Helstone and Margaret, he knew he had been wrong in that assumption.

Walking the property, the fresh air invigorated him and the multiple birds' unstructured symphony was a sweet melody to his hardened ears. He even found a secluded, picturesque spot where he imagined taking his Maggie for a picnic, visualizing their lovemaking under the shade of the trees.

Stepping up into the carriage to return to Milton, his mind was set on its purchase. That night, after Margaret retired, he spoke to his mother about his decision. There were no misgivings that she would be supportive. He had been wrong.

How cleverly she planted doubt and convinced him to let the property go. First, she said that it was too far out. He waved off this saying that it was less than an hour away on easy roads. She reinforced her reasoning implying that leaving Margaret secluded and alone out where he could not get to her quickly was not responsible or sensible.

He countered with his assumption that she would live there as well. Hannah told her son that she would not want to live far from Fanny and sedately situated away from Milton. The dullness of life would oppress her.

While his mother had valid reasons that raised concern, he could not completely decide against purchasing the property. Until she emphasized how much her future daughter-in-law had come to mean to her.

He had believed her.

She pleaded for him not to deprive her of Margaret's companionship and put distance between any grandchildren in her golden years. The final blow was to remind him that she never asked him for anything before and begged not to deny her this request.

How could he possibly tell her no?

Such a deception!

John's jaw clenched and his eyes slightly narrowed thinking on how well his own mother played him. He let out a repressed groan for not seeing through her manipulations.

"John?"

Looking into her compassion-filled eyes he let out a sigh of resignation, "I believe you, Maggie. I'll not keep you from moving out."

"I tried so hard and for so long," she said soberly. "I cannot do it any longer when she takes every opportunity to keep us from moving forward with our future."

She did not need to say any more—the wedding. Reflecting back, in nearly every instance of change and misunderstanding regarding the planning he heard his mother's voice speaking not Margaret's, who always stood in the background, silent. His mother was purposefully stalling the event.

"You have the forbearance of a saint," he said, kissing her tenderly on her mouth, "but I am appreciative that you aren't wholly converted."

John was gratified to see a soft and loving curve form on her lips, and feel her palm slide along his jaw line. Then he balked with a sudden remembrance, siphoning the color from his face.

The wedding dress.

John knew how excited Margaret was to wear her mother's wedding dress. Since her parents were gone, wearing the dress had even more meaning for her; it was like having her mother present in some small way.

During one of their walks, she narrated that when she was eight years of age, right before leaving to live with her aunt, Maria Hale pulled the dress out of the keepsake chest for her daughter to admire.

Smoothing the lacy material, her mother recounted the romantic history of her husband's pursuit. She believed her mother over-romanticized a bit but the story had her sighing longingly for such a romance for herself. That was when mother had held her daughter's face lovingly close; speaking with such strong conviction that God would deliver the one man on earth for her. In him, she will find love and happiness as she deserved.

Margaret believed with all her heart and asked for the honor of wearing the wedding dress. With eyes moist with unshed tears, Maria answered that nothing would please her more.

Seven years later, being home for the summer months, Margaret pulled the dress out and this time tried it on. A little long but the transformation had its effect. It was the first time she truly seen herself as pretty.

John interrupted by scoffing, saying that any man alive would not use such a simple word to describe such a beautiful lass. He certainly did not. This earned him a quick kiss from her on his cheek.

His compliment added to her lightheartedness as they walked. She demonstrated how she dramatically paraded around the bedroom pretending it was her wedding day, dancing with an imaginary groom, around and around.

She was enchanting acting out the memory for him. It transformed the grown woman into a graceful, moonlit fairy. Grinning widely as she waltzed with the imaginary groom, he politely asked the invisible man if he could steal the bride. Receiving permission, he took her hand, wrapped his arm around her waist, and danced.

It was their first dance together. The nightly symphony of insects and stars replaced the musical instruments and crystal chandeliers. Margaret's eyes sparkled with exuberance and his with high spirits. There they danced on the secluded pathway; he twirled her around and out and then back, her gentle laughter rang beautifully in his ears. When they reached a more public part of the path the dance ended bringing both back to a more subdued merriment as their pace returned to a slow stroll.

John took her arm and wrapped it around his asking why not pretend walking down the aisle to her awaiting groom. She answered that the room was not big enough to get the desired results of doing the wedding march down a long isle. He laughed heartily at this assuring her that he will make sure he found the longest isle for her to walk down for their wedding. Margaret shook her head saying that she waited long enough and now desired the shortest isle, adding that her young girl ideals have long since been simplified.

He could not fault this logic and it was at that time that they set the official date, which later, had changed mainly due to his mother's interference.

Now the question of what exactly happened to the wedding dress loomed regretfully before him. Could his mother be a part of its ruination?

John recalled how heartbroken Margaret had been when the dress was accidently soiled beyond restoration. Was it an accident? At the time, he had reservations but he never for an instant considered his mother would do something that vindictive.

Dixon brought the dress over when she arrived to Milton and hung it in a spare room awaiting alterations. She took it out of the box in pristine condition, but when the dressmaker came, an unmanageable amount of dark stains had been discovered over the front of the dress.

Margaret dismissed it as an unfortunate mishap. She had everyone fooled until he found her crying that night. It tore at his insides to see her in tears. He wanted desperately to shield her from every hurt. As he comforted her in his arms, he secretly planned to personally investigate on who could have done this.

His mother told him that she was certain that one of the house staff admiring the dress inadvertently handled it with dirtied hands. It seemed plausible but to John, the amount of soiled material went beyond an absentminded servant with dirty hands.

When questioned, all the staff stayed adamant that they did not know about the dress or go into that particular room. It could not have been Dixon; she handled the dress as if it was the most precious piece of clothing on the earth. Margaret and he were innocent which left only one person left. Even then, he believed it was unfathomable that his mother could have purposely hurt her in such a way.

John's determination was that it must have been one of the factory workers. From time to time, individuals entered the residence to speak to him during their off hours. Waiting unattended was not uncommon. The person must have stolen into the room and fingered the lace and silk while admiring it. Thus concluded, he ended his inquiry and turned his attentions to his wounded bride-to-be.

Shockwaves shot through John at the thought of his mother being that malicious. With Margaret informing him about his own blindness to his mother's disregard towards her, he may have to deal with this inconceivable reality. He wished he pursued the investigation of the dress further, learning the truth and sparing Margaret the weeks of spitefulness after.

John tightened his hold on her. "It is true what is said about true blindness comes to those who think they see the clearest," he spoke hoarsely with emotion, "I didn't want to see but now my eyes have been opened."

"I really believe she doesn't know what she is doing, and I understand why she does it."

"There is no excuse to justify what she has done."

"You are all that she has and I am taking you from her. Please try to—"

"No excuse, Margaret."

His mother knew exactly what she was doing. She was selfishly causing harm to the one person that was the breath in him. Injuring her was striking at him. It was wrong in every sense yet Margaret was trying to paint her in a better light to ease his growing guilt in the matter. John's mood darkened as his mother's voice replayed in his mind.

I'm sure she will take you from me. I hate her. I've tried not to; when I thought she would make you happy. And if you won't hate her, then I must.

He did not take her harsh words seriously at the time but now he thought that perhaps he should have. It was becoming apparent that his mother was not willing to give Margaret an opportunity to redeem herself, and was fixated on keeping him as close as possible.

It pained him to believe that his mother would actually plot to come between Margaret and himself. With eyes wide open, John relived past events where his mother interfered in the planning of his life. Not only with Margaret, but before the Hale's moved to Milton.

He could forgive her interference before—such as it involved no one but himself, but with Margaret installed in his life, he could not be lenient in his forgiveness. His mother meant to cling to him and slowly push Margaret into the background and possibly out of his life. That was beyond unacceptable.

As much as he held himself responsible for falling for his mother's subtle deceptions, he found that for the first time in his life he was furiously angry with her. She did not want his happiness; she wanted only hers, and he was her happiness.

Margaret turned his face to her and spoke quickly, "John, don't. She loves you very much. Don't be too harsh on her."

"That kind of love I can do without," he said sharply. "She doesn't deserve your kindness. I refuse to let you give it!"

Her head dropped and he could feel her trembling with welling emotions. He fought to control his indignation. Taking a calming deep breath, he broached the subject that he could no longer ignore.

"I cannot help believe now that the dress wasn't an accident," he said in a more controlled voice.

She was instantly up from his lap, turning to face him. "John, please don't confront her. Let it go."

Rising he pulled her into his arms. "I cannot. I will need to ask her about it."

Pressing her head against his breast, she clung to him as she stuttered out a meek plea for him not to say anything. Her reaction had him frowning.

"You believe she did it?"

Margaret did not speak causing John to lift her chin to look upon her face. The panic in her eyes answered the question and more.

"No, *you know* that she did it!"

She instantly paled and he knew that she confirmed his suspicion. Before he could speak, she grasped his arm.

"John, you were to never know. I don't want to come between you two any further. I have forgiven her. Please, let it go for me!"

Her eyes glistened with unshed tears as her voice begged. He melted at her sincerity and heartfelt entreaty

He looked at the woman who was to be his wife and loved surged out of every fiber of his being for her. He could not promise her that he would allow what his mother did go unpunished, but he could put it aside for now and concentrate on deserving her and making her happy. Placing both hands on her upper arms, he gently kissed her forehead and rested her under his jaw.

"Do you know how much I love you?" he asked.

She could only respond with a slight nod. He waited a moment to allow both of them to compose themselves before he released her and went to the office door, opened it and waved the man waiting outside in.

"Have a seat, Higgins. Miss Hale and I have a proposition to throw at you."

Cap in hand, "Thank you, Master, I prefer to stand."

John nodded and walked around to his desk chair and sat down motioning Margaret to come stand by him. He reached up, took her hand into his, and gently drew her closer. Looking seriously at the man, John spoke.

"Higgins it seems my future wife thinks I am in need of a partner and she insists it be you. What do you say to that?"

Higgins eyes widen in surprise. A slow knowing smile appeared as he glanced affectionately at Miss Margaret.

"I don't know what to say, but I guess I should say that I don't deserve it."

"She thinks that you do and we both know she is always right."

Margaret smiled down at him in time to see him give her a quick wink.

"I say then that what ever the missus wants, be mindful she gets," he said giving her a friendly wink as well. "You don't want to lose this one, Master."

Looking up into her beautiful face, John spoke, "I couldn't agree with you more, Higgins." Squeezing her hand he added, "I won't risk losing this one." ଔ

Chapter Ten
Evil Intent

Across the dining table, Hannah watched with narrowed eyes as John leaned over to speak to Miss Hale, who responded with a smile and nod. Picking up the decanter of wine, he filled her glass and then his. Placing the bottle off to the side, he took up his glass to drink of it.

Hannah caught his eyes as he peered up from the rim of the glass. He quickly shifted his view, breaking the contact. Putting his glass down, he returned his attention to his plate and the woman sitting by his side. His expression was warm and inviting for Miss Hale, altering to hard and unresponsive towards her. This was the extent of their mother and son relationship, restrained and aloof. Hannah glared at Miss Hale. She blamed her.

Three weeks ago, John announced that he was moving back into the residence, and Miss Hale was returning to the house where she lived previously with the parents. He did not say why and within a week, the source of her daily discontent was gone and her son was back where he belonged.

With Miss Hale's departure, hope abounded like never before. Was the engagement off? They must have quarreled. What other reason would she quit the residence? It would take much for him to allow her to leave its safety, but he offered no explanation.

It did not take long for her hope to be shattered.

Nothing had changed between the two lovers. If anything, they spent even more time together.

Within a few days of Miss Hale moving, Hannah became aware that something had occurred that broke their close, mother and son bond. Miss Hale had gotten to him! John said nothing but his actions spoke loudly.

Previously, after working hours, his routine had been to pour himself a drink, fall back to relax in his chair, and discuss the day and seek advice with her. This time of the day had been dear to her and she welcomed its return. It never came.

John went straight to his study and shut the door, indicating that he should not be disturbed. During the evening meals, when Miss Hale was not dining with them, he was reserved, answered with a terse word or two, and contributed little to conversations.

After excusing himself from the table, he went to either call on Miss Hale or incarcerate himself back into his own thoughts in another part of the house. If she came into the same room, in the span of a few moments, he would remove himself from her presence.

Hannah expected Miss Hale to run to him eventually with her complaints but what she did not expect was her son not to approach her with any of her accusations. She was prepared to defend herself. His silence and avoidance, was not anticipated and left her without recourse.

Her son never displayed such disrespectful behavior before. She resented it and was anxious to set him straight. But first, she needed to find out what exactly Miss Hale accused her of doing, but any attempt to engage him was averted.

A week of avoidance had her on the edge with a mixture of aggravation and despair. That night she found him sitting in the drawing-room buried behind the latest issue of the local broadsheet.

Hannah took her usual place on the settee and occupied herself with her needlepoint. She expected him to quit the room thereafter, but to her surprise, after a half hour, he still occupied the same space. Longing for a natural conversation, she licked her lips with cautious anticipation, and looked up to address him.

"You are not walking tonight with Miss Hale?"

John did not look up from the paper. "No, not tonight. I don't want her out in this air."

Encouraged by the polite tone, she continued, "The evenings have been unseasonably chilled. I hope she is well."

"Very well, thank you for asking, Mother."

The anxious tension eased as she took a few stitches in her sewing. The corner of her mouth drew up into a knowing curve, finally, she thought, her son was done with his childish behavior and coming back to normalcy. Hannah brought her head up again.

"Fanny mentioned yesterday that she would like to call on Miss Hale."

"What about this time?"

"About wearing her veil," she said casually. "We both agree it would look well on her. Shall I arrange it?"

A deep release of breath sounded and the paper dropped revealing John's face, marred with tempered incredulity.

"What did you say?"

Surprised by his reaction, she spoke tentatively, "Fanny's veil. She thought that Miss Hale would like to wear it and wondered when would be a good time to bring it by. I would, of course, accompany her."

His expression turned to one of stony disappointment. "That is what I thought you said." Straightening his paper back up, he spoke in a barely polite tone, "No, Mother, you'll not go and I'll see to Fanny."

"But I...we haven't called on Miss Hale since she moved."

"End of discussion."

Hannah's lips pursed with frustration of not knowing what to say next. Why did his demeanor changed so suddenly? She picked up the sewing only to drop it a few minutes later. In the intermission, she found herself staring at the back pages of the newspaper that he was reading.

Time seemed to go slowly, building a sense of urgency within the pit of her stomach causing it to churn with upset. She had to find out what caused this alienation of affection so that she could bring about its reversal. There was not much time; the wedding was fast approaching.

The deafening sound of John flipping to the next page of the paper startled her to blurt out, "I demand you tell me what I have done to deserve this treatment from you!"

Not in the least affected by her outburst, he peered out from the side of the paper. "I've taken on an apprentice," he said with forced calm. "You know him, Mother, Nicholas Higgins."

"The Union man!"

"He will become master of Hamper's after Margaret and I are wed."

"That goes against Mr. Hamper's and your arrangement!"

"Don't you mean your arrangement?"

"What do you mean by that?"

"It isn't important now. It has been worked out to Mr. Hamper's satisfaction. Higgins will have the opportunity I had in that the profit sharing will allow him to purchase the mill outright in four to five years from Hamper and myself."

"What brought this on? Why would you do such a thing, taking on this Higgins?"

"He is a highly capable man, hard working and a good friend. I'll not have you insulting him."

Taken aback by his tone, she forced herself to be silent. Inwardly she bristled furiously but it wasn't because of her son's impertinence. It was because she realized that there was only one person who could have possibly cause John to make such a rash and foolish decision to make this worthless man master—her soon-to-be daughter, Margaret Hale.

The warning sound of his voice must have stopped his mother from saying anything further, but John could see she was seething by the stiffness of her body and pinched expression on her face. He meant to be civil towards her to ease the growing tension in the house but her speaking about Fanny and the veil threw him off.

What his mother did not know was that he visited Watson that afternoon, ironically enough, to talk to him about another one of his speculation opportunities.

As promised, John discussed the prospect with Margaret first. They both agreed that more information and research would be needed before going in. John thought it was insightful of Margaret to suggest he correspond with Mr. Bell to get his counsel. He did and with Bell's advice in hand, a long list of questions to ask Watson, John endeavored to use good sound judgment whether to allocate funds into the scheme. This time, no payrolls were in danger, and together, Margaret and he approved the amount. If lost, there would be no impact on anyone but themselves.

While waiting, Fanny made an appearance, and spoke of the veil and how Miss Hale admired it. He suggested that it would be a polite gesture to allow Margaret borrow it.

His vain sister's jaw dropped in over-dramatized astonishment that he could even suggest her risking such a treasured piece. Why it was made of the finest and most expensive French lace, and was irreplaceable. When he asked what she meant about "risking", her answer caused his ire to be elevated.

Fanny informed him that their mother convinced her that her precious veil could not be trusted in the care of the chubby maid who allowed the wedding dress be ruined. She went on to say that their mother ordered a veil similar to hers in a catalogue, and they were going to tell Miss Hale of the gift next time they called.

Before he could reprimand Fanny for her callousness, Watson walked in. John shot her off a disgusted look from which he received a nippy view of her tongue.

After the business with Watson, he made a hasty retreat back to his office. Internally he fumed, feeling the weight of disappointment with both Fanny and his mother.

He deduced his mother's real motives behind ordering another veil and gifting it. Catalogue orders took time to arrive and deliveries were often unreliable. It was another effort, feeble as it was, to delay the wedding. John could not fathom her believing that a veil would stop him from taking Margaret's hand.

Unbeknownst to his mother, he vowed to Margaret that nobody or nothing would change the date set. John joked that he was going to be her husband that day even if the sky was falling with fiery hail or thousands of frogs were invading the land. She replied that she preferred the frogs because if the dress and veil weren't ready, she would be wearing a burlap sack, dry straw crown shrouded with thin cotton fabric. Certainly, not recommended with flames raining down. In their laughter, he agreed, frogs, no fire.

As he paced his office, he stopped by the newly mounted picture hanging on the wall. When Margaret presented it to him, beautifully framed, he was overwhelmed with emotions—such a gift he had never received before.

It depicted the likeness of him as he were that day they became reunited, leaning casually against a tree, looking off into the distance amongst the greenery, and natural splendor of her girlhood home. Prominent, to the far side, a blooming wild bush of yellow roses.

He had absolutely no idea that she was such an accomplished sketcher and artist, mentioning that she only recently rediscovered her talents back in London. Fanny could not accuse Margaret of not being proficient in this, in fact, Fanny could have no scruple in comparing Margaret's sketches to hers; his sister's attempts, to be kind, were lackluster and imprecise.

What had further endeared the gift to him was the promise in her signature. She did not mention it, and it wasn't until days after that he noticed it. He had to blink to make sure that he was seeing the signature clearly. Barely noticeable in the lush grasses in the corner— M. A. Thornton. It became his treasure beyond all wealth and knowledge.

That noonday, he broke from his duties, to visit the emporium and ordered every imaginable item to promote her artistry. For his Maggie, it was not in his mind to spare any expense. The supply had yet to arrive due to delays, thus his reasoning behind his mother's purpose in ordering a veil.

Moving away from the picture, he sat down at his desk, grateful for the fresh reprieve of the cherished memories shared with Margaret. These memories, once rare in his life, now became plentiful in his thoughtful escapes.

The pleasure of the moment faded, and his human nature returned to fuel his need to teach his mother and sister a lesson in civility and decency. Each idea was borderline harsh but he considered each one thinking that the anticipated outcome would bring him satisfaction. Then he stopped himself when the virtuous face of his Maggie had him looking to what would please her more.

By the time he sat down to dinner that night, he managed to bury his masculine need to discipline for Margaret's sake. For her, he thought that perhaps he could start repairing his relationship with his mother rather than demolishing it further.

Smashed to pieces were his good intentions when his mother blatantly lied about the veil. He felt total betrayal. Deep down he hoped that what was said about his mother had been a big misunderstanding. He adored her all his life and it crushed him that her scheming possessiveness had all but killed that adoration.

Because of his mother's proven treachery, John could no longer give her his trust and loyalty. He knew what he had to do. It troubled him that the one fear that his mother plotted to prevent, was about to happen—separation.

He lowered his paper. "Mother, I think now is the time to address a few matters," he said in a firm voice. Not waiting for a reply he continued, "From now on, I will ask you to refrain from questioning any further on any personal affairs and business dealings unless I freely disclose them to you first."

Her eyes widened in surprise. "John, why are you saying this?"

"Furthermore, I think it is best that you no longer walk the factory's floor. I have paid overseers to do that."

"I have always walked the floor!"

"I need you to manage the house. That is all."

"But after you marry, when she is living here—"

John gritted his teeth to keep his rising anger from surfacing. "Her name is Margaret, and we will not be living here."

Visibly shaken, she asked, "Where are you going?"

"You never mind that," he answered.

"I thought we agreed that she would…Margaret would remain here with us. I look forward to all of us being in the same—"

"Enough!" Propelling himself up from the seat, he threw the paper down and placed himself before his shocked mother. "Your interfering stops here," he said with restraint, "do you understand?"

Her shoulders slumped but her chin lifted and face became etched with defiance. "I am sure I don't know what you mean."

His jaw clenched causing the cords in his neck to stiffen. Anger threaded throughout his entire body. Not trusting himself to speak any further, he turned and exited the room.

That exchange that night convinced Hannah more than ever that Miss Hale poisoned John against her. It was evident that she was no longer trusted or revered by her son.

John, or that staunch maid, was always present, and never left Miss Hale alone with her or Fanny. All decisions regarding the wedding were left to Miss Hale upon John insistence. Excluded from the goings-on in the mills, she rarely saw her son or interacted with him. As much as she resented these actions, the worse was to come.

The property he wanted to purchase with the cottage was still available and he actively pursued its purchase, which he became successful. Hannah was sure the new Mrs. Thornton would not tolerate her living in their countryside cottage. Her worse fear was about to be realized—she being parted from him.

The ground, sinking in under her feet, continued to draw her into a dark hole from which there was no way out. She glared at the woman sitting next to her son and bitterness well up inside as never before. She despised her.

"Miss Hale, how are the final arrangements going? Do you need any assistance?"

Margaret looked up and gave her a genuine smiled. "Thank you for asking, Hannah, but no. I have the flowers and final fitting of the dress."

"Sandow's Greenhouse is the best for floral arrangements. They do our annual dinner gathering each year."

"I remember. The arrangements were lovely. Thank you for the recommendation."

What a pretty part she played, Hannah thought contemptuously. She resented having to be polite. She was tired of it.

"I suppose, Miss Hale, that you'll take up the planning of that annual dinner as Mrs. Thornton," she said, no longer masking the sarcasm.

"Not at all, unless you wish for my help. It is a tradition in this house that you probably look forward to each year. As for us," Margaret said, looking at John and placing her hand over his, "I imagine we will be starting new traditions."

He did not hesitate to lean over, wipe a non-existent crumb from the corner of her mouth with his thumb, and drop a light kiss in its place.

Hannah felt her stomach churn with nausea at her son's worship over her, and hurried to ease it with wine.

Margaret was not surprised to see Hannah's stern facial expression behind the glass of wine.

Although strained, Hannah's manners remained courteous when John was present and as a result, the evenings usually was pleasantly spent. But this night, Margaret sensed a growing discord; she felt that she needed to put more effort into defusing Mrs. Thornton.

"And to think," she said to Hannah cheerfully, "there will be additional events and gatherings planned with Fanny and myself to add to our enjoyment of the year. And since I am quite ignorant at organizing such occasions, I am sure I will need your advice."

John squeezed her hand acknowledging her attempt to bring about peace in the family. For him, she would not give up in trying to make things better between him and his mother.

"In organizing an event, this doesn't include a wedding," Hannah replied with vehemence.

John's body stiffened next to her. "Mother…" he cautioned in a low voice.

"You misunderstood me. I didn't mean it quite in that way," Margaret stammered.

"Miss Hale, you'll not get such help from me. Your inabilities and lack of breeding will be revealed in good time. He'll learn his foolish worship over you was recklessly given."

"Mother!"

Margaret was incredulous. Hannah spoke as if John was not in the room! She stood up from the table and before John could get up, she put her hand on his shoulder indicating she wanted him to continue to sit.

"No, John, you have guarded me for weeks but not tonight." He reluctantly sat back down but remained defensively rigid. "You have insulted me in every possible way, Mrs. Thornton, but for John, I kept trying to break through to…to show you that by your actions only, you are losing him."

Her voice changed from controlled anguish to a pleading tone.

"If you could only see that you can have him and gain a daughter who is more than willing to love you." Glancing down, she addressed him, "I watched you two grow further apart and it is the last thing I ever wanted. I wish now that I never told you."

"Maggie—"

Hannah interrupted harshly, "Stop with the innocent airs, Miss Hale! I am no fool to think that you did not deliberately plan to pit my son against me." Margaret gasped in disbelief as she furiously continued, "You parade around as a grand lady when you are only a daughter of a failed clergyman and not worthy of my son even with all your undeserved wealth!"

John stood up so violently that his chair went flying backwards as he slammed his hands on the table causing all the dishes to rattle and Margaret to stagger back against the wall.

"Enough!" he leaned forward with palms pressed flat on the table. "The dress! Who ruined the dress?"

"You're accusing me!" she sparred angrily.

"Don't deny it! You dare to hurt her when she has done nothing to you. Now you insult her further in the most disgusting of ways!"

Margaret put her hand on the back of his shoulder. "Please stop," she pleaded, "John…"

She went unheard as John's purest anger echoed throughout the room.

"Answer me! Did you ruin the dress?"

Hannah stood up from her chair and shouted back, "She told you I did and you believed her! She'll say anything to have you turning against me!"

Mrs. Thornton's scathing tone made Margaret flush with humiliation. The pain struck hard in the chest at the extent of Hannah's unjustified loathing towards her. She could no longer deny the probability that she was obsessively mad.

She tried to bring calm but found her desperate entreaties drowned out by the two releasing weeks of pent up bitterness and resentment. Son and mother thundered against each other and she felt helpless in the torrent.

Eyes welling up with tears and finding herself unable to cope with the infuriated confrontation she backed up slowly, turned, and left the room.

Forgetting her frock, she ran out into the night, barraged by the frosty air. Crossing her arms against the cold, she refused to go back into the house. Shivering, she made her way down the darken streets wanting only to reach her residence. Tears flowed freely blinding the way. Taking the shorter route down a narrowed lane, she began to doubt her actions. Should she have stayed and tried harder to bring peace or waited—

An arm grabbed violently from behind, encircling her neck in a choke, cutting off any scream. Seconds had a dirtied palm tightly covering her mouth with fingers biting into the soft flesh of her cheeks.

Dragged deep into a deserted alleyway, she frantically struggled, legs kicking and body twisting, trying to free herself from her unknown assailant. All breath expelled from her lungs as she found herself slammed hard against a brick wall.

In a blink, a knife was at her throat, the blade, cold and hard against her skin. She could feel the razor-sharp edge penetrate slightly as she swallowed against the terror that was invading her entire body.

"One move or sound and that will be the end of ya."

Margaret did not dare nod because of the knife, but her eyes flew open, finding her attacker's face covered with a filthy sack except for big holes where the eyes and mouth were.

Assured that she would not scream, he moved his hand on her mouth to her throat and squeezed in warning. Slippery moisture on her skin had her gasping in fear.

Mouth dropped and lips quivering, she tried to control the trembling as the knife trail down the front of her blouse to her stomach. His face was close and she could smell the stench of his breath.

"I've been waiting for you. Following your every step, I have. Waiting for a chance to finally get at you alone and have a piece of ya."

Lifting the sack halfway, he ran his tongue over her chin then up, saturating her open mouth. She wrenched her face away sobbing for him to let her go.

He used the knife blade to force her face back to him. "Why, so you can go back to Thornton?" he sneered, "Not til I'm done with ya."

"Please…stop."

Lust filled eyes scanned her body hungrily. "I've dreamed of you and me together. What would it be like to bed you, fine lady that'ch are. Too fine for the likes of me they would say. But not Thornton. You'd let him have ya."

Scream Margaret! Scream! Before she could find the courage, his rank mouth covered hers again more violently. His crusted, decaying teeth and thick saliva collided with the inside of her mouth causing bile to rise and her to gag in revulsion. His tongue invaded, forcing its way to the back of her throat causing her to choke.

Her recourse was instinctive; she bit down.

A howl emitted and she experienced a searing pain from the blow from the back of his hand. Head reeling by the violence, she struggled to stay conscious. Her knees buckled, but the wall to her back and his pressing body kept her from falling.

The man spat out some blood and lowered his face close to warn her menacingly that he would cut her if she tried anything like that again. With one hand, he held the knife back to her throat, as the fingers of the other clawed her breast.

"Ripe for the picking aren't you? Thornton is a fool to wait. Now he won't be the first." He reached down to work up her skirt to expose her. Pulling and tearing at material he seethed, "I'd worshipped you, killed for you…by damn, I'm going to have you!"

Horror struck Margaret as powerful as any physical blow as she processed what he was going to do. God help! Please send John she internally cried out.

Her head began to swim with fogged dizziness. The terror was shutting her body down. Any courage she could have mustered dissolved as she fell into a petrified submissiveness.

"He won't want you after I am done!" His grip shifted up on her neck to force her to look at him. Tears fell as he continued, "Nobody will!"

Margaret gasped as his rough hand reached her bare skin below her navel. She heard a growl of satisfaction as his nails dug in and kneaded.

"I'm not just going to have ya," he said sadistically, "I'm going to fill your belly with my bastard." Spittle flew as he laughed out his mockery. "A bastard child! My gift to remind you of our time together. A gift Thornton is sure to hate."

Using his leg to hold up her bunched up skirt, he began fumbling with his belt. His whole body pressed into hers for leverage as he worked to free himself, grunting in eager anticipation.

Shutting her eyes tight, her mind started to shut down to block what was about to happen. A brilliant flash of light went off behind closed eyes. Frederick! His sword raised, he was charging forward shouting commands to fight. His voice pierced her soul and coursed it way through her defeated frame.

"No! Help!" she screamed as her knee snapped up, finding its mark.

He doubled over in pain, giving way for an opportunity to get away. With surfacing strength, she pushed her way forward causing him to fumble out of control. She ran towards the dim light at the end of the alley.

Within steps of the burning street lamps, Margaret found herself fiercely jerked from behind, dragged back, and thrown to the ground. He was on top, pinning her; the knife was back at her throat. She could only sob out her failure to escape.

The man's fury replaced any remaining sanity as he ferociously pawed at material to get to her again. Feebly she tried to push him off but he growled viciously for her to be still or else. When she did not, he slapped his palm across her face; the sudden excruciating pain caused her to black out temporarily, allowing him to gain complete dominance with his entire weight covering her.

She could not struggle any longer and went limp with pain and exhaustion. In her panicked mind, she begged John for forgiveness for not being stronger. The man must have sensed surrender because he rumbled in triumph that he was going to savor taking her.

Margaret held her breath as he exposed her skin. She did not have any more strength to prepare herself for the violence that was seconds away from happening. She now prayed for unconsciousness to come as he lowered his mouth to her breast.

A voice calling her name, Margaret's eyes sprang open. John! Her mouth opened to call out but her assailant had his fingers around her throat, squeezing and blocking air and voice.

"Listen good. Wed Thornton and the same knife that was at your throat will be in his back," he threatened, "but before I kill him, I'll burn the mills and finish you."

Her fingers pleaded with his hand to loosen the hold as she became desperate to get air. Unwavering in his grip, she started to feel herself slip into blackness. Suddenly he released her neck, and his weight lifted off her body. Begging for air in gulps, wide terrorized eyes followed the man as he disappeared into the darkness of the back alley.

A new fear entered her head. He will come back! Shakily she raised herself up off the ground. Hot tears and dim light blinded her ,but she knew from which way John's voice echoed and she ran in that direction.

"Maggie!"

She lifted her head and saw him rushing towards her. Mouthing his name, she labored to reach him. Stumbling she fell to her knees. Weakened, she tried to rise again, managing to get only halfway up, her eyes raised in time to see him diving to catch her. It was then that she collapsed into his reaching arms.

"Dear God!"

John caught her as she was falling. He dropped to the ground with her, his body acting as a cushion for her petite frame.

"I got you," he reassured tenderly. "I got you, now."

He cradled her back into the crook of his arm so he could see her face more clearly. It was chalk white except for a reddening patch on her left side. He struck her! A flash of red had his eyes darting to her neck region. Blood! She was bleeding from her neck!

Deep alarm registered as his fingers spanned out to support her head so he could see the wound to her neck. He let out a deep sigh of relief when he saw it was superficial. Reaching into his inside pocket, he pulled out a handkerchief and pressed it to the wound.

He scanned the rest of her. Fury registered on his face but his low deep voice soothed her as his free hand worked to pull loose and torn material over exposed areas. He could not miss the dirt and red indents on the stomach before covering.

For the first time in his life, he wanted to kill. Teeth clenched, he shut his eyes to ward off the penetrating desire; he must see to Margaret. She needed him first.

Soft moaning from her caused John's attention to return to her. The need to shield and protect her from any more harm overwhelmed him more than the need to kill. He drew her trembling body closer to his chest and moved her head to rest under his jaw. Her warm, fresh tears fell on his lower neck.

Gentled fingers brushed hair back from her face. "Maggie, open your eyes, Love," he begged. "Please, open them for me."

Her eyelids fluttered and faintly speaking his name. That was all he needed. Choked with emotion, he rocked her back and forth in his arms.

"I'm here, Maggie. I'll not leave you." John pressed his lips to her brow and lingered; blinking at moisture forming in his eyes he added a deep resounding, "I found ya."

His voice was like a blanket enveloping her in all encompassing warmth. She allowed his loving hold spread peace and comfort to her fragile state.

God answered her prayer. John came.

Margaret felt him lifting her body and securing her into his strong arms. It was then that she let blackness take her. ☙

Chapter Eleven
Change of Plan

Dixon knocked on the door and opened it to find Mr. Thornton in same position she left him an hour before—chair pulled up to the bedside, holding the mistress's hand in both of his, with head bowed as if in prayer.

"Sir, a Mr. Higgins, and Inspector Mason are here to see you, and your mother, she still is waiting."

Craning his head up, he turned towards her. "Let her wait," he said.

Dixon nodded in approval. It was two hours before when she opened the door to see Mrs. Thornton on the other side. It took everything in her not to slam the door in the woman's face. She was certain that if it were not for her upsetting the mistress this could not have happened.

Mrs. Thornton was a shrew to whom she would never trust for the life of her. Although the mistress never confirmed it, she was sure that the woman ruined the wedding dress in spite. And the sister, Mrs. Watson! Putting up with those two would have been a deal breaker in marrying any man.

Drawing closer to the bed, Dixon watched Mr. Thornton draw up her mistress's hand and run his lips over her fingers, speaking tenderly that he would be back.

Well bless him, she thought. He may have had a slow start with Miss Margaret but he was proving himself a good sort of man. The way he was when he showed up, carrying her, wildly concerned and attentive, he showed his deep love for her. It had Dixon thinking he would have done himself harm if Miss Margaret was taken to an early grave.

One could put up with quite a bit for a man who loved like that.

Dr. Donaldson assured John that she would recover, but the stark reality of nearly losing her left him vulnerable, and not wanting to leave her side.

Long hair framed her pale facial features in the lamp light, creating an illusion of a tragic ending. He wanted to lie down by her warm body and feel the rise and fall of her bosom to reassure him further that she was alive and survived such a brutal attack.

However, the announcement of the two men waiting downstairs flamed his desire to find the man who did this to her. Rage that he temporarily buried began to surface, causing vengeful thoughts to rule his mind.

"Let me know if she wakes," he said, rising from the chair.

"Yes, sir. I'll not take my eyes off her. Not for a second."

He put a hand on Dixon's shoulder after she took his place in the chair.

"Thank you, Dixon."

Closing the door behind him, he found his mother waiting at the top of the stairway.

"John, how is she?"

"Do you care, Mother?" he replied angrily. "Go, she would not want you back with your false concern."

She grabbed his arm stopping him. "John, I did it. I ruined the dress, but I never wanted her to be harmed like this. I know you blame me—"

"Mother, stop!"

His fingers flew up to his forehead and began to rub it in

irritation. He glanced at his mother's pleading look, doubting that in the span of a few hours her harsh disregard for Margaret could have significantly changed.

I watched you two grow further apart and it is the last thing I ever wanted.

If he would have kept a cooler head and not have been so abrasive, perhaps she would not have run out into the street. He recognized that his mother was not the only one here at fault.

"I blame myself," he muttered. "I cannot talk about this now."

Detaching himself from her grip, he descended the staircase leaving her staring after him.

John walked into the sitting-room to see a concerned Higgins standing with cap in hand, nervously twisting it.

"Master, Miss Margaret…"

"Resting, Higgins. She has yet to wake but doctor said she will recover." He was gratified to see the older man's relief. He then reached out his hand to the other man in the room. "Mason."

Taking the hand offered, Mason spoke quickly, "Sir, I am deeply sorry for what the young lady has gone through. I was hoping to speak to Miss Hale but since she is resting, I will ask you what you know."

John nodded and proceeded to go over what he knew of the attack that happened only hours before.

Noticing that Mason was writing little in his notebook, he spoke, "It isn't much as I came upon Miss Hale after the assailant vanished."

"I am hopeful the miss can give us more details."

"In that regard, Mason, I'll question her being I am closer to her."

"I understand, sir."

"In the meantime, I want to be kept informed of everything."

Mason nodded. "A sack was found that we believed was used. Holes were cut out where the eyes and mouth would have been.

Fresh blood was found on it, sure to be Miss Hale's."

John's fists balled, imagining one upper cutting in the hooded man's jaw, and the other slamming into his gut. He wanted to feel the soreness of skinned knuckles and pain in his hands; it would have brought satisfaction.

In its place, he worked out a little of his anger and frustration by interrogating Mason further about the investigation asking about the manpower, witnesses, and further evidence. The inspector was thorough, answering all his questions to his satisfaction, assuring him that they would not rest until the assailant faced justice.

"Mason, I'll be offering a substantial reward for this man's capture," John said, "and I do not want any one to know that there was a knife involved. Leave that detail out."

"Very good, sir," replied Mason. "Can I ask you, does Miss Hale have anyone who might want to harm her, perhaps a previous beau?"

Higgins piped in, "No one could ever want to harm Miss Margaret."

"I have to agree with Higgins, Mason. Miss Hale has no enemies that I know of."

"And you, sir, is there anyone who has it out for you?" he asked.

His head snapped up at the disturbing thought of her being brutalized by a person who sought revenge against him. He had enemies but for any one to stoop to such a despicable low against a woman made his stomach sour. He felt certain it was a random act but he gave the inspector the names of past acquaintances that may wish him harm.

Mason departed leaving Higgins and him in the room alone. Running his fingers in his hair, he felt physically restless, causing him to pace the room, but it was not long before the emotional strain hit him.

"Master, sit."

"Higgins, you don't have to call me master."

"Mr. Thornton, sir…sit."

John's lip curled up, complying with the respectful command, he sat in the nearest chair. Higgins poured him a deep glass of brandy and handed it to him.

"Drink up and don't worry. If I know anything about Miss Margaret, she is a strong one. She keeps a level head about her, that one."

"Higgins, if you could have seen how terrified she was. The brutality of what he did to her—how will she recover?" He put the untouched drink on the table and covered his face with his hands as his body began to shake with a sudden release of powerful emotions. "She came close to being killed. If I had not found her when I did…" He could not finish the thought, and he dropped his head.

Higgins squeezed his shoulder. "When my Bess was dying, she was strong for her. You'll be the same, so have it out before you have to go back to her."

Looking up at his friend with eyes brimming, John nodded. After a few moments, he got control of his emotions and that was when Higgins asked how the miss came to be out in the streets alone. John left nothing out as he told Higgins about his mother's dislike of Margaret, Hamper's, the property, dress, and the argument at dinner.

"As your friend, I wish you would have told me all this sooner, it would have done you good to unburden yourself."

"Unfortunately for me, I am not known to have many friends to confide in," John said, holding his hand out, "Thank you for your friendship, Higgins. It has meant a great deal to me."

The older man shook his hand and nodded towards the glass sitting on the table. "So, are you going to drink that good brandy or must I for you?"

Grinning, John handed the glass over to Higgins. Standing up, he moved to the table and poured himself another glass and both men raised their glasses to their lips with Higgins blurting out, "For medicinal purposes."

John downed the liquid in two gulps and allowed the alcohol to shock his system and spread renewed energy and warmth throughout.

Dixon came running in. "Sir, she's waking."

Glass shattered on the floor, as John shot out the door leaving the two standing with stunned expressions.

Dixon glanced at Higgins frowning, "Was the table too far off?"

Shrugging his shoulders, Higgins answered with a smirk, "At least it was emptied."

Margaret watched in horror as John fought with the hooded man. A glint of a blade caught her eye, but before she could warn him, the man plunged the knife into his rival's stomach. John staggered forward towards her, his pained expression begging her to leave him, shouting for her to run. The wicked man came up from behind and stabbed him again in the back. Margaret screamed out John's name as he crumpled to the ground. The man kicked the body at his feet, it remained motionless, and then turned towards her, approaching with menacing intent. She cried out.

"John, no! John!"

"Open your eyes, Maggie. I'm here."

His voice and his touch! Her lids flew open and eyes focused. John sat on the edge of the bed, leaning over her with his right arm on the other side of her, while his left palm caressed her ashen cheek.

Relief hit her like a crashing wave causing her to spring into his arms and bury her face into his chest. The vividness of the nightmare had her trembling violently.

His fingers threaded through her hair coming to rest behind her head. Directing her face up, he kissed her temple, and spoke strong, soothing words into her ear. At length, she clung to him in silence, as her body absorbed his warmth and security.

Margaret heart strengthened and swelled with love for the man who held her, feeling passionately that in reality, she would not have run away, but gladly risk dying to reach him.

"Maggie, take some water," John commanded gently.

Margaret's glistening eyes looked up to his face as he held the glass to her lips. As she drank, he could see that Higgins had been right, what he saw was strength.

He lowered the glass and kissed her slowly, with a tenderness that he hoped would help erase any of the harshness she experienced. She responded, her arm reaching up around his neck, seemingly more eager for the reunion. Her soft sighs helped to ease some of the anxiety he was feeling for her.

He drew away, wiping the last trace of a tear away with his thumb. "Better?" She gave him a faint smile. "Tell me what else I can do," he said with urgency, "and I'll do it."

She fell back into his arms, hugging him tightly, saying she needed nothing more but for him to be there. He responded by moving her hair off to the side and kissing the delicate curve of her neck whereon he noticed the bruising.

"Do you hurt?"

She moved to test some of her muscles and he watched as her face pinched, "My back, I think, and my teeth or is it my jaw…it aches," she answered.

His eyes darkened with inner rage, but he kept his voice level. "And your throat?"

Margaret reached up to finger the bandage, "I didn't even know it was there. I felt the knife. Was I…hurt there?"

"A small cut, but enough to bleed quite a bit." John lowered to address her more intimately. "Maggie, I need to ask you, did he hurt you in other ways? You can tell me."

She flushed and shook her head. Drawing her head back to his chest, he helped her to hide her embarrassment.

After a few moments, he asked if she could tell him what happened. John felt her fingers dig into his undershirt, clutching the loosened material with her fists. It was as if she was grabbing hold of some additional courage or strength.

"Maggie, you don't have to—"

"He…he wanted to rob me," she spoke quickly, "I had nothing but he didn't believe me."

Margaret started to fidget uncomfortably, and went to move out of his embrace but he strengthened his hold on her.

"I'll not let you go." He waited until she stilled before continuing, "Did you see the man who attacked you?"

"No, he wore a bag with holes."

"Can you tell me anything about him?"

She shook her head, stuttering, "It was dark and he...he didn't speak." Her eyes shifted away.

"Margaret?"

"He smelled very bad."

"You're not telling me everything."

"He tried to...but he didn't, then you came." Her eyes suddenly filled with unshed tears. "You came."

He felt himself sinking into the pools of her adoring eyes, kissing each and then finding her mouth to whisper on her lips that he thanked God that he found her.

Taking her hand into his, he asked if she could remember any detail for the investigation. She said no, and then changed the subject by asking for more water.

John handed her the glass, watching her intently. Her hand was shaking as she put the glass to her lips, and avoided eye contact with him, which helped him to conclude rather quickly that she was lying.

"This wasn't a robbery, Love."

"John, I am tired, we will talk more tomorrow."

She handed him the glass, and laid back down on the bed, turning sideways with her back to him. He reached down and pulled the covers up and over her, letting his hand rest on her shoulder.

"You forget, my Maggie, I know you don't tell the truth when you are protecting someone you love." He felt her flinch, lowering himself closer her ear he whispered, "I can guess who."

Her answer was to pull the covers tighter to herself. He sat back, while his palm smoothed over the back of her head in gentle retreat.

"Sleep now. I'll not leave your side."

She turned her head to look at him. "John, I want you to go."

Her tone was firm but with a touch of panic that told him it was not due to her want for privacy. It troubled him that she wanted him gone for a secret reason. A sixth sense advised him not to leave her. Decided, he pulled up the chair and sat, crossing his arms before him.

"I'm staying."

"John, please, respect my wishes."

"Sleep, Maggie, I'll be here in the morning."

She let out a frustrated sigh but spoke no more and within minutes, her breathing became slow and even.

The trauma of the day had him dozing for some hours. He became fully awake to her moving fitfully in her sleep. He was glad that he stayed. If she had another nightmare, he would be there for her.

John knew from her reaction to the first nightmare that she was protecting him. Whoever attacked her must have threatened him harm.

What she suffered, not only that night but in the past weeks as well, with his embittered mother, his selfish sister, and his own blindness. He vowed to make it all up to her in some way, and if that meant leaving everything and everyone behind, for her, he would do it.

Margaret's restlessness ceased. He stood up and redistributed the displaced covers over her, and then stretched some of the stiffness out of his joints. Pulling out his undershirt and unbuttoning it halfway, he prepared for more hours in the uncomfortable chair. Sitting back down, he thought that there was no place he rather be.

She turned to her side, facing him. Shadowed eyes, renewed by the sleep, traced every line of her shape, settling on her peaceful expression. Leaning forward to where his elbows laid on his knees, and hands folded together in front of him, his thoughts focused on the best way to keep her safe and ensure no further harm came to her.

He wanted her out of Milton, away from the danger, and sadly, away from his mother. Her conduct went beyond incivility and passive aggressiveness. When he spoke to Mason that Margaret had no enemies, it frightened him to think that perhaps he should have mentioned her future mother-in-law.

Margaret turned onto her stomach and drew in the pillow to hug it closer to her head, murmuring softly with the corner of her mouth twitching up.

Masculine softness and relief crossed his face as he realized she was having a pleasant dream. John wondered if he was in that pleasant dream. He liked to think so. For him, there were still a few weeks of dreaming of her before he could have her safe with him, day and night, tucked away together in their—

Abrupt clarity had him sitting up straight in the chair. His mind worked to formulate the possible change of plan. Nodding to himself, he knew what to do.

No grand ceremony, and no more waiting!

"John, wake up."

Her soft voice drew him out of his fog, groaning from the inflexibility from sleeping in an unconventional position. Streaming sunlight pouring in from the window had him blinking awake and focusing down on the woman before him on bended knees. One of her hands rested on his leg and the other contoured to his whiskered jaw.

Remembering, he gripped her upper arms and stood up taking her with him, blurting incredulously that she was out of bed. The sound of light laugher had his jaw dropping.

"You'll not catch me sleeping until noon again," she said, "and you aren't a sensible man to stay all night in that chair."

"Maggie, not this soon. Please, back in bed with you!"

"I am bruised and a little out of sorts John, but that is all. I believe there is more of Frederick's courage in me than I imagined."

He stared, not knowing if he could believe her. She was talking as if nothing happened. Taking her face into his hands, he examined her for any signs of distress. He was relieved to find color back and the bruising faint. Her expression was relaxed and rosy. Finishing his appraisal, he sealed it by teasing her mouth with his lips until she smiled, and then kissing her fully.

Breaking, he looked at her with over-exaggerated skepticism. "Any other woman would have been in bed for days after what you experience yesterday."

"Fanny for weeks and even months."

He broke into a full smile, shaking his head in wonder at her incredible fortitude.

"There…I am done for this day. You smiled," she said.

The only way he could answer her was to take her into his arms. John could feel her cheek resting above where his undershirt had been unbuttoned. What she did next had him closing his eyes and drawing in breath at the same time—she breathed velvety kisses on his exposed skin. He luxuriated in the feel of her sweet boldness.

This gave confirmation that she was comfortable with him and no longer had any hesitancy. He knew, with no reservations, that she was ready to become his wife.

She did not know what came over her. After the initial surprised of finding hair on his chest she turned her cheek away to escape the tickle it was causing. The warmth and feel of his bare skin, and his close embrace drew her into a singular need to touch the spot with her lips.

"Maggie, as much as I enjoy you doing that, you must stop."

"I'm sorry, John."

"Never apologize for what you just did," he said, "but we have to talk."

"I agree. I need to tell you about yesterday."

His expression went from serious to concern. Leading her over to the bed, he sat her down and sat next to her, taking her hand into his.

"You were right, the man wasn't a thief."

"Can you tell me what happened?"

Margaret, feeling brave, nodded and gave her account of what happened, leaving no detail out including the threats on him and herself. She thought she was doing well but she began to shake.

As he soothed her trembling, she could tell he was raging inside and it frightened her. Given the chance, John would not hold back if he got his hands on the man who attacked her. The result could be her nightmare coming true.

Last night it was in her mind to leave John and never come back because she feared for his life, but he refused to leave and opportunity was lost. Hours later, she was to have another dream but this one was vastly different.

Hand clasping hers, and grinning proudly, John led her briskly out of the church. Their friends and family were all there, even Mamma and Papa, Frederick, and Bessy, cheering and showering them with the traditional handfuls of grain.

As they made their way pass the crowd, there in front stood Mrs. Thornton. The tears that were streaming down her face were not tears of anguish; it was tears of joy. A beautiful smile lighted Hannah's expression as she approached her new daughter-in-law, embracing her warmly and kissing her cheek, then turning to her son, to do the same.

Laughter and shouts of approval surrounded the couple as John lifted his bride up in the air and twirled her around, and then bringing her down to kiss her passionately.

Margaret woke knowing what she wanted. She wanted those tears of joy, the laughter, and her husband; she was going to fight to have it all.

This man was obsessed with Margaret and hated him so much that he wanted to violate her to get her with child. John felt physically sick to his stomach. He could not fathom a more evil plot for revenge. He was dealing with a madman and it struck more fear in his heart for her safety.

"Thank you for telling me," he said as he pulled away to look at her, "but you weren't. You were planning to leave Milton and me behind."

Her eyes lifted to his. "That was my plan if you hadn't stayed last night. I thought to go to Spain or Argentina."

"What changed your mind?"

With tears threatening, she told him about the nightmare, and that she could not leave him behind even with the man approaching.

"The devil would have his victory whether I ran or not," she said. "To die by your side or live life without you. I made my choice."

"Maggie, without you I would have welcomed that knife in my back."

"John, don't."

"It is true. The knife would be the lesser of the pain."

She stood up. "Well, John Thornton, I have come to the conclusion that I simply won't marry you until he is caught if that is his only demand."

He stood and put his hands on her upper arms. "No, it isn't. This man knows how to wound me and he is mad which makes him more dangerous and unpredictable. Remember, he knows us, but we don't know him."

Margaret went to protest but he put his fingers to her lips to stop her from speaking. "So, I propose a different solution that I hope you'll favor."

She remained silent but her eyes told him to continue.

"Margaret, I purchased the dirty cottage in the wilderness."

Her face lighted up. "Oh, John, you did?"

He took her hands into his. "I know you'll love it. Are you happy, Maggie, that we won't be living in Milton?"

"I would be happy with you in a thatched hut. A dirty cottage would be living in splendor to be sure."

"I was going to present it to you after we were wed, but now, I hope to do it before the wedding."

"Before?"

"Yes, Maggie. Please trust me." Framing her face with his hands, he looked deeply into her eyes. "Marry me…tomorrow."

"Tomorrow!"

"Yes, we'll go secretly to the parsonage in Trentside. We will make it seem like you broke the engagement and left town because of the attack and because of my mother."

"I don't like to be deceitful and it is not because I am unskilled at doing it."

"I know it makes you uncomfortable, but Maggie, Mother confessed to me last night that she did ruin your dress. I feel she is regretting, but let her believe that you are out of my life," he said firmly. "Her reaction will settle it on where we stand. If she wants a relationship with her son, she will have to humble herself and atone for her conduct towards you and myself. She will need to show me that she truly wishes for my happiness."

"If she doesn't, what will you do," she asked with trepidation.

John knew he had to be straight with her. "There can be no compromise. I'll have to walk away from her until she is able to receive help."

Margaret nodded sadly. "You'll stay with her at the house?"

"Yes, when I return. Tomorrow, I will leave under the guise of searching for you to bring you back. As you said, that could take me to Spain or Argentina. We will only tell Higgins and Dixon for you both will need to leave tonight for the cottage. I do not want to chance this man following you. I will be gone for some days but in reality I'll be with you, as my wife."

Margaret bowed her head, smiling to herself, thinking of the dream. Her face flushed pink with excitement at the thought of finally becoming Mrs. John Thornton. His voice broke her thoughts.

"Maggie, if his attack on you in any way…we need to marry but if you need time to heal from last night, well, we don't need to know each other in that way. Do you know what I mean? It doesn't have to be…" Clearly agitated he flew up his hands in defeat. "Ah hell!"

"You're blushing again."

He cracked a smile and shook his head, "Ah, Maggie, my love, only you can turn me into a stammering fool. What I was trying to say was that I'll wait as long as you need."

"I know little on what happens between a husband and wife but I know love is kind and gentle nothing like what I experience last night. I trust you, John, and will not fear what is to happen."

"Then you agree to marry me?"

"Will you be safe when you are here? When will I see you?"

"I will be careful and there will be no doubt that I'll find excuses to leave from time to time to be with you. I'll not be kept from you long. We will declare us married when your attacker is caught and brought to justice."

"What if he isn't caught?"

"If it is one thing I have learned, money is a powerful ally. A reward will be posted that would tempt Satan himself."

"He wants you dead. I heard it in his voice. How can I leave knowing that?"

"You endanger me more by staying. I need you safely tucked away in our home with Dixon. I have in mind someone to guard the outside and help around the property." He sensed she was still unconvinced. "I had my warning and I'll heed it. I will not risk leaving you a young widow."

She was most likely thinking hard and fighting in her mind between what was right and wrong, safe and unsafe for him. He knew it was improper what he was asking her to do, but he felt that this would be the best course of action. He must persuade her.

"We've been wronged—by my mother and this man. They both jeopardize our life together and happiness we both deserve." He bent his head to capture her troubled far-off gaze. "I will not lose it if it means I have to scheme and plot. I know you are fighting a battle within." He gripped her arms tighter. "Don't think of others for once in your life." His voice elevated with emotion. "What do you want, Margaret?"

He watched her eyes lower to think of her answer. After an endless moment, her face lifted, the expression on it displayed an air of calm confidence. In a level voice that was without doubt, she spoke the one word he wanted to hear.

"Tomorrow."

John's heart jump and face lighted as he grabbed her up and hugged her tightly. He could not contain his excitement. Pulling her back, he saw her shining with animated elation.

"Guess you get your way, woman. Weren't you the one who wanted me to drag you to the church without ceremony?"

Her lips curved up. "Yes, but I do not think you should use the word drag. I was always willing."

He grabbed her around her waist and brought her flush against his chest. "Yes, you were," he chuckled.

Kissing her quickly, he let her go and turned enthusiastically serious. "There is much to do. I need to get you and Dixon out tonight and see to—"

"One promise, John." He stopped and took her hand, waiting for her to speak of it. "If he isn't captured, will you leave Milton?"

Placing her palm flat on his chest where his heart was, he held it there.

"Feel that, Maggie? It's beating and I am human again," he said. "In a heartbeat, yes, I will leave with you." ☙

Chapter Twelve
Coming Home With Me

After deciding that the marriage would happen the next day, John sat Margaret down to write the fictitious parting letter. Standing by her side with his hand on the back of her chair, they corroborated on the content and tone. She sealed it with his name elegantly written on the front, and gave it over to him with no misgivings except for having to deceive Hannah. John reaffirmed that this was the only way to know where his mother stood in their future.

Higgins came around, with Dixon included, and all four conspirators sat down to plot the details of the hours ahead. It was noonday when he kissed his intended for the last time as Miss Hale. When he saw her the next day, she would become Mrs. Thornton.

Under the cover of night, Nicholas escorted the two women to the cottage. As much as he would have liked to see her reaction to his rather sizeable wedding gift, John had to play the unsuspecting soon-to-be jilted groom, going about his business. This included a stop to speak to Mason with details from Margaret on the attack and inquire about the investigation.

Back at the Thornton house, he stayed in his study most of the evening to avoid his mother. Dinner was uncomfortably silent until she asked after Margaret. Short and to the point, he told her that she was well but the ordeal had her requesting her privacy.

As planned, noonday had him stopping by the house to pack. Coming down the stairs with his baggage, his mother came out of the drawing-room with a look of surprised alarm.

"John, where are ye going?"

Dropping the bags in the entrance hall, he walked pass her to the liquor table and poured himself a glass, downing it quickly then pouring another.

"John?"

"She left, Mother. Are you satisfied now?"

"Left! When?"

"Last night." He took the opened letter out from his inside jacket pocket and waved it angrily before her. "There is to be no wedding. She left Milton and I have no idea where she has gone. I cannot see that I blame her."

Hannah came over to put her hand on his arm. "What excuse does she have but that she must not have loved you to leave you like this?"

John jerked away, as disappointment flooded his expression. Perhaps he had been wrong; she felt no regret.

"Does she need an excuse? I tell you she doesn't, not after the way you treated her," he snapped. "She loves me more than you can ever understand. Here read for yourself."

Hannah read the words, and her face paled.

"Yes, you understand now. The man threatened to kill me if she became my wife and burn the mills down," he said. "It is because of her love for me that she left. She would sacrifice her happiness for me. What would you sacrifice, Mother?"

"Where are you going?"

"After her."

"What about the mills. How long will you be gone?"

"Higgins and as long as it takes." He turned towards her and crossed his arms. "Here I tell you of her leaving and with her all my hopes for happiness and all you can think to ask about are the mills and how long I'll be gone, but this is what you wanted."

"No, John, I didn't want this. I never wanted her to be—"

"Didn't you?" He walked pass her and picked up his bags. At the doorway, he stopped and turned, eyes glaring at her. "You are a fool to believe that we will go on as before. It was you who killed our bond, not Miss Hale."

The slamming of the door echoed throughout the house.

John's words had Hannah's head ringing and the memory of her running the blade over a draped wrist. The pool of blood and her husband's lifeless face flashed in her mind; thereafter, another flash and she was looking into the lifeless face of her son.

Lightning struck her violently and the stark realization of her words and actions over the past months hit her all at once. Symbolically, did she draw the blade over John's wrist, and bleeding any love that he had for her out?

Hannah dropped to her knees and buried her face in her hands. She knew the answer and cried shameful tears.

No wedding dress or veil, not even the burlap sack and crown of straw; Margaret wore her favourite dress of pale yellow with white lacy embellishments. Her soft brown hair was down, pulled back, and weaved with thin ribbons allowing wispy ringlets to escape to the edges of her graceful neck.

Nicholas and John waited outdoors by the carriage for her to come out of the cottage. The sound of the door unlatching had both men turning. The fading rays of light created delicate shadows, and softened the hue of her flawless, pale skin. Nicholas clamped his hand on John's shoulder, non-verbally letting the younger man know that he was a lucky man.

John's smile broadened in awed approval; she was the wild rose he stolen away that day in Helstone. She bloomed with simplicity and grace. His Maggie was the fresh air that taken his breath away.

The sun was moments away from setting when John and Margaret arrived at the small parsonage in Trentside. Nicholas opened the church door for the couple, and followed behind, honored to be the only witness to the joyful occasion.

Because of the darkening hour, lighted candles flickered, casting a warm glow throughout the quaint place of worship. With her arm secured around his, John walked his bride down to the waiting parson.

Lowering his head a little sideways, he commented on how short the aisle seemed. Margaret beamed up at him and hugged his arm in response.

The kind-hearted parson smiled and nodded at the man and woman standing before him, and opened the book.

John woke to a symphony of birds waking at the dawn's light with his wife cradled in his arms and her slender body laying alongside the length of him. Closing his eyes, he could feel every touch of her body—her palm rested on his ribcage, a smooth bared-leg draped over his with the tiny foot contoured to his lower calf, and her warm breath on his collarbone. Only she was not as he left her when she drifted to sleep. He felt the soft material of her nightgown; she had put it back on.

In her modesty, she must have wakened while he slept and dressed. He would savor her shyness for he was sure that it would fade with time as she got more at ease with their intimacy. He grinned, wondering if she closed her eyes tight to his nakedness upon returning to bed, or did curiosity get the better of her? He would have to ask her later.

Drawing in a rejuvenating breath, he was ready to love her again. Kissing the top of her head and fingering her soft tresses, he decided he could wait. Neither received much sleep the night before in anticipation and excitement of their nuptials, and with the attack most likely still fresh on her mind, he wanted her to rest.

Turning his head, he looked out of the nearby window, thick branches, and greenery from the huge English oak kept the room dimmed from the brightening day. It crossed his mind that he would have liked to have such a climbing tree outside of his window as a lad.

It would have helped in making a quick escape from his father and at times, Fanny.

A faint grin appeared as he imagined catching his son up in a tree, while his cross mother, hands on her hips, scolding the boy down before he hurt himself. The vision of having a son was pleasing.

Margaret shifted to her side, enough for him to be able to stretch out his arms over his head and elongate his torso, exhaling a long sigh of contentment. John's eyes settled on her, as a finger move some of her hair off her cheek so he could study her face at rest. Beautiful.

His eyes then roamed the length of her. Although she was back in her gown, he remembered vividly her idyllic proportioned, unclothed body and smooth, soft skin that covered its entirety. Undeniably, he could say with absolute certainty, that she is the handsomest woman he ever beheld from top of her head to her pretty toes. Finally, she was now his, under that sacred and binding union. He would forever thank God for her.

He could not help compare how different this morning was compared to all other mornings in his lifetime. The sights, sounds and freshness in the air, made an entirely new world for him. Even the bedroom, with the antique empire bed and furniture, rugs, and fresh flowers, had a different feel of comfort and hominess he never experienced before.

Along with waking with his lovely Maggie next to him, created the best morning of his life, and the night before, was everything he imagined it to be and more.

John expected her virginal shyness and tentativeness the first time and did everything to stimulate her gently into complete womanhood. His hands and mouth glided over in gentled worship, as he prepared her for his coming need.

When they came together and she gasped at the sudden stab of pain, he stopped. In their intimate attachment, his eyes locked on hers, looking for a sign for him to continue.

"That cannot be all there is to it," she exclaimed innocently with flaming cheeks.

"No, Love, I was waiting for the sting to go away," he said, trying to hold back his passion. "Can I continue?"

Still a little frightened and not knowing what to expect, she bravely nodded. John released his hold and took her mouth passionately, then moving downwards to bury his face in her neck, while purposefully moving to take her until that momentous height when he felt her quake and shutter under him, and finding his fulfillment that left them both breathless.

At length, he asked her how she was and she could only look at him with wide beautiful eyes filled with wonder. Her pleasure was evident without words. He luxuriated in her afterglow and his gratification of making her completely his, to have and to hold forever.

Any shadows of darkness or uncertainty across her heart, were now gone. She felt blissfully happy, fully alive in her husband's arms. Unable to speak, and wanting to desperately blend into him, she held him as closely to herself as she possibly could.

John rolled taking her with him so she was lying on top of his chest. The sudden draft made her conscious of her own nakedness. Blushing, she drew the sheet up between them. Her husband chuckled as he moved some of her hair from blocking his view of her face.

It was perplexing that she did not know when the nightgown left her. Did it get up and walk away? No, it was there, over by the chair. Even though she now knew the mystery of "knowing" one's husband, she wanted the gown back on. Feeling her husband move beside her, she remembered why the gown had to be removed.

Apart from the brief pain, the experience was beyond description, leaving her utterly speechless. John's pleasurable administrations brought out a different kind of ache that was neither unpleasant nor unwelcome. How his eyes hypnotized her into complete trust, luring her down into his command. He left nothing unexplored with his fingers and mouth. She needed him but she knew not in what manner, until he moved…

Oh, what he did to her!

Her palms went flying to her enflamed face, and his laughter sounded. Lightly kissing her shoulder blade, he assured her that time will erase her blushing. Shaking her head, she replied that was not possible, and that she would assuredly start blushing in every shade on the color pallet.

His laughter recurred with more resonance, lighting her face with pleasure. Toppling her over onto her back, he pulled the sheet out, his hand moving between their bodies, smoothing up her stomach to the soft mounds above. He positioned his mouth close to her ear.

"Let us see what shade this time around, Mrs. Thornton."

Her nervous laugh had him looking up at her. "What is it, Maggie? Tell me."

"Will it hurt again?"

He grinned, shaking his head. "No more pain, Love. Only the first time."

A look of relief crossed her face. "I am glad of it." Feeling much more relaxed, she touched the side of his face, noticing the color of his stunning eyes. "I'm thinking blue."

Later, John was unsuccessful in achieving the desired color in her cheeks, but Margaret thought that it was not for the lack of trying.

Margaret's restful languishing by her husband's side renewed her energy allowing her curiosity to find courage to ask him if they created a baby. He said possibly. In a couple of months, they should know with the absence of her monthly cycle.

Her mouth drop wide in shock at him mentioning such things, let alone knowing about the workings of a woman's body. He grinned, reminding her that he lived in a house full of women and that, as husband and wife, there was little they would not know about each other. Nodding, she saw how that could be true. Taking that as an invitation, Margaret endeavored to explore her husband's anatomy.

Propped up on the headboard and pillows, his arm draped along her back, he observed her every expression and movement as she went on her exploration.

Sitting half up with the sheet covering her front, her hand journeyed over his shoulders, chest, and ribcage, then down his stomach, stopping when she reached his lower half that the same sheet covered.

He spoke huskily, "Don't stop there, Maggie. I'm all yours, in body and spirit."

Her eyes lifted to his. "I cannot. I guess I am not yet prepared to go any further."

Unable to help himself he reached up, gripped her upper arms, and laid her on her back while looking down into her surprised face. "Then we need to practice."

"John, you're the devil, throwing that back at me at such a time."

Together they laughed but within minutes, the friction caused by touching skin, caused desire to take over.

His body laid heavily on the whole length of her but to Margaret it was a pleasing weight. She felt acutely the heightening warmth emulating from his body that sent currents of anticipation to register in her mind. He kissed her deeply, creating stirrings, and then he moved down. She gasped as he nipped and touched areas sending unfamiliar strange sensations to course through her body.

Something was building up inside her and she wanted to give back to him in some way but did not know how. So as calmly as she could, under the circumstances with him doing delightful things, she simply asked.

"John?"

He looked up. "Too fast for you, Maggie?"

She shook her head, as she brushed hair away from his forehead. "John...what can I do?"

He nuzzled her neck, his breath warm on her skin. "In time it will come to you but until then, allow me to love you and take you up." She gave him a bewildered look. He whispered on her lips to clarify, "Be prepared to fly, Love."

How could she have possibly forgotten? She had compared it to a lightning strike from her thundering Mr. Thornton but she could see how it could compare to soaring. Wrapping her arms around her husband's neck, anticipation started to build as she readied herself; John was about to give her wings to fly.

Margaret groggily began to wake and as her custom was, she mentally listed things she wanted to do for the day. The dress, its final fitting, a basket for Clara who was recently widowed, poor thing, letter to Edith and…

A sudden movement had her eyes flying open in alarm. Springing up she turned quickly to find a man sleeping in her bed! Then she remembered, and her stiffened body relaxed as her heart thrilled. Her husband!

"Good morning, Mrs. Thornton."

He is awake! Frantically, knowing what a sight she must be, her hands flew up to her hair and tried to comb through the tangles.

John chuckled as he reached around her waist and drew her down to the top of his chest and pulled her up so their faces were within an inch of each other.

"It's no use, it's a mess, and you still are so beautiful," he said lazily. "I've been waiting for you to wake, Love."

Before she could respond, he kissed her long and hard, tumbling her over until he was on top. Breaking the kiss, he fingered the lacy collar of her nightgown.

"Did you get chilled?" he asked smirking.

She looked up at him with a guilty expression, "I'm sorry, John."

"Don't be. I enjoy unwrapping a gift," he said as his fingers reached down to pull the nightgown up, "even if it is the same gift over and over again."

She felt an overflowing spring of joy and contentment as her new partner in life adored her with his lips and hands. As he loved her, she gained the courage to do something she always wanted to do and her fingers threaded fully through his ebony hair, luxuriating in the smooth coolness. He lifted his head and blue eyes met her mossy hazel as he gave her a pleased grin.

"That is what I meant when I said it would come to you on what you can do for me."

"My fingers in your hair?"

"More will follow. I'll try to be patient in waiting for you to discover these little acts in pleasing me."

"Can you not tell me?"

"I like for you to discover them on your own, but I may find myself giving you hints here and there."

He started to pull his head from her fingers and she did not allow it. She drew his head down to return his kiss but to deepen it as well in a manner that she never attempted before. When their mouths parted, John's eyes, darkened with fresh desire, locked with hers.

Pleased with his reaction, she ran her hand up his chest. "There…no hint was needed that time."

Clearing his throat, he found her neck. "You're a quick study, my wife."

"I'm glad of it for I do not like the idea of my husband doing all the work."

"Work!" He descended to move his lips over her collarbone and inch his way down and across her covered bosom. "Maggie, loving you'll never be considered a labored undertaking. It gives me life like the blood that flows in my veins."

Hands still embedded in his hair she lifted his head up higher. "John Thornton, you sounded like a poet right then."

He groaned lightheartedly, "You have me a poet now."

She gave him an apologetic smile; drawing him back to her and coaxed him to take in more of the area he was previously uncovering. She drew her leg up in-between his, fueling the fire he was building for her. When she heard him groan in pleasure, she felt like breaking out in song herself and could not wait for him to unwrap her over again.

Turning her head for him to explore more of her neck, she noticed the time; it was half past ten. She smiled to herself. Miss Margaret Hale would have been aghast at the lateness of the hour and jumped out of bed, but as Mrs. John Thornton, she most certainly, would not.

Dixon watched out of the large kitchen window at the mistress and her new master walking the grounds. It was quite late when they came down and eaten. Afterwards, he led her outdoors to introduce her to the rest of the property.

The day before, while waiting for Mr. Thornton to arrive from Milton, the mistress and she explored the inside of the charming cottage together. The mistress was the picture of happiness itself, revering every thing from top to bottom. The appraisal took all morning for the place was not small, twice as big as the parsonage in Helstone, complete with fine servant's quarters and a small livery yard.

When the master arrived, the mistress had forgotten herself, bounding out of door and into his arms as he climbed out of the carriage. Surprise lighted his face as he grabbed her up.

"It's the best place on earth!" she exclaimed, as he twirled her around.

With hands on her waist, he lowered to meet her smiling eyes. "You love it? Truly, Maggie?" he asked like an unbelieving boy.

Flushed with joy she nodded emphatically. "Oh, yes, we are going to be happy here."

"Fine place you got here, miss. If ever you need someone to work a spade—"

"Nicholas!" Margaret escaped John's embrace and hugged the older man standing behind him.

Dixon watched all this happening with a contented heart and smug expression. It was hard to believe that only two nights before her mistress was nearly killed. As for herself, she could easily learn to like the place if master kept to his promise that she would have more help and a dedicated cook. Yes, she could like it very much indeed.

Raising her head to glance again out the window at the mister and missus, her jaw dropped. He had her up high up in the air, her hands on his shoulders and smiling down at him as he smiled up. The master then brought her down to kiss her, dipping her slightly in his arms. Dixon snorted, a little over dramatic in her opinion but such as they were only just wed, not surprising.

That aside, Dixon snickered. Back in Milton, they would not even be able to have such shows of affection. Yes, Dixon was glad to be out of Milton, and she was sure that Mr. and Mrs. Thornton was glad as well.

Only a week into their marital retreat, Margaret was in a simple dark green, country dress, her hair worn down with a ribbon containing most of the unruly strands in back, and him in basic brown trousers and white shirt. They marveled at each other's transformation.

You would not believe, as a casual observer, that he was a hardened tradesman and she a prim and proper lady of one and twenty. They both had an air of young, first love. Basket in hand, together they both embarked on a pleasant afternoon together.

After they ate and drank wine in the picturesque spot, they found themselves contented. Margaret sat up with legs tucked behind her on the side while his head was pillowed on her lap. One of her arms rested over his shoulder while her other hand played with his thick black hair.

John could not help closing his eyes and letting a deep sigh of contentment escape him. He now knew why she coveted Helstone and the South's peaceful and slow-paced living. He would gladly get lost in it with her forever.

"You are quiet. What are you thinking?" she asked, kissing his forehead.

His eyes opened slowly and lifted to hers. "I want to paint the shutters on the house green, like the color of your dress."

"Now that is something I will need to see, John Thornton."

"You don't think I can do it?"

She laughed sweetly, "I am sure you would do well but I picture you in your black jacket, armed with a brush and your topper filled with paint."

John laughed heartily, his full smile made him look all but seventeen. She will never get over how his smile altered his appearance completely.

"Is there anything you would like done to the place?" he asked.

She thought for a moment and shook her head, "Not a thing to our dirty little cottage." His grin widened remembering Fanny's disingenuous description of their home. "However, I do want to try my hand in a garden."

His brow rose. "A garden…in the dirt. You?"

"Really, John, you sound so surprised. We had a small garden in Helstone. Mamma loved her garden, and we spent many happy hours there, talking and," bending her head closer and giving him a beguiling look, "getting dirty."

"If it is a garden and dirt you want, that is what my Maggie will get, but I insist upon a wide hat and gloves."

"Even now you are negotiating."

"You knew what you were getting yourself into."

"Yes, but I will have to draw a line at signing contracts for muddied shoes and allowable amounts of perspiration."

John's fingers rubbed his chin in thought. "I'll have them drawn up immediately."

She rolled her eyes and he drew her in to give a reward for her tolerance of an over-protective husband.

Margaret became enthusiastic at the prospect of having a vegetable and flower garden and chatted animatedly about it. She spoke on how nice it was to add fresh vegetables and floral arrangements to charitable baskets to go along with the breads. His wife, all ready thinking of others, he thought admirably. John imagined the whole of the county would be falling for her as he did.

He could picture her digging in the dirt and weeding. He would not begrudge her the activity and glad that it would occupy a lot of her time while he was away during the day. He promised to speak to Samuel, a local widower he hired to be the property keeper, to till some ground for her.

Their conversation turned to talk about getting a single-horse carriage and horses for him to drive back and forth into Milton during the week. Margaret thrilled at the thought of having domestic animals, and soon had him agreeing to chickens, but commenting that he was not too keen on the idea of the rooster abruptly waking them each morning.

A mischievous smile appeared on her face as she whispered in his ear causing him to prop up on his elbow with intense astonishment written on his expression.

"Early morning activities?"

"It is customary for southerners to rise with the first light to start chores. I do not see why it cannot apply here."

"You were not talking about gathering eggs and feeding livestock!" he laughed.

"No, I see no reason to keep it mostly a nightly pursuit. Do I have your agreement in that?"

"Most heartily!"

"Then it is settled, until that is," her eyes sparkled again, "we get the Jersey cow, you can do the early morning milking."

John grabbed her and rolled her over with a mock scowl, "There I must draw a line, Mrs. Thornton!"

He tried to stay serious but her comical expression had him bursting and her following. While hugging each other in their shared humor, they listed nonsensical chores that each would be assigned. In the end, they both agreed that Dixon would get the unsavory responsibility of catching, decapitating, and pulling of feathers off the dinner chicken.

The couple found themselves in all easiness, basking in the perfectly warm, early August afternoon, under the shade of an ancient elm. John laid himself out flat on the unfolded quilt, with hand behind his head, looking up into the blue heavens. Margaret found her head's pillow on his breast, sighing restfully, as his free hand roamed up and down her back.

She loved the sound of his heart under her ear but found the material of his shirt muffling the sound and the buttons pressing into her skin. Her fingers made the way up to rid her of these irritations. Successful, her husband's steady heartbeat, quickened.

Only a week into their marriage, her modesty was still present but she felt it was time to take some responsibility in pleasing her husband. The thought of him loving her in the daylight stirred her insides. On God's carpet, under the shadow of His wings, she deeply desired her Adam to know her.

Not affronted by the birds and wildlife that would witness their intimacy, she worked to further undress him while trailing behind with her lips. Her want was consuming her.

John used a considerable amount of control as her hands found the barrier to his lower half and fumbled with the buttons. Her hands were not steady as her eyes looked up with pleading for his help. Appreciating her attempt, he kissed her hands, and took command of ridding himself of the rest of his clothes for her.

With her husband anatomy fully exposed, she proceeded with her exploration and attentions. John delighted in her inquisitiveness. After all, it was in the light of day and not a dimmed bedroom. Curious on what she was thinking, he asked.

Margaret did not blush this time, but gave him the most sincere look, telling him that he was created beautifully and perfectly, and considered herself blessed by God for bringing them together as husband and wife.

Then something singular came over her. Her head fell, and she started to tremble, causing him to grab on to her arm with concern. Lifting her face he looked into her beseeching eyes asking her what was wrong. Her fingers dug into his upper arm with urgency, as she pleaded for him to make them one flesh.

His wife's need for him was great and he exerted to fulfill that need, for it quickly became his as well. Taking full control, desiring her bared, he swiftly removed her folds. Flamed desire had him crushing her to him and bringing her down on the quilt. Black hair fell forward shadowing his concentrated stare, making his eyes the darkest of blues. He was impassionedly serious when he spoke.

"Maggie, in a few moments we will be one but I want to say this is when our child was conceived," he said lowering himself to draw his lips over her belly, while speaking against her skin. "In April of next year, I hope to hold our first child in my arms. My love," he said hoarsely, looking up, his eyes probed into her soul, "allow me complete you as my wife by making you the mother of my child."

She gasped at his words and her body started to quiver with passion and eyes watering with erupting emotions. Her fingers reached to grab his hair, drawing his face forward to be close to hers. Tears poured from the corners of her eyes, her voice full of fervent entreaty.

"I want your child growing inside me," she cried softly, with longing. "Complete me."

He took her mouth with ardent force and thundering heart, pushing aside the guidance and hints, taking full command of her womanhood. He worked her to that peak of possession and she acquiesced eagerly to his every demand.

Holding her face, he commanded her to look at him. She complied and their passion-filled eyes locked and he spoke with authority, "Maggie, remember this moment." She nodded, as he possessed her completely, she crying out his name as they reached that earth-shattering climax together. They clung to each other, breathing heavily, allowing the breeze to cool their hot skin and refresh their bodies.

After many moments past, he loved her again, gently this time, and reverently. Hands entwined together above their heads, they stayed as one under the Eden of their own making. Parting himself from her felt unnatural, but his concern for her tender areas had him rolling over and sheltering her with his solid frame.

"John, I did not know how to…to stop," she whispered breathlessly, "I didn't know myself."

He gently caressed her cheek, looking deeply into her luminescent eyes. "You are a passionate woman—beautiful, spirited, and very capable to feel complete abandonment. Don't fear it, Maggie, embrace it."

"It felt like a miracle."

"Perhaps it was. Do you think we accomplished what we set out to do?" he asked.

She moved herself so she was squarely in the center of his chest, her arms up over his shoulders, fingers again, in his hair. "Yes, I am sure of it. You were determined."

"Yes, I was," he said, "and you, my love, opened yourself to me fully. You allowed me to embed so deeply inside you. We truly were one flesh."

"I'm overwhelmed with love for you and what we did."

He rolled slightly to his side, taking her with him. His strong arms moved her up so he could reach her stomach to kiss its flat smoothness, whispering huskily with emotion how much he loved her and the child he was sure they created.

Picturing Margaret, belly swelled and his hand roaming over its fullness, feeling their baby moving inside, elevated his longing. He was going to be a father like no other. His children would not experience what he had with his. With Maggie as their mother, exceptionally blessed they will be in that as well. Wrapping the quilt over their bodies, he held her close, and they rested peacefully, bodies still entangled.

Margaret was the first to come out of their light slumber, and she began to move to free herself from the quilt. She could not get out; the edges were under John. She wiggled, and he, coming awake, threatened that if she did not stop she would be forced to address his needs again.

Her hand smoothed down his cheek, telling him that whenever he reached for her, she would always submit. He kissed her tenderly saying that he was concern that further exertions may cause her discomfort later and he would prefer to wait. Nestling into her husband's neck, she sighed at his loving care for her.

After a moment, she giggled. He gave her an inquisitive look. Lifting her head, she shuffled up to meet his gaze.

"John, we're cocooned."

"So it would seem," he laughed. "Well, Mrs. Thornton, shall we break out and fly away."

She kissed his lips quickly. "But, sir, you've took me to such heights before, where else am I to go?"

"Ah, Maggie," he said kissing the closest part of her, the top of her nose, "I guess you'll have to come home with me."

She hugged him to herself, whispering, "With you, I am home."

It was late day when they walked back. They both discussed that on the last weekend of each month, when weather permitted, that they would picnic in their designated place under the big tree, even when they were overwhelmed with a dozen children and troubles at both the mills.

Holding out his hand as if closing a business dealing she took it. "Then it is agreed, Mrs. Thornton."

"Agreed."

John did not let her hand go but used it to pull her to him to give her an impassioned kiss of promise. ༀ

Chapter Thirteen
Parting & Revelations

"Maggie, wake up, Love. Wake up."

Breathing heavily, Margaret's flickering eyelids opened and focused on John's face as reality cleared the dark dream.

Trembling, she clung to him. "John…oh, John."

"Ah, hush now," he coddled while smoothing away the damp hair from her tortured expression.

"I reached you but I was too late," she cried, "your blood…my hands were covered."

Rocking her while his low voice soothed, he pressed his cheek to hers and held the back of her head to control some of her shaking.

Sobbing into his nightshirt, her arms wrapped around his neck like an iron padlock, as extreme anxiety and anguish weighed her down. Lifting her face, he planted kisses where her tears were trailing, tasting the saltiness, and feeling her frustration.

It had been the first nightmare since they were married three weeks before. John could only attribute its sudden appearance because that evening he informed her that he would be returning to Milton in the morning.

Finding Margaret sitting on the sofa in the main room, he walked over to where she sat, and bent to greet her with a kiss, asking what she was reading. Smiling, she closed the book so he could see the cover.

Straightening, his head tilted to regard her. "Gardening and Botany. Determined to have a successful harvest, Love?"

Opening the book again, she nodded. "You can only reap what is sowed correctly," she said. "I want to do it right."

Lowering again, his finger reached under her chin to direct her attention up. "In spring, we may be reaping what had been sown a fortnight ago."

She flushed with remembrance, as he fused a gradual kiss of hope on her mouth before rising and walking over to pour a drink. Placing himself by the fireplace, he stared absently into the low flames. Taking a sip from the glass, he set it on the mantle, so he could rub his forehead. Lowering his hand, he glanced at Margaret, so lovely and serene, peacefully engrossed in the book. Head dropping, he forced his attention back to the fire.

"John, what is it? You're restless tonight."

He let out a sigh and turned towards her. "Maggie, tomorrow I go back."

Their eyes locked from across the room, but her face remained passive. As she saw him approaching her, she responded by nodding but not saying a word.

Reaching her side he asked, "Do you want to talk about this?"

Lowering her eyes, she shook her head as she flipped to the next page of the book. He knew she was no longer reading the words; she was most likely withdrawing into a place of dread from separation. He had arrived there himself when he made the decision.

Reaching down he took the book from her, closing it and tossing it to the side, while holding out his other hand for her to take. Her fingers folded over his and he fluidly helped her rise and led her up the stairs to their bedroom.

Margaret stood silent as he undressed her and pulled her nightgown over her head and then he dressed in his nightshirt. Lifting her up into his arms, he carried her to their bed. Spooned together, he placed her head close to his center, allowing his heart's beat lull her to sleep.

John was relieved; she seemed resolved and accepting. Until, that is, he awoke to her thrashing and crying out for him.

"Maggie, I will be safe. I'll return to you."

"No, stay. I do not want you to go. If I could beg for one thing from you, it would be to beg you not to go. Please, another week."

"Don't make this any harder for me." He eased her down on the bed with his arms securely locked around her. "I have to see to the investigation and Higgins needs my help."

"I know, I am being selfish."

"Selfish! You are the least selfish person I know. You fear for me. That is not selfish," he replied.

"I fear for you, but more I cannot be without you."

Margaret now knew what her parents had in their marriage, that pure love that two people could share together. Her mind wandered back to her father speaking to his dead wife lying on her deathbed as if she was still alive and listening. John could not guarantee he would be safe and she agonized, would that be her talking to John lying on his?

"If that be the case, I am selfish as well," he said.

"John then—"

His tone hardened slightly, "Don't ask me again, Margaret. I will go."

Her open mouth clamped, and she swiveled her head away. He recognized that his own struggles with his raging emotions were starting to reveal themselves, and it was having its effect on her. He sought to release them in a more precious way.

His hand found the small of her back, while the other found

the back of her head, raising her up; he found the soft fullness of her mouth, huskily whispering his love and want of her on her lips.

Margaret's arms raised and he lifted her gown off. With all gentleness and devotion in the entire fiber of his being, he brought their bodies together in exquisite harmony with one another that left her clinging to him not wanting their intimate bond to be broken.

Exhausted with her own emotions, he managed to sooth and caress her to sleep. While she filled all of his physical desires, he allowed her to tear apart his soul, leaving him unable to endure seeing the pain in her expression and hear her pleading words. There would be no sleepy smiles for him, or her cuddling against his body as they leisurely welcomed the morning together.

At the first rays of light, he kissed his wife's peaceful face then extracted himself from her sleeping form. Dressed, he returned to the bedside to pull the quilt up to compensate for the absence of his warm body. For a moment, he stood looking down as she slept, detailing every inch of her including the fading wound on her delicate neck.

His countenance turned serious, as his purpose and responsibilities magnified. Bending down he touched her exposed cheek with the back of his fingers and whispered in a low voice that he loved her.

Picking up the black suit jacket, he flung it over his shoulder, turned and walked out of the room.

Margaret woke to find him gone.

Inundated with shame of her begging, she regretted causing him more heartache in having to leave. Why could she not be strong and supportive in his decision? A fine wife would have sent him off with a reassuring smile and words of encouragement. Wiping the tears angrily from her eyes, she busied herself to prevent more from spilling.

After dressing, she worked to make the bed, noticing his head print in the pillow. She grabbed it up, and hugged it to her face, taking in his familiar masculine scent. Lowering herself to her knees by the bedside, she spoke fervently in prayer for her husband and for him to come back safely.

Write him was the first thought that came to her mind after her finished prayer. Sitting at the writing desk near the window, she looked out, her mind searched for the words to start with.

Her mind wandered, wishing that she could think of a way to help find her attacker. If only she could talk to her father. What would he say? He was so analytical in his gentleness. He meditated over things that many would overlook making his memory practically faultless.

My dear, go for the smaller details, it will help fill in the gaps that complete the picture.

Dipping the pen into the ink, she mentally prepared herself to relive that horrible night in every detail.

John's letter would have to wait.

John walked into Hamper's office to find Higgins sitting behind the desk bent over some papers.

Looking up he stood. "I didn't know you would be coming back this day," he said, coming from behind the desk.

"Higgins." John stepped forward and the men clasped hands. "Is all well since your last update?"

"Yes, at both sites. I take it by the look on your face you've seen Mason."

John nodded. Mason described in detail all that transpired in the investigation. The search was extensive and yet, his frustration elevated with the inspector informing him that they were no further along in the case than they had been that first night.

Leaving Margaret darkened his mood, but hearing about the lack of progress in the investigation all but made it volatile. Furthermore, he had yet to see his mother.

His head began to ache at the thought. At least the mills seemed to be doing well with Higgins as master. As he conversed with the man, John continued to be impressed by him.

Higgins caught on remarkably well without a formal education. His experience in working in the industry was vast which was two-thirds the battle. Ironically, his Union leadership helped him to transition well into the role of master. The man could delegate and pass out authority when needed. It was the book work that Higgins still needed his further instruction, but it was passing muster.

Again, Margaret did a good thing by sending the man his way. At times, he believed that the woman had more business sense than he did.

"And the missus, how is she?" Higgins asked.

"She is well, but she'll not be in good spirits this day."

"I imagine she is not all together glad to be separated from such an attentive husband."

John nodded with a faraway look on his face and replied absently, "She woke in the night fearful for me. First time since we've been married."

"Cannot see that I blame her considering his threats. Master, sit." Higgins indicated to the leather-backed chair behind the desk. "I have something that may be of some interest."

This immediately broke his vision of his wife waking up alone in their bed. Seeing where Higgins wanted him to sit, he shook his head.

"Higgins, as I said before, the day I wed is the day you became partner and master. That chair is now yours. You earned it."

"Master, I don't—"

"Thornton or John. We are equals now."

Higgins grinned still not believing his good fortune. "Well, forgive me if it takes some getting used to the new title, sir." Both men grinned. "But master or not, I don't feel myself in these clothes. And the hat, I'll take my cap over it if I could."

"We all have a part to play, Higgins. I got a taste of country living and more casual dress. I found it hard to don the necktie and master's jacket as well."

Higgins chuckled and shook his head. "Shirt and trousers

perhaps, but a cap, that I cannot see."

"No cap. Margaret even has the topper permanently attached to my character," he said with the corner of his mouth rising, "filled with green paint."

"Sir?"

"Higgins, sorry I was remembering."

Nicholas smirked, "A bonnie face perhaps."

He nodded speaking, "Higgins, you said you needed to speak to me about something. About the mills?"

"Not the mills. All be running well with little worries there. It's Mrs. Thornton, sir, your mother that is."

"Mother? She is no longer allowed on the floor."

"Yes, sir, but she come by yesterday. Asked if I heard from you saying she needed to talk to you right away. I was going to come out after hours to speak to you about it."

Frowning, John shook his head. "I don't want to deal with her ploys right now."

"Well, may be you do." John looked up at him as he continued, "She wanted to find you because she said she knows who attacked the missus."

"What? I find that hard to believe."

"That is what I told her after speaking to Mason only hours before about the investigation's progress myself."

"What did she have to say?"

"That's just it. She wouldn't say. For your ears only."

"I question why she didn't go to the authorities if she wants Margaret's attacker caught? Another of my mother's games, Higgins."

"Perhaps, but what harm to hear her out? Not like there is anywhere else to go."

Nodding, he had to agree with him there. "I will speak to her later at the house."

"She'll not be there. Said she moved to your sister's home. That is where you'll find her."

He was stunned but did not trust his mother's motives, what ever it may be in moving in with Fanny, and he told Higgins as much.

Getting up from the chair, John walked over to the desk and looked down at the pile of papers in front of Higgins.

"First let us take care of business. I notice the books open."

"Worse part of the job."

John put his hand on his partner's shoulder. "Leave it to me, Higgins."

"Gladly, Thornton."

The two men worked straight until early afternoon and made their way to the luncheon hall. It being towards the end of the hour, the place was clearing out. Both sat as a middle-aged woman, stout but comely, came by to serve them.

John could not help noticing the smile the woman gave to Higgins, and he returning it warmly. Picking up the fork, he started in on his plate.

"Finally got around to getting extra help here, I see," he said casually.

Higgins dropped his face more to his plate. "Clara…Clara Browne, fine cook, and very capable. Lost her husband about a month ago."

"She's on her own?"

He nodded. "Five children, all grown. I knew the father. He was a good man and friend."

"I'm sorry. Why didn't you tell me?"

"Glad I didn't, seemed to have your hands full."

John nodded, and felt a little body take place next to him. Grinning, he glanced down, as Thomas was glancing up.

"Where'd ya go?" the boy asked fearlessly.

"Away." John replied as he put his arm around him. "What book are you reading?"

The little boy's eyes lighted as he regaled to tell him about the man, Robinson Crusoe, stranded on an island.

"What no Foster's Industrial Revolution yet?" John teased. The expression on the boy's face caused both men to laugh aloud catching the attention of the straggler patrons.

Higgins reached over and tousled the boy's hair, "Don't mind him lad. I'll let you read it when you are having trouble getting to sleep," he said glancing at John. "Works every time."

"Glad you are getting some use out of reading it, Higgins."

Both men were still enjoying their amusement when Clara walked by. Higgins waved her over.

"Clara, Mr. John Thornton," he introduced, "John, Mrs. Clara Browne."

John went to stand but Clara motioned him not to get up. "Don't, sir, finish your meal. I am glad to meet you. Nicholas speaks highly of you."

He sat back down, "I am sorry to hear of your husband, Mrs. Browne. If there is anything I can do."

"Thank you, sir. I am doing well," she said glancing at Nicholas, "I've found a nice fit here, and I have the master here to be thankful for. If you excuse me, I'll get back to work." She put her hand on Thomas' shoulder. "Come away, Tom, let the men be."

After the two walked away, John smirked at Higgins. "One moment she is calling you Nicholas, the next master, which one is it?"

"Noticed that, you did?"

He nodded adding, "And the looks going on between you weren't hard to miss."

Nicholas gave him an appalled expression. "It's only been a month since she put her husband, my friend, in the grave, and you think we could have moved on so quickly?"

I'm afraid Miss Hale and I met under less than pleasant circumstances. I had to dismiss a worker for smoking in the sorting room.

I saw you beat a defenseless man who is not your equal! A gentleman would not use his fists on such a pathetic creature, or shout at children.

Placing his hand on his friend's shoulder, John nodded, "Higgins, trust me when I say, it can happen within days under any unpleasant circumstances."

Looking over at the woman crouching by Thomas, going

over numbers on his writing tablet, Higgins chuckled, "Well then, I think I am in trouble, sir."

John entered the opulent parlor of his sister's and frowned with distaste. She outdid herself he mused. Watson's fortune, no matter how huge, was in jeopardy with his sister's expensive gaudy taste.

"John! Where have you been? Mother and I were worried sick!"

Turning, he found his sister by his side. "Fanny," he greeted, kissing her cheek.

"Well? What happened with Miss Hale? Frankly, John, I all together think she really wasn't the one for you but with her wealth and all—"

"I did not come to talk about Miss Hale, Fanny. I need to speak to mother. Where is she?"

"Really, John, you disappear for weeks without a word and come back with no explanation—"

"Mother, Fanny, now."

Affronted, Fanny frowned, "You dare treat me this way in my own house."

He let out an exhausted sigh forgetting his sister's need to have an air of superiority. Patience wearing thin, he decided it was better for her to have it this time.

"Forgive me, Fanny. I am out of sorts and need to speak to mother immediately. It is urgent."

"Really, you can be so rude. She is upstairs."

"I'm here. John, you're back." Hannah brushed by Fanny and embraced her son who stood stiffly.

"Mother."

"John, may I ask about Miss Hale?"

"She has not returned here. That is all I am going to say."

Yes, he thought with a pained expression. She was there and he was here. He was feeling their separation acutely.

Putting her hand on his arm, Hannah looked up at him with beseeching eyes. "Tell me where she is. I'll go to her and do whatever I can to bring her back to you."

He looked into his mother's face and saw sincerity but tested her still. "I was right, I never did deserve her."

Hannah's eyes watered. "Yes, you did. It was I who didn't deserve the both of ye." Grabbing her son's arm tighter she turned him to face her directly. "I was a foolish, old crow. I know that now. Tell me what I can do to make it up to you both. Please, John, I did this to you and her. I should be the one to bring about reconciliation."

Fanny piped in, "You did nothing, Mother! Why should you—"

John spoke abruptly, "Fanny, leave us."

"No, I am mistress here."

"Fanny, please," Hannah said flatly.

"You always take his side!"

Both mother and son looked at her expectantly. Her face contorted in disgust as she swiveled angrily and stomped out of the room, mumbling.

Alone with his mother, he felt an awkwardness that had him moving to the other side of the room.

"Son, I know you don't believe me."

He turned towards her. "You would be correct. I find it very difficult."

"I have done some things that I am not proud of to keep you tied to me. I want to tell you, and get it out into the open."

"I'm listening."

Walking to his side, she took his hand and squeezed. "Please, John, promise me you'll not hate me although I will deserve it. It was an obsessive love of a foolish woman who had little love herself in her life. Know that I have come out of it, ready to make amends."

Her expression was marred with guilt and his compassion had him telling her that he would try.

Hannah walked a little ways from him and turned, taking a

deep breath, she released the words as she exhaled.

"During the strike, I let it be known that you were bringing in the Irish workers."

"What! Why would you do it?"

"I knew it would be the breaking point in ending the strike. I couldn't bear to see you fail."

"You put people at risk and some got injured!"

Margaret's limp body and bloodied temple materialized in his head. Carrying her into the parlor, his love for her already deeply embedded, he laid her on the sofa, finding his lips on her forehead, along with a prayer in his thawing heart that she would be well.

"And I am ashamed, but there is more. That is the least offense."

"There is worse!"

Tears started running down her face as she nodded. "A week before Miss Hale was attacked, I sent out a letter," she paused, wiping the tears with her palms, "to the military authorities speaking of Miss Hale's brother being here during that time of the mother's death."

John's heart stopped and he paled. Margaret! Storming over to her, he grabbed her arms. "Do you have any idea what you have done!"

"It's alright, John," she spoke rapidly, "they came to question Miss Hale but she was gone. They came to me and I told them I was mistaken."

His anger was fierce, shaking her. "What did you tell them, leave nothing out!"

She was looking into the eyes of her husband, staring at her with icy blue daggers, and a dangerous prelude. John's iron grip had her choking back harsh memories. It was her own doing in bringing to light this side of his father out in John.

Hannah spoke on how she convinced the investigators that she thought Leonards was Frederick Hale using a false name, and that she learned only after the letter was sent that it was truly Leonards.

"Inspector Mason confirmed that Miss Hale had been proven to not have been at the station that night. They left, reassure that it was only a strange notion from an old, senile woman. They know nothing more."

He abruptly let her go, having a need to be away from her. He moved to stand by the fireplace. His head fell trying to control some of the fury inside that was causing his stomach to knot and twist.

If his mother did not defuse her treachery, Margaret would have been interrogated vigorously, accused of harboring a fugitive, and bring great danger to her brother. The thought of her going through that extreme distress and anxiety had his blood boiling to the point of eruption.

With jaw clenched, he turned. "You lie so well, Mother," he said with barely controlled rage. "We were fortunate they believed your tale. If any of this gets back to harm her or her brother—"

"It won't, I promise you," she spoke with wide-eyed certainty.

He turned back gripping the mantle, his mind racing on what he needed to do to protect Margaret and her brother further. After a few moments, by all accounts, brother and sister were safe, but his bitterness for his mother remained.

Closing his eyes, he allowed Maggie's sweet voice to speak inwardly to him, bringing self-control and restraint. She helped him to release his anger by exhaling and inhale deep breaths of calm. The room remained silent for the longest time allowing him to come down to a manageable level of civility.

Sensing his dissipating anger, Hannah came up behind him and put her hand on his shoulder.

"John, I am telling you this now because I need you to trust me. I've seen the error of my ways and want to make it right."

"Why did you move here?" he asked flatly, without emotion.

"Call it self-affliction as punishment for my interfering in your life."

He could not help cracking a grin even in his temper, "Move back to the house."

"No, John. Do what you want with it. I'll not go back. I am

moving on."

"I'll not stay there alone."

"Lease it to your partner. Let him have it."

"Higgins?"

"Yes, he seems to have a need for a larger house."

That never occurred to him. Margaret would be pleased. However, as much as he wanted to embrace his mother for it the idea, some doubt in her motives prevented him from doing so.

"Higgins said you know who attacked Miss Hale. Why didn't you go to Mason?"

"This is why I need you to believe me," she said, "I didn't go because I knew that this man was interviewed and cleared."

John remained silent. She sparked his interest but his trust was still an open sore where he still expected her to rub more salt in.

"Son, hear me out at least."

"Tell me everything," he said decisively, "but I'll not tolerate any further deceptions or you'll not see me again."

She nodded and they both sat down.

"The day before yesterday, I was approached by a man who showed concern for Miss Hale and asked after her. I recognized him as the man who you threw out for smoking."

"Stephens!" He became concern. "What did you tell him about Miss Hale?"

"I said nothing except that I knew who he was and that I had nothing more to say to him. He became contrite and imparted how badly he needed work and asked me to appeal to the new master, Higgins."

"Why do you think he was the one who attacked her?"

"As he was talking I saw reddish-brown smears on the side of his shirt. I know dried blood when I see it. I decided to test him, remembering what you said that he threatened you harm if she became your wife. I said to him that you were his partner and would not authorize taking him on again but if he appealed to Miss Hale perhaps, she could convince you. His face became inflamed but he held his anger in check and said he would do just that, go to her."

John's heart began to thunder and his jaw clenched at the mere thought of that man near his Maggie.

"What he said next convinced me that it was him. He asked me where she was and I told him that she was away in London visiting family and recovering from her attack but she would be back soon. He said he was interviewed but he had an alibi," she said, pausing to grab his arm, "and hoped that her neck injury wouldn't leave a scar."

It was Stephens! Nobody on the outside knew that the knife to her throat drew blood except the attacker.

Hate pure and simple shot through John's veins and blocked all rational thought. Twisting away from his mother, he stormed to the door only to have Hannah rush to stop him.

"No, John! Don't!"

"Move away!"

Barricading him with her body, he moved to push her aside. Rage would not allow him to stop. Devil had him and he wanted nothing more than to squeeze the life out of the coward that tried to do the same to his second life's blood.

He felt the sting of her palm across his face, stopping him cold. "I'll not let ye become as your father was!"

"Mother—"

"Think John...think! The last thing Margaret needs is for you to be imprisoned or worse, killed!"

Fanny came running into the room. "What is happening here?"

Breathing heavily, he stiffly turned away from both women and went to the liquor table, downing a glass of amber restraint. The power of his mother's actions and words began to sink in.

Lifting his head up, he looked at the ceiling, letting a vision of his beautiful wife, possibly soon, full with their child, to take over his tumultuous thoughts. Dropping his head, he nodded resolutely; only because of them will Stephens live to see another day.

After much coaxing, Hannah managed to free the room of Fanny's presence once again. John was subdued but had an impatient energy that worried her.

She knew her son. He fiercely protected those who he loved and depended upon him, whom she benefited, but she abused it, and took advantage, assuming it was only hers to receive.

It took him saying that it was she who killed that love that woke her up sharply from her obsessive sleep. It snapped her out of her hate of Miss Hale as well.

Her hate was not because Miss Hale was taking her son away. No, it was because John loved her completely. She never experienced that kind of affection from her own father and her husband. Jealousy ruled her mind, hating the woman who had the love of a man, so deep and right.

She moved over to John who was now staring out of the window. Putting her hand on the back of his shoulder.

"Son, what can I do, please tell me."

He absently spoke his thoughts. "If he has been cleared, there is no proving his violence against her. I cannot let him get away."

Hannah turned him around to face her. "Then let us put our heads together and work this out," she said. "Let us bring her back to you."

John nodded, and for the first time in weeks, he embraced his mother. ☙

Chapter Fourteen
A Thundering Storm

John walked out of the factory door and out into the square when he noticed Mary Higgins approaching him. She had a look about her that alerted him that something might be amiss. Quickening his pace, he took off his hat as they met.

"Mary, what is it?"

"Sir, all is well, but please can you come with me."

Even with her reassurance, he was alarmed. It was rare for Mary to speak to him, so he followed without question and found himself led to the Higgins' newer residence in Princeton.

Mary opened the door. Upon entering, he saw Margaret rising from a chair and rush towards him. Opening his arms, they embraced while Mary herded the three children that were not schooled out the door to give the couple privacy.

The sound of the door shutting had them ardently kissing to make up for the weeklong absence from each other. The joy of rediscovery came to a sudden halt with John breaking first.

"What is it, Maggie? What is wrong?"

Catching her breath, Margaret stammered, "I had to…to see you. It was that man, that first day I saw you at the mill, the one that you were…harsh with. He attacked me."

John gripped her shoulders and peered sharply into her eyes.

"How do you know this?"

"The morning you left I woke feeling powerless to help. I became determined to go over every detail of the attack. I spent the next day's reliving each moment and writing down every detail as father did when trying to recall something specific."

"Details, like what?"

"His voice it was, how should I say, well nasal and weak, not as a man ought to talk. I knew I heard it before. He wasn't tall as you, but shorter and thin. And his odor, it had something familiar that I could not quite make out," she said, her eyes lifted to his face, "until last night. It was pipe tobacco. It all fell into place from there. It was him but I do not know his name."

"Stephens."

John's jaw clenched, hating that she forced herself to re-experience the brutality repeatedly. He wished to have the power to wipe it out of her mind forever.

"You do not believe me?"

He took her into his arms. "My clever Maggie. I know that you are right."

"They caught him! Oh, John—"

"No, they haven't. Come here and sit down. I need to explain."

Directing her to sit in a chair, he pulled another close and relayed the events of the first day he returned, leaving out his mother's confessions and the plan to catch Stephens.

She was pleased about the change in his mother and the idea to move Higgins into the larger house once their marriage became public and details settled. To be sure, it would be a rather large culture shock for the prospering family. The house did not seem to fit them but she had no qualms that they would adapt.

Upon confirmation that Stephens was the one who assaulted her and that no evidence was available to place him in prison, Margaret began to shake with fearful apprehension. Pulling her across his lap to sooth her, Margaret quickly responded.

After a few moments, she pulled out of his arms, looked

directly into his eyes, and spoke sternly, "John, you are being calm about this. You're not telling me something."

He was silent, weighing his answer before speaking.

"I wanted to kill him for what he done to you, and would have if mother hadn't stopped me." His hand ran possessively over her stomach. "She reminded me that I do not want blood on my hands and bars between us."

Margaret took up his and put it to her cheek. "I am grateful to your mother. I am glad John…so very glad," she said earnestly. "But what is to be done about this man?"

"There are things that are happening that I cannot tell you about."

"Is it dangerous?"

"Maggie, you must not worry."

She seized his jaw to command his attention. "Is it dangerous?" she repeated louder.

He found himself unable to speak and inadvertently she got her answer. John did not have a chance to react as she pushed herself off his lap and angrily stood over him.

"John Thornton, you either tell me or I am going to step out into that sun and go to Nicholas and find out myself," she threatened.

He jumped up. "No you will not! I'll not risk you."

Unyielding, she answered, "And I must stand aside and allow you to place yourself in danger? If you think that I will allow that then you'll learn something new about me this day."

"What! That my wife refuses the protection of her husband!"

His elevated voice had no effect as she firmly replied, "No. That she refuses to be a widow."

Two pair of eyes flared angrily at each other at the sudden impasse. She broke the glaring by letting out a short sound of exasperation. Grabbing her hooded shawl, she hurried to put it on as she moved towards the door, only to have him pull her back and turned her to face him.

"Margaret, don't make me—"

"John, let me go! I am not one of your laborers under your

command," she said with tempered restraint. "This marriage isn't one-sided. You cannot expect me to step aside to survive on the hope that you come home to me. That is for a soldier's wife. You stopped treating me as a child but now I am a porcelain doll to be locked away in a glass cabinet. I won't have it."

The speech had him dropping his hands to his sides. After a moment of silence between them, she continued in a depleted but determined voice.

"You either include me or not. Which is it going to be?"

"You are giving me a choice?"

"Not really, but I want to give the impression of being rational."

His lip twitched up, "Womanly wiles again."

"My parents and I waited for months while we suffered Frederick's unknown fate. I refuse to do that with you for any length of time."

"I'd forgotten about your brother." Encircling her waist, he peered down into her saddened face and spoke in a low controlled voice, "I will tell you what is happening, but you are not allowed to try to stop us from our course. Do I make myself clear?"

She shook her head. "In this I cannot agreed, John. Another mind may be useful. If I think there is a better way that will prevent you and others from being in danger, I expect to be heard and taken seriously."

"You must be the most stubborn of women."

"A trait I learned mainly from my husband."

Sighing heavily, he placed his hand on the nape of her neck and drew her forehead to touch his. "Trying to be master over you is a losing battle."

"I do still pay your wages. You haven't officially declared what is mine is now yours with us being wed."

"I declare it now. So tell me, does it change anything?"

"Not in the slightest."

He shook his head chuckling, "I thought not."

Taking up her shawl, he wrapped it around her, lifting the

hood to shadow her face.

"What are you doing?"

"Taking you home to tend to your needs, Mrs. Thornton."

"And what about your needs?"

Kissing her skin right under her ear, he spoke in a low, seductive voice. "Your fulfillment will bring about mine. In this, I know I am master."

Margaret's face went all warm and a shiver course through her body at the thought of him taking command of her in that way. Her fingers reached up and threaded up into his hair.

"Yes, you are," she whispered as his lips trailed across to her mouth. "Take me home."

He let out a groan as he kissed her deeply. Breaking suddenly, he hooked her arm with his, picking his hat off the table, he made for the door. Putting his hand on the handle, he paused and turned to her.

"I will say this now, Love. I am going to have my way with you before I speak another word about any strategies. I'll not chance that fiery temper of yours depriving me of intimacy."

Margaret felt a thrill shoot through her frame. "Husband, in that regard you have no cause to worry. I can guarantee you that you'll not be denied."

"I'd like to get that in writing."

Her light laughter was music to his ears. Using his arm as leverage, she raised herself up to kiss his grinning lips. "Always thinking as a business man."

He returned her kiss lingering to add, "Wait until I get you home. I assure you that trade and industry will be furthest from my thoughts."

Less than a mile from the cottage, John turned the single-horse carriage down an overgrown path.

"John, where are we going?"

"Maggie, forgive me," he said leaning over to speak more intimately, "My need for you is great. I cannot wait."

Her eyes widened. "It is going to rain. The sky is about—"

"Let it rain, I need you," he said with urgency. "Now."

Her mouth dropped at the tone of his low husky voice and the intense craving in his eyes. As the carriage dipped and tilted on the rough trail, she began to feel a thrilling sense of intrigue. She knew what her husband wanted to do, but the pressing question needed to be asked.

"But where, John?"

The thunder clapping drown out the question, and raindrops started to pelt the top of the carriage. He pulled the horse up to a small clearing near a grove of trees, and sprang out. Coming around to her side, he did not wait for her hand for help out of the carriage. Hooking his arms under her, he raised her out, carrying her purposefully, to where, she did not know.

Margaret's feet touch solid ground and John took her mouth fully, hands clasping the sides of her waist, he slowly backed her up until she felt the rough bark of a tree on her backside.

She gasped at the delayed answer to her question. How was it possibly to happen? Her cheeks burned hot, but not because she was feeling mortification; it was because of the intoxicating excitement shooting through her body.

His hands anxiously labored on the barriers of fabric. "Sweetest Maggie," he mumbled against her skin, "I need to feel us whole again. I need to be inside you."

John's passion induced words and exertions had her wanting him as desperately and her fingers searched for the buttons to help.

For an instant, a flash of the man, forcibly trying to take her against the brick wall, came to mind. But the thought was fleeting. This is not the same. John's lovemaking erased all that. Her husband was taking what his wife wanted to give. As eccentric and avant-garde the position may be, she would submit to satisfy his masculine hunger.

He must have read her thoughts and blue-flamed eyes found hers. "Forgive me…forgive me," he begged.

"I want…I need you, John, please," she said wildly, not

hearing his appeals.

His want was full and ready. Finding her core, he probed to see if she was prepared. Wrapping her arms around his neck, she was anxious for him to move to take her.

"Hold on to me," he instructed impatiently.

Margaret instinctively brought her leg up to rest on his hip to give him more access. Moving tenaciously he found her velvety space and filled her thoroughly. Moving slowly, he groaned in the pleasure of possessing her.

"Maggie, I missed you," he panted as he stroked.

"Please, John, please…," she breathed out for his ears only. "Yes, I feel you inside. Oh…please," she pleaded with eyes closed, feeling him deep, but wanting to be filled by him more.

Her imploring energized his slow tempo and he became vigorous and strong. She heard herself making light sounds as each upward jolt brought a wave of building pressure. The sounds turned into the calling out his name and cries of encouragement.

The ecstasy heightened with the downpour, lifting her face to the storm above, her mouth open to taste the rain as he brought her higher and higher until the flash and thrill of mini lightning strikes hit them both.

Laughing freely, feeling his power and strength, she rejoiced in her thundering Mr. Thornton.

By the time they reached the cottage, they both were soaking wet. Dixon did not understand how and grumbled over the pools of water each made on the floors. John patiently dismissed her, informing her that they did not want to be disturbed for the rest of the day and night.

Dixon grasped their meaning immediately, glad for the respite, and retired to her quarters without another word.

Margaret giggled, "Do you think she was embarrassed?"

"Not at all. She's a funny one, tough as a rock, stern as a master but with a heart of gold."

"But not fallible," she said with a knowing smile.

He looked at her puzzled. "What do you mean?"

"John, really, you haven't noticed?" His head tilted, eyes asking her to continue. "Samuel. He has an affection for her and I believe she is welcoming it."

Shaking his head he smiled, "I picked up on Higgins attachment straight away, but missed this one."

"Higgins?"

Nodding, he told her about Clara Browne and their conversation in the meal hall. Hugging him, she thrilled for their friend.

Feeling her shiver, he drew her attention away. "We got to get out of these wet clothes," he said, taking her hand to lead her upstairs. "You look like a drenched kitten."

Halfway up the staircase her soft voice sounded. "John." Stopping he turned to her. "I want to thank you."

He wrapped his arm around her waist, "Thank me. What for?"

"For giving me the most exhilarating moments of my life." His mouth curved up. "Not only for what we did back there, but every time. It is as if you give a piece of yourself to me every—"

He did not allow her to finish as he crushed her to his chest and backed her against the wall to kiss her deeply. He broke only to switch the angle of his head in taking her mouth, soon leaving her breathlessly stunned and tingly.

Lifting her chin, he gave her a serious look. "I replied with my actions. You are welcome my sweet wife." Nuzzling her neck, he added, "But next time you want to thank me, remember, actions speak louder than words."

She blinked, and rapidly recovered her composure. Picking up his hand, she brought it to her lips in the same manner as when she did on the train station's bench.

Lifting her eyes to his, she gave him an enchanting smile. "In speaking of actions," she spoke while running her mouth over his knuckles, "you remember who did it first."

His rich laughter echoed in the stairwell as she took charge and led him up the rest of the way.

John's face contorted with concern as Margaret rushed to the bathing room. She became physically ill to her stomach. Waiting for her to return, he got up from the bed and paced back and forth. He would have never expected this reaction from her. He put himself by the door and knocked for her to open and allow him in. Requesting her privacy, she sent him away.

When she did return to the bedroom, she was on the edge of angry hysterics, puffed up and hissing vehemently like that drenched kitten. He did not think it was in her nature to be that disconcerted but he obviously been wrong.

He was certain that it wasn't only the highly dangerous plan that caused her upset, but that there seemed to be no other alternative to capture their prey. She was the picture of frustration and who could blame her?

The trap had been set to spring shut, and sitting on the trigger as the bait, her husband.

Her attacker was working at Hamper's!

Nicholas was instructed to make mention that Thornton is to marry her as planned, and now they waited for him to make his move to come after John. Margaret's worse nightmare was set up to come true!

She found little comfort in learning that Mason and his men were in on the scheme. To her the plan is way to simplistic for the degree of danger to her husband and to the workers at Hamper's Mill.

What astonished her most was his mother. She came up with the plan and put her son in such peril. The same woman, who clung to her son with all her might, was now so readily dangling him on a string in front of a murderer. Hannah, who still believed her son was unmarried, was to give the impression to people that the ceremony was to happen when Miss Hale returned from London.

Hannah Thornton, indeed, went through a transformation!

Ironically, she wished that the short rope her mother-in-law kept tied to her son were still tightly knotted.

Upon hearing this plan, she got physically sickened and ran to the outer room to retch. John knocked at the door wanting to come in but she was too embarrassed and told him she was well and that she would be out. What he said about there being nothing that husband and wife would not shared together, she never considered this.

Dipping her face in water, she refreshed herself to do battle. She was determined to let her husband know that in no way is this plan acceptable and the man needed to leave Hamper's at once and John, leave Milton.

Her pleas and demands were ineffective and John witnessed for the first time, utter frustration and angered panic in her countenance.

Lying in bed with his back propped against the headboard, his head followed her back and forth in her heated pacing and verbalized anxiety.

Seeing her this way might have been amusing at any other time but her last words left him greatly affected when she asked him how he would feel if it was her being used as the lure into a trap? How would he feel if the image of her with a knife in her back and she crumbling to the ground haunted his every waking and sleeping moment?

He knew how he would feel, and he could no longer find her fit of temper entertaining. She was right, he is in grave danger, but the only alterative seemed to be killing the man with his own hands. Murder is a hanging offense; he could not put his family through that pain, humiliation, and ruination.

She ignored his cajoling for her to return to bed. She kept repeating that there must be another way. His attempts to offer reassurances infuriated her more and she shot him silencing looks, reminding him not to patronize her. Not getting through to her uncharacteristic ranting and mumbling he acquiesced to wait until she exhausted herself. She should be weakening by now.

After a week apart, their lovemaking had been enthusiastic to say the least. Taking her during the storm created the single most gripping and invigorating moments in his life, and it seemed to be for her as well. Drying each other off, had him recalling it vividly in his mind, arousing him to swipe her up and carry her to their bed. It was right after that he told her.

Yes, she must be tiring soon. Guiltily, he watched as she went through the myriad of emotions. His hand flew up to rub his eyes hating to see her go through this, wishing he could spare her, but that porcelain doll kept on flashing back in his mind. He realized now that keeping her ignorant of everything was not fair to her and to their marriage.

Dropping his hand to see where she was he found her standing still at the end of the bed looking like that porcelain doll complete with soulful eyes and pouting lips. She stared at him with a beautiful but defeated expression written over her face.

Heart melting, he held out his hand to her. "Ah, Maggie, come here, Love," he softly commanded.

Dismayed eyes looked up to try to stop the tears from falling. Unsuccessful, she came around and took his hand letting out the first sob. He drew her down to him.

John did not offer any words of comfort, guarantees, or try to convince her that things will be well. He simply held her tight.

John woke before dawn to find her not in bed. Stretching his muscles, he looked to the corner to find her sitting at the small desk.

"A little early to be writing a letter."

She did not respond and continued to write. He frowned. She is up to something. This time he asked her firmly what she was writing. She put the pen down, picked up the letter, and waved it in the air to dry the ink. Turning, she rose out of the chair, walked over to the bed, and handed the paper over to him.

"John, I got this idea and wanted to put it in writing for you to read. Please, let us discuss its possibilities before you tell me no."

No was on his lips to say, but not two sentences in, he clamped his mouth shut. As his eyes took in the rest of the words, he began to see that not only was he married to a remarkable woman; he is the husband to one of the most surprising.

John took the letter and she watched his face intently waiting for the dark clouds to roll in. The clouds never came. His face remained stone with only a slight widening of his eyes for a second.

After a few moments, he put the paper on the bed, gazed up at her, and calmly spoke.

"I would have never believed an idea like this would have come from you." He reached out and took her closest hand into his, "I do see the possibilities and will discuss them with you but as far as your role in it I will say absolutely not no matter how much you plead with me."

"Who else if not your mother and myself? Surely it is better than waiting weeks, perhaps months for him to make a mistake."

"Maggie, I know you both would be willing to play the parts but it is out of the question to involve two women, one being my wife. But…" He pulled her down and laid her across his chest, their faces within inches of each other.

"There is a but?"

"But, there may be another way." His hand rose to his chin as he became thoughtful, and as if speaking his mind aloud, "If we move the characters around a bit this could work."

"No, use me! I won't be in Milton remember. I'll be here. I won't be in danger."

"That is what one tends to think until it is too late. No, as I said before, I'll not risk you."

He was putting her into that glass cabinet and he knew that would anger her but she kept her composure and said nothing. Drawing her close, he kissed her, and then propped her up so he could climb out of the bed to dress.

She was crestfallen. What had she done?

"Maggie?"

"You're going to use yourself."

After pulling on his trousers, he sat on the bed and took her hand. "Yes, I won't lie to you. It is a good plan. No, it is a better plan and I will be careful, I promise. Higgins and—"

"Nicholas! Oh, John, no!"

"Higgins just became a partner. It is more advantageous for him with me gone. Stephens is more likely to believe him wanting me in the grave than my mother wanting you."

Putting his hand on her shoulder, he felt a shiver of apprehension course through her body. Moving his hand to her back and clasping her waist, he leaned her close to his side so he could tilt his head to rest on hers.

"He has yet to agree to take part. He said that if there is anything he could do to ask him and give him an opportunity to say no. He can still say no and that will be the end of it."

"You know he will not. What about Mary and the orphans?"

Moving his hand to the nape of her neck, his thumb directed her face to him. "Look at me, Margaret." He waited for her downcast eyes to raised to his. "If we determine this plan is doable, and I say if, we will go to the authorities and tell them everything. Set the trap up proper. They will be aware and be sure that all involved are watched. You plan, my clever wife, gives us much more control. Does that ease your mind a little?"

She nodded but John saw that she was thinking hard. Forehead furled in deep thought, his eyes narrowed and brows drew in.

"Whatever you're thinking, put it out of your mind," he warned.

"I will not. I am coming back with you," she blurted out, standing and moving to get dressed. "With us married, he will be sure to accept the offer. We will live in the empty house before Nicholas moves in. It will enrage him more with us married. Don't say no, John. I mean what I say, I'm coming back!"

Standing, his voice barely controlled, "Margaret, you don't

know what you are saying. He may carry out his threat against you."

"Yes, I am aware of that. We both will be in danger but we have the upper hand and, as you say, constant protection from the authorities. We'll be ready for him and chances are he will go after you first with the thought of being compensated." She turned and looked at him. "I refuse to be far from you when you are placing yourself in such danger."

"Then I won't do it!"

Finishing buttoning her blouse, she looked up at him. "I understand, but either way, I am still coming back," she said. "This man needs to be captured. It is going to be a matter of time, John, and I prefer sooner so we can move on with our lives."

"Margaret, your safety is not open for discussion," he cautioned.

"I am your wife, and I will stand by my husband's side. I cannot hide and if something is to happen to one of us, we will be there for each other as husband and wife as it should be," she said, walking up closer to him. "Either I go back to Milton on your arm to announce our union or I go back on my own. Which will it be?"

Grabbing his undershirt, he put it on with fury in his motion, turning he gripped her upper arms.

"Neither! You're staying here!" he roared.

He was incensed, but it was more because of the fierce fear he had for her and his inability to give reason against her wanting to stay by his side.

Defiantly, her eyes met his. "With or without you?"

"You would disobey me!"

"In this…yes," she said in a raised voice.

For the longest moment, their eyes locked in a heated cease fire and he felt his resolve crumble with her beautiful, but steely look. She is not going to give in. What could he do? There wasn't an underground dungeon where he could lock her safely away.

He frantically searched for words to convince her but he could not find them and in the end he emitted a loud groan and crushed his mouth to hers, taking all his frustrations out on her lips.

Pushing away from his chest, she breathlessly asked him more resonantly for him to choose.

Letting out an expletive, he shouted out a loud, "With!"

Margaret knew what it took him to give in. Raising herself up she kissed her husband's cheek and hand threaded through his hair.

"John, do not misunderstand me, I want to obey you as a good wife should but you must allow me to be selfish this time." Her chin lifted as her lips found his and kissed him. Pulling away her eyes met his, "I love you and will stay by your side even if I have to use my wiles and cast spells."

His face softened as he whispered her name under his breath and tucked some of her hair behind her ear. Tilting his head down, he touched his forehead to hers.

"Maggie, you are more than a good wife, you are my life. If anything happened to you, I wouldn't know how to exist."

"You would carry on as I would if something was to happen to you," she said softly, "but we won't worry about that because Dixon is coming back with us and will guard me like a bulldog when you are at the mill."

His head turned sharply and his eyes shifted as his brain worked. Breaking from her, he walked over to the desk and fingered the neatly organized papers and the many broken pen nibs and empty inkwells.

Turning to her he stated, "You enjoy writing."

Her brow furrowed in puzzlement. "What a strange thing to say at such a time but, yes, I do."

"Since Higgins doesn't seem to like the bookkeeping aspect of running a mill, I may need additional assistance in writing correspondences and updating of records."

She saw where he was going with this and she smiled, "What are the chances a woman would be considered for such a position?"

John grinned as he walked back over to her. "None, but since I'm in very well with the owner, it may turn in your favor. Do you wish for me to speak on your behalf?"

Only the sparkle in her eyes gave away her true feelings. "Please do. It is worth a try if I can be close to…of assistance to you."

Wrapping his arm around her waist, he pulled her to his chest. "Mrs. Thornton, may I talk to you about taking on an assistant?"

"Mr. Thornton, you forget yourself. You are owner as well but hire whomever you wish with my full approval."

As his lips descended upon hers, he whispered, "I will do exactly that."

John was more at ease with this plan but he still did not want her to return to Milton. After their lips parted, he spoke seriously.

"Maggie, remember you said that if he wasn't captured that we leave Milton and start a new life elsewhere?"

"Yes."

"If he isn't captured by this time next month, we will do it. What do you say?"

Eyes glistening, she nodded. ଓ

Chapter Fifteen
Choices & Sacrifices

The banners announced that Miss Margaret Hale was now Mrs. John Thornton to the people Milton and beyond, eventually reaching all the way to London.

Stunned, tittle-tattle regarding the secretive elopement died down within days, and heartfelt congratulations began to replace the banter. Soon life seemed to resume back to a normal pace. However, as simplistic it would seem on the surface to be well and good, underneath that veil of happiness of the couple was the danger and apprehension of the truth.

Billy Stephens agreed to murder John Thornton for monetary gain.

Margaret found herself clinging to John thinking that Stephens would not dare kill him in presence of another. She refused to be far from his side. This suited John just fine because he did not want her far from him as well.

His concern was mainly for her health. Stressed nearly beyond her limit, it affected her sleeping and eating habits negatively. She suffered, not only physically, but mentally as well. On the nights when she managed to sleep, agonizing nightmares plagued her.

No amount of persuasion could influence her to return to the cottage. She shook her head and turned away from him in determined silence.

John fervently wished that he did not give in to bringing her back to Milton, but the end of the one-month agreement neared and the plan was set. His role was imperative to its success and he could not turn his back on ridding the streets and back alleys of such a demented and vile character like Stephens.

Stephens was to waylay him on the outskirts of town under the guise of meeting with a new buyer. Situated nearby, Mason and his men would lie in wait, ready to catch him in the act. The last meeting between Higgins and Stephens, to give him the down payment, went smooth, but Higgins warned that the man was anxious, displaying a crazed eagerness to strike at Thornton before the arranged place and time.

Margaret's continual decline and perceived condition had him fearing for her. He needed her home, happy and safe, in their Eden. This needed to end. Mason confirmed that Higgins was successful; he arranged with Stephens that the day be move up. Tomorrow was that day.

He dreaded what he needed to do next—inform his wife.

Margaret sat in the cushioned chair monogramming the linens. Entering the room unnoticed, John was able to watch her in her retreat.

Smiling to himself, he recalled him walking in a few days before to see her sitting close to his mother as she demonstrated the stitching technique. The lighthearted talk and pleasing smiles were genuine and warm. He turned away because the sight profoundly affected him. This is how it should have been from the beginning. He was saddened with the wasted weeks but after the business with Stephens, all their futures would be bright.

Together, they asked Hannah to move to the cottage with them, but she declined with the main reason being her penitence of her impropriety towards Margaret. He could not convince her, but later, Margaret reassured him that her challenge was set before her—to change his mother's mind. Once challenged, if memory served him well, he had no doubt she would be victorious in her pursuit.

"Maggie, Love…" he spoke announcing his presence.

She looked up, offering him a light smile. "Did things go well with Inspector Mason?"

Mason left moments before, and he knew she was always anxious when he stopped by to discuss details.

"He enjoys his reading and borrowed a few of my novels."

"I'm glad of it, although it's hard to imagine him relaxing," she said, returning her attention to her sewing. She let out a light laugh adding, "Really, John, we will need to take on a Librarian for your literary grotto."

His upper lip jerked up into a crooked smile. Her wit always seem to blow greyed clouds away and allow sunrays to come down. However, he knew her clouds were dark and ever present.

She startled as the needle pricked her finger. Briefly, she raised her eyes to him to see if he noticed, a little embarrassed of her domestic blunder.

He did notice. Forehead furrowed with deep concern, he saw how exhausted she was. Walking up to her, he held out his hand for her to take. Drawing her up, he examined her finger, kissed it, telling her that she needed more practice. The smile he expected did not come. Instead, she folded into his embrace, and he engulfed her to add strength to her fragile state.

Holding her, he endeavored to brighten her outlook. "When we move all the books to the cottage, you are the only Librarian I want to catalogue one of my treasured escapes," he said, running his lips over the side of her face, "can you guess what the other escapes are?"

"Picnics and thunderstorms?"

Laughing, his fingers found the underside of her jaw to lift her face up, fusing his mouth with hers, he kissed her for the "exactly right" rejoinder.

Sighing, her body relaxed in his comforting hold, making it even harder to bring up the distressing subject. Pleasantries aside, he could not avoid it any longer.

"Love, we have to talk." The seriousness in his voice had her going rigid. His hand smoothed over her cheek as his soften eyes sought hers. "Plans have changed and you cannot accompany me tomorrow," he said. "Do you understand why?"

Inhaling a shaky breath, she nodded that she did. As the news was absorbed, her trembling started and he felt her legs giving out. He swiftly lifted her up to cradle her in his arms, soothing her with his low voice as he carried her up the stairs.

Reaching the top, he glanced down to see her staring at him with glistening eyes.

"John, I cannot leave you. Please, do not make me stay here."

"You can and will, Maggie. He will not try for me with you around. We have to give him this opportunity."

Her palm spanned his cheek, "I was wrong. I won't be able to go on if something happens to you."

Reaching the bedroom, he lowered her down on the bed. Sitting on the edge he leaned over placing one arm on her other side entrapping her as his eyes captured hers.

"I'll not patronize you and say I will be safe but I will tell you this. You'll go on because of our child growing within you."

Eyes widening, she sprung up into a sitting position. "Our child! We've only been married a short while."

A slight grin formed on his face. "Seven weeks but when was the last time you went through your cycle?"

He watched with amusement as she turned a light shade of pink at the mention of her monthly confinement and waited as she counted in her mind. Her lips opened in surprise at the realization that it was over nine weeks since.

"I've forgotten and didn't notice I hadn't had my...I didn't count the weeks before we were married. Oh, John!" she said with excitement in her voice.

"Your mind was preoccupied and I imagine it is common to forget the weeks before. And I saw you having the morning episodes."

"Is that part of being with child?"

"It is normal, Maggie. Most women experience it."

"You noticed. I believed it was a stress related condition. I didn't want to worry you."

Holding her chin while his thumb ran over her lower lip, his eyes lowered and voice commanded, "Don't try to hide anything from me again, Love. You could have averted much anxiety."

Obediently she complied and he said that he would do the same, kissing her to seal their shared pledge. She wrapped her arms around his neck and his face found its favorite resting place, the crook of her soft neck and shoulder.

"Oh, John, I'm complete."

"Maggie, it could be all the stress. Let's have Dr. Donaldson confirm first."

"Oh no, I am sure it isn't. I feel it now."

He knew it was too early to feel movement, but seeing her cover her stomach lovingly with her hands and see the sheer wonderment in her facial features, kept him from saying anything. He did not want to quell the joy he was witnessing in her for the first time in days.

"John, when did you know?"

"About a week ago. That is why I tried harder to get you to return to the cottage. All this strain on you is a big concern for me. Miscarriages are common the first time and if it wasn't for the workers livelihoods, mother, and Higgins, I would be escaping back with you before the end of the month."

"You would have left all this behind?"

"Yes," he said without reservations.

She kissed the corner of his lip and drew her mouth across his cheek up to his ear to whisper, "My husband has his flesh and blood heart back, and ironically, it is the one time that I wish it to be a steel drum."

"Ironic, yes. I cannot ignore others. That is why I have to go through this plan. And for our child's sake, why you must stay here. I cannot go through tomorrow knowing you," his warm hand covered hers that still rested on her stomach, "and him are endangered."

She put on a brave smile. "He could be a her."

"Madeline Maria Thornton."

"Why Madeline?"

"So I have my Maggie and Maddie."

Her brow rose. "You've set your mind on this before consulting me," she accused, crossing her arms. "If it is a boy, am I allowed to name him?"

"It would be a fair assumption."

Her face lighted up and proudly announced, "Reginald Gaylord Thornton. Yes, I like the ring to that very much."

He struggled to hold his tongue. She could not be serious!

Giggling at his discomfiture, she added, "Or we can name him after his father."

Sudden relief crossed his face. "Woman, you were teasing me."

"Yes."

"How did you come up with such a name?"

"Can you guess? Fanny. She informed me that is the name of your pending nephew."

He laughed aloud and pulled her to him. "I should have known."

"She said it is a mature and regal title."

"Dare I ask, if it is a girl?"

"I asked her the same thing and she insisted that giving birth to a girl is not an option."

"Then I will pray for a niece for I wouldn't wish that name on any child."

She nodded in agreement. They both were glad for the lighthearted moments from their troubles, and they held each other close in silence.

At length, he shook his head, abruptly questioning again, "Reginald Gaylord. Really?"

Her laughter was the sweetest melody to his ears.

Basking in his strength and warmth, Margaret prayed that he

never let go of her. She was about to express her thoughts when it suddenly came to mind how she had been the night before he returned to Milton. How she begged him not to go and how he left her before she woke.

"John."

"Yes, Love."

"You go and do what you have to do tomorrow. I will stay here," her eyes rose slowly to his, "and if something happens, I do not want you to worry. I will be strong and raise our child with all the love I have inside me for you."

"My sweet Maggie. You don't know how much that means to me to hear you say that."

John's thumb stopped the tear that trailed down her cheek and he kissed the other one away that fell on the other side. Drawing her face forward he kissed her lips with all the gentleness and devotion inside him, which melded her to him not only physically but spiritually as well.

Margaret was not able to be strong any further and she began to cry softly into his shirt. His voice and arms created a sheltering warmth around her causing her tears and sobs to stop and a comforting void to lure her away.

John held Margaret close while speaking of his love and his vision of their future together with their children. Her crying and sobs ceased suddenly, he imagined so she could hear his voice.

She once spoke on how his voice, when he wasn't shouting the walls of Jericho down, was like soaking in heated water, tranquil and comforting. He felt the same about hers, a delicate calming, breeze, cooling him from his heated assertions.

It did not take long before her body relaxed and went limp. Laying her down, he pulled the afghan over her. Bending down he kissed her cheek and rose from the bed, standing straight, his eyes lifted up praying that no nightmares would haunt her this night.

After he stoked and fed the fire in the hearth, he left the room shutting the door behind him. Turning, he ran into his mother who was standing near.

"Mother!"

"I came in as you were carrying her upstairs. I was concerned and followed."

"What did you hear?"

"Everything. John, please leave here with her. Go."

"What? You want me to leave?"

Hannah stepped forward and grabbed his arm in desperation, "Yes. Make a new life for yourself and your family. Don't risk yourself. Just go!"

A rush of tears came spilling from her eyes, assuring him of her sincerity.

"Mother, I cannot."

She grabbed his arm and drew him to an emptied room, shutting the door behind her. He looked at her in confusion as she motioned him to sit.

"Son, I need to tell you another secret I kept inside."

His eyes darkened. "Another confession," he said, rising from the chair.

Hannah put her hand on his shoulder pressuring him to sit. "No, this happened years ago. It is the reason why I wear black."

John's anger immediately resided and he went calm. "Speak of it, Mother."

Restless, she moved about the room, coming to a stop at the window to peer out absently. Taking a fleeting glance at him, she turned back to the glass frame and spoke.

"I ran the blade over your father's wrist. I killed him," she said without any trace of emotion.

"I know."

She gasped, turning sharply to him. "You knew!"

Nodding, he rose and walked over to his stupefied mother. "I watched you from around the corner, and hid when you left the room. I went in after and he was still alive, although barely," he said, taking her hand, "but I turned my back and walked out. I don't think that there was much that could have been done at that point."

She fell into his arms and he held her. "So, Mother, don't lay all the guilt on yourself, I could've stopped it from happening," he said, "but I allowed you to go through with your choice as I did with mine." Raising her tragic face up, he asked, "Why tell me now?"

Pulling out of his arms, she took a few steps back from him. "You spoke once about what we sacrifice for the ones we love the most. I thought I did that for you and your sister, but after, I made myself entitled to your love because of it. When Margaret threatened that entitlement, I reacted in a shameful manner and will forever look upon my conduct with abhorrence."

"We both—"

"Allow me to finish," she interrupted, "I know what must be done to qualify for redemption as well as make amends to Margaret and yourself."

"You have."

"Son, I have not," she declared, "but I will and it will bring me great peace." She walked up to him and put her hand on his arm. "Remember that."

John, confused by her words, continued to tell her that she redeemed herself in his eyes, and she had his love as well as Margaret's.

"John, listen, time for you to make a choice. Leave Milton. You have the means to be a distant owner like Hamper. Do it for her and your child." She hung her head with shame, "After all that I have done to her, she holds no bitterness or malice towards me. She has accepted me, but like you, I feel I don't deserve her. So go, please."

"There are workers and their livelihoods at stake, and this man, he is a danger if he stays free. If it was only Margaret and I, yes, but now I cannot." he said, squeezing her hand. "Perhaps this is my chance for redemption for turning my back."

"Please, I beg of you."

He took her upper arms and kissed her forehead and stood back to look at her. "No, Mother, I'll not change my mind but I am proud of you."

"What if something happens to you?"

"You know the value of your daughter-in-law now." Hannah nodded. "Then for me, be mother to her. That would be my last request if I were not to come back tomorrow. Keep them safe and love them as I would. Promise me."

"With all my heart. I know what to do."

John pulled his mother to him, and hugged her tightly. "I love you," he said with emotion. Breaking his embrace, he walked to the door, turning towards her he gave her a reassuring full smile, "Everything will work out."

Opening the door, he walked out.

Hannah heart swelled and stood for the longest time with tears streaming down her face. Nodding to herself, she agreed with John, everything would work out. She would make sure of it.

She hoped that she could have convinced him to leave but it did not matter. One way or another, her son's future and that of his family would be bright.

Entering the room where her daughter-in-law laid sleeping, she moved quietly to the bed's side. Looking down at the sleeping woman, Hannah knew that she could have never regained John's love if she had not given her unconditional forgiveness first.

After what she put Margaret through, she still opened her arms wide to her. It was not long that Hannah became fully conscious on why her son loved her so much. She vowed that she would not interfere in their lives again. However, the learning of who Margaret's attacker was caused a resolution to come to her and she comprehended that she could not keep that vow.

She would interfere one last time.

By divine intervention, she learned of the sudden change of plan, and of her grandchild. Touching Margaret's cheek, loved surged inside for her and then another wave of shame. Tears spilled down as a small sad smile appeared on her face. Bending down she kissed her new, beloved daughter, turned and walked out of the room with chin held high and determination etched in her expression.

It was time for her deliverance and their liberation.

Where was that woman going so late?

Dixon watched as Mrs. Thornton pulled up the hood on her cloak and disappeared into the shadows as a thief in the night. The shrew did not fool her!

It was all a ruse, pretending to be all-remorseful and humbled for her past doings. Grabbing her own cloak, Dixon donned it and slipt out into the night to follow the woman. She was certain that she was up to no good.

She'll catch her in the act this time. She would!

John's eyes flew open as he registered a hand shaking him out of his sleep.

"Higgins!"

"Sir, don't wake the missus."

Margaret propped herself up, with wide eyes blinking, "Nicholas, the children! What is wrong?"

"The children are fine, Miss Margaret. I didn't want to wake you. It is your husband I need to speak to right away. I knew no other way to—"

"What is it, Higgins. What has happened?"

"Sir, can we talk alone?"

"Yes, wait for me downstairs."

Higgins nodded and left as John threw the covers off, got out of the bed, and hurried to dress. Glancing over to Margaret, he could tell she was alarmed.

"John, the mills, do you think he carried out his threat?"

"We would have smelled smoke here but perhaps Hamper's," he said, looking out of the window while buttoning his undershirt. "No, I don't see any smoke out that way. The additional guards are keeping to their duties."

"What could it be? Something is terribly wrong."

Dressed, he saw that she wanted to come with him but his eyes told her to stay as he gave her a reassuring kiss. "I'll come back,

Love. Wait for me."

She nodded as he left the room.

"Dead!"

"We believe so, but that isn't all. Your mother done it."

"What!"

"There is no easy way to tell you. She is at my house with Dixon. She found out where Stephens lived and went there tonight to do him in. They struggled and according to Dixon, she managed to stab him with a broken bottle."

John was incredulous. "Dixon! What does she have to do with this?"

"Dixon followed her thinking her up to no good. Sir, brace yourself, but Stephens fought back and your mother received some serious blows."

"Has a doctor been called?"

"Your mother refused, insisting on seeing you and the missus first."

"Go and get him now! I'll go to her."

Higgins rushed to do his bidding as he took the stairs two at a time to the bedroom and was grateful to find Margaret sitting on the edge of the bed, dressed and ready.

Seeing the distress in her husband's face, she stood as he grabbed her hand. "Maggie, we must go to Higgins place. My mother is injured."

With restrained calm she asked, "What has happened?"

His voice cracked, "She went out tonight to kill Stephens."

"No, that cannot be true!"

John did not reply; he was finding it unbelievable as well. Grabbing her shawl, he wrapped it around her shoulders and grabbed her hand.

Out in the deserted square, no carriages could be found and John cursed aloud. Margaret sensing his frustration pulled him in the direction of Princeton Street at a hurried pace.

"We don't need a carriage."

He was grateful for once to have his wife take the lead. His state of shock and disbelief had him mumbling.

"She begged me tonight to leave with you. To disappear rather than face Stephens," he choked. "It's my fault she did this, Maggie."

Margaret came to an abrupt standstill and turned him around to meet her gaze. "John, listen to me. Your mother has a mind of her own. If she has done something rash, it must have been for love. Hold on to that and calm yourself for her. She'll need your strength, not guilt."

Her words sparked his memory.

I know what must be done to qualify for that redemption as well as make amends to Margaret and yourself.

You have.

Son, I have not, but I will and it will bring me great peace. Remember that.

"John?"

"She planned this!" Angry tears dropped from John's eyes. "She is sacrificing herself for us!"

She drew him into her arms. "Be of good courage, John, and God will strengthen your heart," she whispered while smoothing the back of his head. "Let us go to her."

The words she spoke and the life force of her person and their unborn child seem to emulate throughout his body, renewing his purpose and strength. Taking her hand into his, he went to do as she instructed, only this time, he took the lead.

Dixon was so relieved to see Higgins burst into the room with the doctor trailing right behind. Getting up from the chair, she moved aside to allow the doctor take her place by the bedside.

Higgins turned to Dixon. "The master…he isn't here yet?"

"No."

"He should have been here by now."

Concern struck Higgins; by carriage or by foot, he should

have arrived long before him.

"Dixon, you stay here with the doctor. I am going back to find the master."

Dixon nodded and watched as Higgins departed.

Crossing her arms before her, she turned to the woman in the bed and the doctor that administered to her. Mrs. Thornton was in a bad way.

When she first arrived and Higgins left to fetch the master, she discovered that she had been stabbed in her lower abdomen. Her heavy cloak probably preventing the blade from going in deep but did not stop her from bleeding profusely.

Miss Mary herded the children next door under the guise that Higgins was intoxicated and been brawling. Dixon managed to get the bleeding slowed but not stopped.

The doctor turned to her, "These are stab wounds. How did this happen?"

"I'll leave all the explaining to my master, if you don't mind. He'll be here shortly."

The doctor nodded and ordered her to boil water. Grateful to be useful she rushed out of the room to the kitchen area. The fire had gone down in the stove and she stoked the embers, blaming the smoke for the tears that were falling.

She had been mistaken about Mrs. Thornton.

Mrs. Thornton was determined and had no fear as Dixon watched in stunned disbelief at the purpose of her nightly venture.

How she knew where the man lived, she did not know but she went straight to the door in the worse part of Milton. Mrs. Thornton knocked, it opened a crack, and after a short discussion, she entered. Dixon did not hear what they said, or saw to whom was on the other side, but at this point, she was more certain that the woman schemed.

Creeping up to the window, she was not able to see inside because of the layers of dirt and grime. A crash reverberated causing her to jump back startled, and then a piercing male voice sounded.

Her eyes widen as she realized a violent struggle was happening inside.

Like the woman or not, her Christian upbringing compelled her to help Mrs. Thornton, but before she reached the door, it opened and she stumbled out, dropping a bloodied broken bottle, her arms wrapped around her stomach. Dixon grabbed on to hold her up, glancing inside, she saw a man, slumped on the ground, motionless. Quickly she led her away into the darkness to the nearest place she could think of—the Higgins residence.

The woman had gone mad! And why did she want to kill that man? Dixon half carried and half dragged Mrs. Thornton. The injured woman labored to speak, pleading to Dixon to tell her children that she wanted this and to be happy for her sake.

Pounding on Higgins' door, she knew now what Mrs. Thornton had done. The man must have been the one who attacked the mistress. It had to be him.

The shortcut through the cemetery proved to be rigorous with the brisk pace and steep hills. Hearing Margaret's labored breathing, he remembered that he held her hand and was practically dragging her along in his urgency. Stopping, he steadied her with his arm on her back, allowing her to catch her breath.

"Maggie, I'm sorry."

"I'm fine, John. I am as eager to reach your mother's side as you."

He touched her cheek and went to continue down the deserted path at a slower pace. Finding the road, he turned onto it. A shadowy figure appeared from the corner of his eye from the edge of the beaten path.

Margaret screamed, as an unknown force pulled her violently back and out of his grasp. John turned sharply around.

Stephens!

Fear mixed with rage, stark and vivid, impaled John. Stephens held Margaret forcefully to him with his arm around her neck and knife directed to her stomach. His voice was rigid and boding evil as he stared down his nemesis.

"Ya knew all along it was me didn't you, Thornton? It was all a set up, Higgins and you."

John's eyes blazed loathing and narrowed dangerously, as his hands folded into iron fists.

"And the police, Stephens. They know about you," he seethed. "You harm her, I'll kill ya myself, and no one would blame me for it." There was no mistaking the dead seriousness in his voice.

"I'm done for one way or another, so I want to see your face as I gut the one you care for the most. You ruined my life, I'm going to ruin yours," he sneered. "I'll go to my grave willingly knowing that!"

Margaret's face was pure white and John saw that she feared the worse with her mouthing the words that she loved him. He would not let panic to set in. He needed to stay calm and bargain her away from him. He had to stay level headed and sharp.

"You don't want her, Stephens. She defended you and cared about what happened to you. You want me. Let me trade places with her. Take your revenge on me and my mother, not her."

Stephens' lips quivered with hostility. John could not tell if it was working. He had to try harder to convince him.

"Why do you think my mother tried to kill you tonight? I am her only son. You were right. It was a set up. She knew I'd be in danger. It would destroy her if anything happened to me."

For a moment, it looked as if Stephens wasn't going to do the trade and he prepared himself to attack, hoping the surprise will deter him from sticking the blade into Margaret's belly. Then Stephens spoke.

"On your knees, Thornton!"

Hopeful, he complied raising his hands and entwining his fingers behind his head.

"John...no, please," Margaret choked shakily.

His eyes set solidly on hers. His voice was strong and steady, "Remember what we said earlier, Maggie."

Please remember, my love, he thought. If anything were to happen to him, continue on. She stifled a sob, as tears spilled from her eyes. Then he saw it, she nodded. She remembered.

Disturbing visions flashed in his mind—the blood on her neck, bruises, and the torn clothes. If he had not reached her in time, he knew what the lunatic would have done to her. John's eyes hooded like a predator on the prowl and his back went ramrod straight.

No, he could not leave her. He must survive!

John's eyes seized on her terror-stricken face; her pleading eyes moved to lock with his. Willing her to read his thoughts, he implored her to find courage and to fight if given the opportunity.

Stephens moved forward with knife still pressed to her side. "One move, Thornton, and I'll kill her as easily as I killed Leonards and Boucher."

She gasped at the disclosure but he stayed passive.

"Yes, I killed them both for harming her. I loved her because of what she did for me and how she hated you, but now that you had your way with her, Thornton, she is as soiled as the ground I stand on. You think that I'll let her live to be with another man? No, I'll kill her and then you. You'll see her—"

"No!" Margaret exclaimed, shoving the arm holding the blade.

She gave him the seconds needed to take action. Lunging forward, John plowed into her legs and toppled her off to the side. As she landed, he rose speedily and rammed his body into the stunned man and they both flew backwards in combat. As the two men struggled, John managed to shout out for Margaret to run.

Rising from the ground she shook her head, "No, I will not!"

"For our child! Go!"

Higgins rushed to the woman who was racing up to him. Grabbing her arms, he brought her to a complete stop.

"Nicholas!"

"Margaret!"

"John," she panted, pointing from where she came, "needs

help…please hurry."

That was all he needed to hear and he rushed ahead in the direction from which she came, quickly coming upon the two men fiercely combating.

Rage and health gave Thornton the obvious advantage as his fists hammered the weaker man to the ground. Higgins raced to help when he saw the glint of the blade. Shouting out, he watched in horror as Stephens plunged it forward, finding its target. Higgins tackled the man to the ground, and pounded him into unconsciousness.

John staggered two steps back in shock by the shooting pain coursing through his abdomen. His legs buckled and he felt himself falling to his knees. He heard a scream pierced the night. Maggie!

"John! No!"

He slowly turned his head towards her voice, to see her rushing to his side as he fell sideways to the ground. Anxious hands were on him, grabbing, and pulling his heavy weight desperately to her.

"John, I'm here. Stay with me. Please, my love…"

Feeling raining tear on his face, he opened his eyes to she her beautiful face, contorted in agony. Her nightmare came true. Her soft lips were on his, begging and pleading.

"Be strong, my Maggie…be strong," he managed to say.

Her tragic face faded as his eyes flickered shut. He drifted away with one thought in his mind.

If I am dying…please let it be here in her arms. ☙

Chapter Sixteen
Tears of Sorrow and Joy

"Go to her, Nicholas," Clara urged. "She'll listen to you."

Patting her hand hooked on his arm, Nicholas glanced at the woman by his side and nodded.

Kissing her quickly, he replied, "You go back, I'll catch up with you later."

Clara gave him a smile and walked down the hill to where Mary was waiting. The two women took to the path leading them out of the cemetery.

Nicholas' attention turned back to the woman ahead of him, standing at the freshly covered gravesite. A chilled, autumn wind played with her cloak and skirt, but she was motionless, head bowed with hands clasped together in front as if in prayer.

He was worried for her. The strain of the past days was overwhelming and weakened her first resolve to be brave. The death further brought her down to where she collapsed. He feared she would have a spell again. As John's friend, he would see to his wife and unborn child's care in his stead.

Stepping up behind her, he put his hand on her shoulder. "Come on, Margaret. The mourners have all gone and you shouldn't be here alone."

"I wanted to…to say goodbye for the both of us. How will I tell him?" she said sadly.

Higgins squeezed her shoulder. "You'll find a way. Come let me take you back to the house. He'll be awake soon and want to see your bonnie face first thing."

She offered him a small smile. "I guess seeing Dixon would not improve his health."

Higgins chuckled, "Oh, I don't know about that. If I woke to see Dixon as my nursemaid, it might frighten me back into health rather quickly. Now, you as the nurse, I am sure he will want to stay in bed for weeks under your care."

"Nicholas, should I tell him right after he wakes? Perhaps I should wait."

"It won't ease the pain by waiting," he said patting her hand. "It will be a blow but coming from you it will be easier."

"I am concern it may hinder his recovery."

"Let me put it to you in another way. If you don't tell him right away, most likely his sister will."

That did it, Higgins mused. Her eyes widened and her pace quickened.

Margaret appreciated Nicholas' humor for it was true, Dixon's bedside manner is rather firm and domineering.

Right before Hannah's funeral, the doctor declared John out of danger, but for the first three days, he feverishly teetered on the brink of death.

Margaret's vigilance by his bedside was unrelenting, praying and pleading in his ear to live for her and their child, and those who depended upon him.

Remembering her father speaking to his dead wife on her deathbed, she adamantly determined, she would not be like him. She was resolute to speak to her husband in life. Holding his hand, she spoke of their future together, their child, making love in the rain, painting the shutters, even chasing chickens, and milking cows.

Late into the second day, all tried to coax her away from him to rest and eat. After refusing vehemently several times, she loss her temper, pointing to the door, speaking harshly for them to go away. She did not know herself! As his wife, she would not leave his side.

Until, that is, Hannah asked for her.

Margaret did not turn around knowing it was Doctor Donaldson that entered by the squeak his shoes made.

"Mrs. Thornton, may I have a word with you?"

Tired eyes lifted up to glance at him, giving a slight nod, and then turning her attention back to John lying, ashen and still as death. Only the slight rise of his chest and warmth of his skin gave her any indication he lived.

"She would like to speak to you," he said, putting his hand on her shoulder, "It won't be long now."

Telling him that she would come shortly, he left the room. Fighting tears, she knew this would be her last conversation with Hannah. Thinking of Frederick, he had that precious opportunity to say goodbye to his mother.

John would not.

Clasping his hand to her heart, with tears escaping, she leaned closer to his chiseled face.

"John, tell me what you want me to say to her," she beseeched, "I'm listening. Please, my love, tell me."

Closing her eyes, she let her mind open to allow his spirit address hers. A moment of complete silence past before a light smile appeared on her face. Opening her eyes, she brought his hand to her lips.

"Yes, John, I will tell her."

Margaret walked into the bedroom.

Dixon outdid herself. The room wasn't draped with the gloom of pending death. In its stead, multiple candles flickered, illuminating the vases of colorful floral arrangements, giving off a fresh, light fragrance in the air. It was a fine thing to see, and she knew that this is Dixon's way of apologizing to Mrs. Thornton for judging her so severely.

John's last words before he went unconscious echoed in her mind—to be strong. Resolved, she lowered herself to her knees by the bedside, and took Hannah's hand into hers.

Her head slowly turned. "I waited for ye," she said in a voice that was fading and weak.

Kissing her hand, Margaret moved it to her cheek. "I'm here, for your son as well."

"He'll see himself straight…he always does, but he'll want to blame himself."

"I will not allow him to do so," Margaret assured. "Hannah, I want to…"

"Call me mother…let me hear it…"

Moving in closer to her ear, she affectionately did as requested, and then spoke the words that in her heart John would want her to say to his dying mother. After, Margaret brought her head up slightly to peer into Hannah's face. Tears trailed from the corners of the woman's eyes.

"Thank you…thank you," she labored.

Margaret's eyes filled, and her palm tenderly cupped the side of Hannah's face. "Dearest Mother, you will live on. That is our gift and promise to you."

"Stay with me."

Squeezing her mother-in-law's hand, "We are all here." Margaret leaned over and kissed her for John, herself, and their unborn child. "There…three kisses goodnight for you."

"I'm…at peace. Tell him."

"I will."

Hannah used the last remaining strength to touch her daughter's cheek with the back of her hand. The hand dropped, and her last breath escaped as she closed her eyes and gently went into that final sleep.

Dixon came in and stood by her side. "Mistress?"

"She is gone, Dixon," she said sadly. "Where is Fanny?"

"Downstairs, she fainted and the doctor is with her."

"I will go to her."

Two hours went by before she was able to return to her husband's bedside. Her strength and courage sapped, she allowed her tears to dampen his nightshirt. Still believing the worse, she prayed she would not have to say goodbye to him as well.

Another sleepless night past with John's fever returning. His voice shouting incoherently at times, and wild thrashing had Nicholas coming in to hold him down.

Early morning found him still as death, but still the fever burned and his body perspired profusely. The doctor warned her that the next twenty-four hours would decide his fate.

Nicholas tried to get her to come away to rest and eat, but stubborn she remained, until the health of their unborn child came to her mind. She took in nourishment but refused leave his side.

Late into the day, Margaret rose to refresh the water basin. A powerful wave of vertigo washed over her and she quickly set the bowl aside as she became more unsteady. Taking two steps forward, her legs gave way causing her to slump to the floor. She heard Nicholas' alarmed voice and felt his arms lifting her as the fog turned pitch black.

"John!"

She sprung up in the bed, frantically looking for him. He is gone! A spasm shot through her as she remembered. Blinking out the sleep, she turned sharply to look at the time. Her mouth dropped as she flew off the bed.

The door open with Dixon carrying a tray. "Mistress, you're up. I have good—"

"Dixon! How dare you!" she snapped angrily as she flew pass the stunned maid.

Reaching John's bedside she shakily touched his face, a deep sigh escaped, he was still warm.

Dixon rushed into the room. "Mistress, the doctor came by while you slept," she said tentatively. "He's out of danger. He is going to recover."

Smoothing her palm over his forehead and brushing back his hair, she choked back sobs as Dixon's words registered. The flood of relief struck her so powerfully that she fell to her knees. Overwhelmed, she buried her face into the covers to release the torrent of emotions racking her body.

By and by, she was able to compose herself to ask Dixon if he had wakened.

"No, mistress. We're hoping since his mum is to be buried noonday…but no, not yet."

Turning towards the woman, she gave her an apologetic look. "I'm sorry, Dixon, for my behavior."

"Oh, I understand. You've become as dear to me as your mother. You won't find me holding a grudge to easily where you are concern."

"Dixon, Mr. Thornton and I, we care for you a great deal."

"Never you mind that. I know," she said with a smug expression, "Can I get you anything?"

She shook her head and Dixon left, closing the door behind her.

Resting on his chest, she luxuriated in her head rising and falling, and hearing the beating from within. Closing her eyes, she let out a calming sigh, whispering his name on her lips.

Margaret laid there waiting, sounds outside were muffled but active, with the mill working full force. Raw voices and endless clanging, hardened lines and faded colors, all made up John's muddied world for so long. He could have died and, yet, life would continue as before.

The line that separated the North from South would still divide the bright colors from the dark. Like love and hate, happiness and sorrow, and good and evil, every person, at one time or another in his or her life crossed each line.

Some, like Stephens, crossed over the line of hate and evil, never to find a way to cross to the other side. It saddened her that many, like Bessy and Hannah, did not go far beyond that line of love and happiness with someone by their sides, as she had with John.

Her hand ran up his chest, grateful that he had been spared. Her life would have gone from light to dark, clinging desperately to that part of him that she had in their child.

She understood Hannah, now, why she always wore the grey and black colors. She could not cross over that line because of something so dark that happened in her life, but she was grateful Hannah had her children.

Strong fingers and a palm topped her head and smoothed down to touch the side of her face.

"Maggie."

It was not a question, but an endearment. Joy leaped into her heart as she looked up to see his head turned to her with drowsed eyes, opened and focused. A rush of emotions flooded her as she sobbed out his name and buried her face in his neck, wrapping her arms around his head allowing the fingers of one hand to thread through his black hair.

"Ah, Maggie, Love…I'd told myself, I'll not leave you."

Lifting her head, she kissed her husband's whiskered face, whispering her love for him.

Running his fingers over his jaw, he tried to reassure her with an offhand comment.

"I need a shave."

It worked. Her expression lightened with glistening eyes.

"I find it most agreeable," she sobbed happily.

Putting in motion her lips up his jaw line, she trailed around his face ending at the corner of his mouth, kissing and speaking softly for him to rest.

He let out a deep breath and drifted back into a healing sleep. Margaret heart then dropped. She did not tell him about his mother, but perhaps, it was for the best.

Walking back with Higgins, her mind was struggling with how and when she should tell John. It weighed heavily on her.

She knew him. He would lay all the blame on himself for her

death even though her dying wish was for him not too. And there is no doubt that he would find those regrets as most did with a tragic loss.

Margaret thought of Fanny telling her brother that their mother was dead sent a chill up her spine. She had not been surprised when Fanny confronted her when she and Dixon came to her outside the church. She allowed Fanny's angry words place blame on her for Hannah's death. She believed her grief fueled her anger.

Dixon did not believe that for one moment but she managed to hold her tongue with her mistress's hand squeezing her arm reminding her to restrain herself from saying a word.

Fanny then lashed out on her dead mother saying how she dare leave her behind to give birth and care for a baby all alone. Margaret had to admit, when Fanny called her mother selfish for dying, well, she was relieved for the first time that John was not present. It would have been an eminently ugly scene to play out on such a sad day.

While her brother's absence would spare Fanny his wrath, it would not save her from Dixon. She of all people became Hannah's fierce protector and vehemently told the daughter that she should be ashamed of herself. Once started, the buxom woman's tongue-lashing hit on harsh truths and revelations that had Fanny going pale and silent.

Thinking that was enough, Margaret pulled Dixon back and laid a hand on Fanny's arm. She then told Fanny, if she wished, she would be there for her when the time came for the birth or any other time she needed her. Such as they were now, sisters, she would be glad for it.

Fanny looked dumbfounded at her sister-in-law. Letting out a loud sob, she crumbled into Margaret's arms, crying out how much she missed her mother. Lifting her face, Margaret gave her a consoling smile, while dabbing her tears with a handkerchief. She then passed the distraught woman over to the care of the hovering Mr. Watson. Self-seeking as Fanny was, she loved her mother dearly.

Even with that realization, Fanny telling John of Hannah's

death, her unconscious lack of tact and delicacy, well, she would not allow it to happen, and the need to return to John's bedside became more hurried.

John forced his eyes open with the sound of her sweet voice directing him out of the fog. She and their child is safe, his mother—his eyes went wide as he turned his head sharply, bringing Margaret quickly into view.

"Mother?"

Her expression went somber which alerted him that not all was well.

"How badly is she hurt?" he asked urgently.

She laid a hand on his chest, rested her head on his shoulder, and spoke softly, "John, she loss too much blood."

He moved his hand to cup her face and brought it up so he could look into her eyes. They were moist with unshed tears. He knew without further words.

"She is gone."

Margaret laid her head back on his shoulder as tears spilled. His voice was steady and low, "Tell me what happened."

"You were right, she planned it all. She paid to have the man followed so she knew where he lived. She left a letter addressed to Inspector Mason with every detail of her plan in her room so we would not be implicated."

"Did you read it?" She nodded. "What did it say?"

"John, she meant to poison him. She learnt of his love for the drink and took a bottle with her—a peace offering of sorts while she tried to bribe him to leave Milton. Once he was dead…oh, John, I cannot finish."

"Maggie, I need to hear it."

She took a deep breath and continued, "She said in the letter that it was her intention to…to take the—"

"To take the poison herself," he finished.

She placed her hand on his arm. "She knew that she would

face a trial, life in prison or worse," she said sorrowfully. "She didn't want to put us through that burden or pain."

"It didn't go as she planned."

"He guessed rather quickly and drew the knife on her and they struggled," she said. Shaking her head, her eyes lifted upwards as a singular notion overtook her. "Oh, what was she thinking!"

"She was thinking of us, Love."

"But to…to take such desperate measures!"

The tone in her voice of not understanding had John thinking that it was the right time.

"Maggie, she had made extreme choices in her life before."

Her eyes questioned and he calmly disclosed his mother's past actions in regards to her husband's death and his part as well. He wanted no secrets between them so he included his mother's confessions about the riot and her sending the letter. Alarm crossed her face and he quickly assured her that Frederick was safe. No further inquiries had been made since. To the rest, her reaction was of shocked dismay, but then her deep compassion flooded her countenance.

"Margaret, from this day forward, we will not speak of any of this again."

"Never again," she promised.

He changed the subject quickly, asking her what happened after he went unconscious. She described in detail including Stephens' arrest, his mothers passing and burial.

"Were you with her at the end?"

"Yes, I was," she replied softly, "and you were there as well."

John let out a deep sigh of contentment. Eyes softening he ran his palm up and down her arm.

"With you by her side in a way I was there," he said, as his hand moved to the nape of her neck. "You are a representation of me in every way, in body and in spirit. I said my farewell through you and I am satisfied."

"Before I went to see her, I knew that you would not be able to say goodbye, so I put your hand to my heart," she said, picking up his hand to demonstrate, "and asked for you to speak the words you wanted to say." A tendered smile appeared on her lips. "Can you guess what your spirit said to me in your sleep?"

He shook his head and her smile widened and whispered secretively into his ear, and then spoke of his mother's reaction.

What she told him had moisture welling up in his eyes and a broad smile forming. Taking her beautiful face into his hands, he looked deeply into her eyes.

"Maggie, yes. Perfect," he muttered with emotion, as is mouth found hers.

His eager kisses greeted her, and she moved to lie along the length of him, her hand smoothing up his chest, over his shoulder to conform to his face as he deepened their connection. To him, there is nothing more therapeutic than tasting her again and feeling her safe by his side.

He predicted him fighting future nightmares of that knife plunging into her stomach and into her womb. He thought of the sharp edge going into his mother. He knew first hand what she experienced. Breaking, he asked Margaret.

She rested on his shoulder, assuring him that she had felt little pain. The loss of blood is what eventually robbed her of life. He flinched, thinking about the irony that like his father, his mother would share in the same fate, not only with the blood loss, but by another's hand.

Margaret told him how Dixon made her room as fresh and colorful as a flower garden right before sunset. She describe the last minutes of his mother's life and her last words. He listened intently, feeling the turmoil of emotions building and evolving regrets. Then she spoke of the three parting kisses and the final goodnight.

His arm flew to his face to hide the grief that began to surface. Her hands gripped his arm and pulled it down.

"Don't, John Thornton. I made promises to your mother and I will keep them. I'll not allow you to hide your grief. You'll not mourn alone. You have any regrets we will share them and work through them together," she lectured adamantly. "And you will not blame yourself. This was her choice and you will accept it. We heal together. Do I make myself clear?"

Dumbfounded, he simply answered her by nodding. What did he do to deserve such love from this miraculous woman?

"What, no argument or reproach?"

"No chance for gainful actions this time around. I have no defense to speak of."

"Well, I will provide it all the same," she said, giving him a lingering kiss on his mouth.

He savored and returned her attentions, moving his hand to the back of her head so he could deepen their intimacy. Lifting his upper back and head, he enthusiastically possessed her compliant lips.

His exertions caused a sharp spasm in his abdomen and a wave of dizziness to strike. Along with the dulled ache, fatigue hit him, causing him to groan. His head dropped back on the pillow in frustration of being forced to abandon his pleasurable pursuit.

Margaret's concerned voice piped in, "You are tired. You rest now, and I will bring you some broth."

Giving him a quick kiss, she pushed herself up and climbed off the bed, but he grabbed her wrist, stopping her.

"I don't want food. I'm hungry for more from my wife," he muttered.

With a stern, motherly expression, she shook her head, "And you think that you have the strength to even attempt to…no, sir, you have no choice in this," she said. "It is either take *real* nourishment with me or I get Dixon."

An irritated grimace appeared. "I suppose I could take some broth."

Her face relaxed into a smile as she bent over, brushing hair off his forehead, and kissed the bared spot tenderly.

He gave her a forced frown. "Now who is treating one as a child?"

Margaret drew away slightly to lock her large luminous eyes on his as she gave him a whimsical upturn of her lip. Bending closely she whispered one word in his ear.

"Practice."

As his sharp azure eyes followed her out of the room, a large boy-like grin appeared on his face.

He was well enough to testify at Stephens' trial two weeks later. As much as he wished to avoid it, Margaret had been placed on the stand as well.

She was brave and clear in her details of her attack and his admission of murder. Even with Stephens sneering and glaring at her, she stayed calm and collected.

The defense drilled her heartlessly but she remained solid as a rock. Later, she told him that speaking the truth was preferable in its simplicity. No amount of badgering could make her stumble.

But Margaret prayed for the man, which John found humbling. He knew what outcome she wanted, insanity or life in prison, but in the end, Stephens guilty verdict led to the sentence of death.

The day of his hanging, John visited his mother's gravesite, laid flowers for her, and then took his Maggie home.

"Ah, Thornton, I see you are in much brighter spirits this time around."

John clasped the older man's outstretched hand, "Bell, glad you were able to make it."

"Wouldn't miss it for the world," he said looking over the younger man's shoulder. "Does she know?"

Before he could answer, her voice sounded loud and clear.

"Mr. Bell!"

John turned to see Margaret, face lighted with surprise, rushing to affectionately greet her godfather. "What are you doing here?"

"I had to see this Eden you described in your letters."

Wrapping her arm around his, she drew him out of the cold entryway to the warmth of the main drawing-room.

Concern crossed her face. "Your health…you were not well in October. You look thin."

"Don't trouble yourself, my dear," he replied, patting her hand, "I had to make the trip back to fulfill an obligation to a dear friend. I'll be back under my Argentine skies soon."

Margaret noticed a passing look between the two men and John's suppressed grin.

"You two are up to something."

"Thornton, I didn't think she could get any more glorious, but in her present condition, I see that I was wrong," Mr. Bell said, "Sixth month?"

"Fifth, complete with an extremely healthy appetite."

Her face flushed. "Don't change the subject," she insisted.

The two men laughed and the talk turned to a manly conversation, leaving her frowning at their apparent avoidance of her inquiry.

At length, Samuel made an appearance, nodding once to John then exiting. Having poured Mr. Bell a drink, he handed it to him, forcing Bell to relinquish Margaret over to his care. Offering his arm, she took it, giving him a suspicious look.

"John, what is this all about?"

"Maggie, Nicholas and Clara are not the only guests I have coming over tonight," he said. "There is one more."

She looked expectantly at the other man in the room. "Mr. Bell, you are staying."

"Oh, of course, but he is not speaking of me."

At that moment, Dixon came into the room. Her face was rosy and flushed with excitement. "Sir, your other guests have arrived."

"Thank you, Dixon," he said, looking down at his wife's bemused face, "show them in."

"John, who is it?"

His handsome full smile appeared as he nodded towards the

entranceway. She lifted her face and a shocked gasp sounded.

"Frederick!"

"Margaret!"

John watched as brother and sister rushed to embrace and their happiness filled the room. Margaret's laughter became mixed with tears of joy.

Nicholas came in from behind with Clara as they both move to stand by John and Mr. Bell.

"Well isn't that a sight?" Higgins' said looking at John. "This Lennox sure came through in a pinch."

"Called it his belated wedding gift," John said. "He's a good man." Turning to Mr. Bell, he held his hand out again. "Thank you for your part, Bell."

Taking the young man's hand, he smiled. "Ah, well, I promised his father and with the aid of excellent representation, he is finally able to roam this earth a freed man."

John turned his attention back to his wife who was coming down from her exuberance. Even though her tears were drying, her eyes still sparkled brightly with elation. Arm hooked around her brother's she moved forward and made introductions.

The atmosphere in the room became animated, full of lively conversation on how Frederick's liberation came about and of his family in Cadiz, youthful memories and plans for the future. Dixon and Samuel joined in the merriment.

Across the room, John caught Margaret's eye and she smiled brilliantly for him. She was so incredibly beautiful in her happiness. Striding to her side, she linked her arm with his, squeezing it affectionately.

As she looked up to her husband's face, he looked down into hers. Simultaneously they moved to meet in the middle for a tendered kiss. The people in the room disappeared as they shared their deep love for each other.

For John and Margaret, no words were needed.

John was home.

Margaret's light smile appeared for him as he approach the desk where she was sitting. He did not bend down to give her the usual greeting kiss; in its stead, he got down on one knee, and turned her around in the swivel chair, with the pen still clasped in her hand.

"John, what are you doing," she asked, baffled.

His expression fixed with purpose, and eyes flashed mischievously, as his hand roamed over to the strained buttons of her blouse, undoing each one.

Her smile flowered. He had this strange fascination with her swelled stomach. When the baby began to kick and fidget, John would span both palms over the mound and patiently wait to feel for himself. She loved seeing his face light up in wonder when his child made his or her presence known.

"And where are you going, sir?"

"To say hello," he answered, as his hand found the opening.

She startled at his touch. "John, warm your hands!"

"Sorry, Love."

As his palms warmed on her swelled belly and his lips kissed her exposed protruding navel, she laughed sweetly.

"Well, say your hellos and be gone before someone walks in. I want to finish this letter."

"I gave them all the day off."

"Now why would you do that on a Wednesday?"

He looked up with a huge grin. "I ran into the good doctor this afternoon." Margaret gave him a bemused look. "I asked him a specific question, worded carefully, mind you."

"What was the question?"

"Stems from me not wanting to risk having intimate relations with you," he said, kissing her belly again, "during your advanced, delicate condition."

She let out an exasperated sigh, "John, you didn't. That poor doctor."

"You'll not ask me what he said."

"I can guess with you giving the day off to the staff."

John's mouth smiled on her skin as he spoke to their unborn child, "You have a beautiful and perceptive mother, little one. I cannot wait for you to meet her."

Her curiosity on how her husband was going to perform such an intimate connection with her joyful burden remained to be seen, but she was decidedly willing, and trust that he would succeed in this undertaking.

With her own passion rising, she threaded her fingers in his hair and brought him up from his kneeling position, kissing him fully. She stopped to catch her breath and to ask if the doctor gave any prescription.

Nodding, he brought her up standing from the chair, took the pen and placed it on the desk, then swept her up into his strong arms and moved purposefully towards the front door, bypassing the stairwell.

"John, where are you going?"

"Do you think I am going to even attempt to carry you upstairs?"

"That heavy?"

"That heavy. It is unseasonably warm this day and the carriage waits."

She took his jaw into her hand, "But it isn't going to storm."

"Believe me, Mrs. Thornton, we don't need a storm."

Margaret's eyes sparkled with excitement and merriment as her husband loaded her into the carriage and ran around to the other side. Looking in the back seat, she saw that he thought of her comfort, complete with quilts and pillows.

"Where is the basket?"

He glanced over as he snapped the reins. "Are you hungry?"

His question brought back a memory that made her smile bloom. Wrapping her arm around his she looked up at him as he peered down at her.

"Yes, but not for food," she answered flatly, "and I expect to get my full portion."

"Not just satisfied, eh?" She shook her head. "What the missus wants, be mindful she gets."

"Oh, but John, our child may get hungry later," she said rubbing her enlarged stomach.

Etched deeply in his expression was desire and want for his wife to whom he had not had intimate relations with for weeks.

Frowning, he shook his head. "We're not going back," he said decisively. "If hungry, I'll catch a chicken." ଓ

Chapter Seventeen

Always

Coming out of a deep sleep, John knew she was not by his side and his eyelids slowly fluttered opened knowing the reason why.

His eyes focused and found her in the dimmed light as the first rays of dawn were appearing. She was sitting in the rocker next to the bed, tenderly nursing their daughter.

Every morning for the last three months, he woke to such a picture, simplistically beautiful in its design, forever to be engraved into his consciousness. Treasuring these moments, he watched every loving expression that crossed the young mother's face as the child took hungrily of her breast.

Hannah Marie Thornton was born in early May, along with the brilliance of the wakening summer season. As promised, his mother's name would live on through her granddaughter.

Before the birth, they both agreed that if their first child happened to be born a male, he would prevail to father again, sowing the seed until they became successful in fulfilling that pledge. John concluded that he would have to break the promise made to his mother after the fourth or fifth son. Margaret adamantly disagreed, saying whether on second or by seventeenth, Hannah was going to get her namesake.

Fortunately, God endeavored to bless them with a daughter straight away. After kissing his exhausted Maggie, they both huddled together on the bed, admiring their little Hannah. John had to admit, he was greatly relieved. Knowing how he was in his youth, he did not think he had the fortitude to handle many sons.

Needing her rest, Margaret passed the newborn to him. Holding his little girl in his arms for the first time, he kissed her tiny forehead, and whispered her name on her soft skin, picturing his mother holding her namesake, smiling in her joy.

Fatherhood was a role he found as fulfilling and rewarding as being a husband. Whereas he completed her by making Margaret a mother, she did for him by giving birth to their child and making him a father.

As the baby nursed, Margaret played with her tiny hand, bringing the tiny fingers up to her lips, whispering a hushed lullaby of endearments.

The window allowed in enough of the waking light to give one side of her face and long loose tresses a warm soft glow. She was so beautiful and his heart could not stop the masculine sigh of contentment from escaping, alerting her that he was no longer asleep. She looked up at him, their eyes met, and her lip curled up gracefully as her eyes lowered to the child's face.

"Papa's awake," she cooed.

The baby, responding to her mother's new tone, detached herself with little arms flaying in excitement causing Margaret to laugh softly as she looked back at John.

"I think she is done. Do you want her?"

Propping himself up against the headboard, he grinned back at her.

"Every day, as her mother."

His simple answer made his wife's smile come alive and she drew up her nightgown, padded over to his side of the bed, and placed their daughter into his waiting arms.

He took the opportunity to bid his wife a quick good morning by kissing the cheek closest to him, anxious to give attention to his Hannie girl.

Frowning, she stood up straight and crossed her arms. "Do you call that a proper kiss for the woman who spent eleven hours in labor?" she asked with mock annoyance.

"Come back after I am through with her and I'll be more than obliging," he grinned with a promising wink.

Her hidden smile appeared for him, turning on her heel, she went over to the bassinet to tidy the contents, commenting that Hannah will soon need the larger crib.

John gave an exaggerated frown as Hannah's tiny hand played with her father's lower lip. His voice adored as he addressed his daughter with babying sternness, "Listen, my girl, no growing up to quickly. I won't have it."

Margaret turned with a glint in her eyes. "John, it is no use trying to be a domineering master to our daughter."

"I know this," he said, kissing his daughter's forehead. "She will be as her mamma, beautiful and stubborn." After a pause, he looked up at his wife and added, "Thankfully."

"With her dark hair and your eyes, I cannot say she is entirely like me."

"Appearances excluded. Come back to bed, Love."

She moved to the other side of the bed, hitching up her nightgown she climbed on the mattress, moving over close to her husband to watch as he mouthed Hannah's wiggling fingers. They both laughed at her many sweet expressions and baby smiles.

John looked down at his daughter and then to the face of his Maggie and felt this sudden surge of love that threatened to overwhelm him.

"Maggie."

Concern crossed her face at his tone. "John, what is wrong?"

"I don't want to remember my life before you," he said, looking down at Hannah, "and her."

Margaret's eyes went soft and she raised a hand to draw his face towards her to get his complete attention.

"I do not think you would have loved me as much as you do now if you forgotten the path taken to get here. No, John, I want you to remember so you never allow yourself to go back."

He thought for a moment and had to agree with her statement. The remembrances of what his life lacked before he had her to fill the empty spaces brought clarity to him as a man, not the machine; he will never let the past repeat itself.

"You are right, Love. The story of my life may have started at birth but I didn't begin living it until the chapter when you appeared in the words."

She smiled, "I did make a rather sudden appearance."

He leaned slightly forward and confirmed, "Yes, you did. I was never the same after that moment."

"I'm glad of it even with me believing at first you were the villainous character."

"And you the feisty heroine."

Laughing sweetly, "As much as I like being called a feisty heroine, I think blind mouse is more appropriate description but," looking at the drowsed child in his arms, "I think the story turned out rather well. Do you not think so?"

"There are many chapters left to go, Mrs. Thornton, and if I wasn't holding her right now, I would be writing one without the ink or paper."

"I cannot imagine what you mean, Mr. Thornton." Her blushing cheeks told him otherwise.

"Can you not," he said. "Now, since you are in such close proximity, let me give you that proper morning kiss."

Freeing one hand, he did not allow her to speak as he drew her to him and possessed her mouth with committed enthusiasm. His fingers threaded through her hair, gripping a handful to announce his complete control. Pulling away, he regarded her with desirous eyes. She was breathless and wanting.

"John…I need you."

"I know, Love."

He moved to kissed her more tenderly. Her hand went up and touched where their lips fused causing him to move his mouth over to kiss her palm and move down to her neck.

After a minute of nuzzling she spoke, "John…"

"Mm…"

"You know what part of the week this is?"

"The end," he murmured against her skin.

She moved away and slipt off the bed causing him to emit a disappointed groan. Padding around the bed, she took the slumbering baby from his arms.

"Yes, and we are at the end of the month, as well," she whispered, glancing over at him as she reached the bassinet. "It is looking to be a warm and beautiful day."

His brow rose and his crooked grin appeared. "Looking for help in harvesting vegetables?"

Drawing a light blanket over Hannah, Margaret rose and turned towards him with hands to her waist.

"No, think again."

His grin grew into a smile. "Oh, you don't like the green. You prefer blue?"

She could not suppress the full smile. "You did remember."

"I am a man of many contracts and agreements. Do you think I could ever breach this one?"

"Well, I am glad of it," she said, walking over to her side of the bed to crawl in. "I would have been thoroughly affronted if you had."

John reached for her arm and gently pulled her over to him, tossing her over onto her back, pinning her down with his weight.

"Love, I would like to add a clause to the contract, if you are in agreement."

"Then speak of it. I am open to suggestions."

He lowered his lips to her ear and whispered as his fingers moved to draw up her gown. Her expression lighted with pleasure.

Nodding emphatically, her arms encircled his chest. "That is most agreeable. Twice a month when weather permits. Where do I sign?"

"To validate this amendment, no signing, or handshake will do," he said while positioning his wife for his need. "It will take more to seal this deal."

Languishing in her husband's arms, Margaret found her courage to ask the question that had been pressing on her mind.

"John?"

"Yes, Love."

"I've been wanting to ask…well, since we began to be intimate again, I cannot help but notice that after, you do not…finish." Face reddening, she moved to hide between the apex of his chest and arm. His deep chuckle had her pressing even further into the mattress with embarrassment.

He lifted her face. "Forgive me, Maggie, I thought you knew the reason," he said, bringing her face up into view. "I do not want you with child."

Her eyes widened with surprise. "Isn't that a decision that we both should make?"

"You are delicate and I do not want your body to go through such stress and strain so soon."

"I am strong," she exclaimed with eyes flashing. "I'm hoping to give you a son."

"And I have every confidence that someday you will, but not until much later."

"John, I am disappointed," she mourned, moving herself away, she turned her back to him.

Normally, this was his queue to grab her up and start in on his begging for understanding and forgiveness. Her prettied pout would not have its effect on him this time.

With their wedding anniversary only days away, his idea for her gift had since been brought into fruition with the aid of her brother. In the Spring of the coming year, she will not be burdened with a pregnancy or birthing if he had a say, which he admitted took considerable restraint.

No, she will be traveling abroad for an extended tour. She could be unhappy with him for a few more hours. His plan was to surprise her during their outing that afternoon.

It was all set up with Higgins and Hamper for him to be gone for the five months. Mary Higgins was elated that Mr. Thornton personally asked her to accompany them as companion and help to Margaret and Hannah.

The itinerary included sailing to Spain to spend two months with Frederick and Deloris. Together, the two families would travel along the African coast. After stopping back to Cadiz on the way back, the last month was reserved for his family to stay on the northwestern coast of Saint-Pol-de-Léon. There, in the picturesque countryside of France, it is his hope that he could endeavor to conceive their second child.

Margaret moved and propped herself up near him. "John, is there any way I can change your mind?"

"No," he said firmly, "I'll not risk your health."

She frowned. "When?"

"Perhaps, next autumn."

"Next autumn! That is too long to wait."

"Enough said, Maggie."

Her mouth clamped shut. He closed his eyes with a slight grin on his face. A mulled silence entered the room. By-and-by, he felt her hand run up his bared chest, and warm breath on his ear.

"I'll allow you to name him," she sweetly bribed.

Opening his eyes, his head turned to her. "Reginald Gaylord is still available."

"Thankfully, Estelle Regina is not."

They laughed heartily. Remembering the sleeping child both covered their mouths to muffle their amusement. At length, they subsided into a peaceful contentment of holding each other with legs and arms entwined.

John recognized a profound truth recently about his wife, and that was that motherhood was her true purpose in life. She would fight to advance that natural inclination. He waited for it and sure enough, a few moments later her voice, as soft and inviting as a cool breeze on a hot day found his ears.

"John, I know you are a reasonable man," she said tentatively. "Can we negotiate?"

Grabbing her around the waist, he positioned her on her back. His ebony hair fell forward and dark long lashes could not hide his smiling eyes.

"I'll tell you what, let us compromise," he said, trailing kisses over her face. "You let me have my way with you and in return I will agree to discuss future children this afternoon."

Margaret allowed his lips to inch downwards. She still had little hope of changing his mind but she did not want to stop his course of action by denying him. His seductive tone had her not wanting to pass up this opportunity to partake in his rising passion. Every opportunity of his loving could have him faulting at his determination of abandoning his fervor at his finish.

At that thought, she fictitiously relented. Hearing a sound of satisfaction coming from him, her arms flew above her head in blissful defeat.

Sighing dramatically, she said, "Always being ones master."

Peering up from nuzzling her neck he grinned at her and with all seriousness, he responded.

"No, Love," he said, lowering his lips only a breath away from hers, "you were the one who assumed some kind of rule over me from the beginning. This leaves me with this conclusion. I'm a father third, husband second, but my Maggie, I will always be yours, first." ଓ

Epilogue

"Papa, pick me up, pick me up!"

John looked down at the little girl hugging his leg. Reaching down he lifted her up, little arms encircled his neck as he cradled her with one arm.

Peering into the angelic face, he asked if she was frightened. She shook her head but her wide eyes told him otherwise.

The ominous black head of the whistling train approached slowly into the busy London Station. Looking back at Margaret sitting on the bench, playing with their fourteen month old on her lap, he strolled over to sit down beside her.

"Right on time," he mused, "but it should be another half hour before we can board."

Margaret nodded and offered a reassuring smile for the clinging daughter. "Do not be afraid, Hannie, your papa and I have ridden on a train often. Think of it as a rather large, noisy carriage without the horse."

"How does it move, Mamma?"

John answered for her. "Thousands of little elves underneath running along those," he said pointing to the steel tracks. "You have to look hard."

"Where, Papa!"

"Have to wait to see. When they stop the train, you'll see the sparks, and when they start up, they blow big puffs of steam."

Their little girl gasped in wonderment as her large eyes stared at the wheels of the train coming into the station.

Margaret shook her head. "The pictures you put in her head. I would not have believed you to be so imaginative."

"It is none of my doing," he said leaning a little closer to her, "I was enchanted by a chance meeting, a captivating woman, and a bench such as the one we are sitting on now. It forever changed my world from grey to one of color and light."

Her eyes sparkled with remembrance but before she could reply, their daughter sounded for her father to take her closer to the train wanting to see little elfin legs, sparks, and steam.

"I'll take her," Mary said coming up from behind, returning from bidding farewell to her beau.

"Mary, Mary, there are elves under the train!"

Mary took the little girl from her father, while acting astonished at the news. Both John and Margaret laughed at their little girl's animated face.

Draping his freed arm along the back of the bench, his fingers absently drummed on his wife's furthest shoulder, catching the attention of the child in her arms, and provoking little fingers to grab at them.

"Looks as if we are going to lose Mary soon," he said looking at the young woman ahead of him.

Margaret nodded, pleased that her efforts had come into fruition with Mary and Henry's cousin. The two met two years before when the family went to London to visit her Aunt Shaw and Edith.

"I am glad of it. She certainly has blossomed. I see much of her sister in her."

"Maddie and Bess will miss her."

"I am sorry to say, but I am grateful we left them over into Nicholas' and Clara's care while on our visit here. The twins are a handful. I wonder if I should feel guilty."

John glanced at her while two of his caught fingers toyed in his son's grip. "As I always said, Higgins' is to be admired for taken on another man's children. Next year, when we go to Argentina, let's take their two oldest boys. They both could use some real adventures." Enthusiastically, she agreed saying she would write to Frederick immediately.

She looked forward to the trip. Mr. Bell's death had not been a surprise but the fact that the man was much wealthier than he led them to believe, was. Being godfather to Frederick, as well, dear Mr. Bell left the remaining balance, villa, and the property to him. It was considerable. Frederick's family was happily situated under Mr. Bell's glorious Argentine skies.

"Tom is now the age when I had to take to the docks," John reflected, "I am grateful he will see fewer hardships in his life."

Margaret's reply was a softened expression. The conversation stalled which gave her opportunity to examine her husband's profile as he casually observed the goings-on in the station.

After six years, he aged little except for the creases in the corners of his eyes had deepened with laughter, and a slight greying of his hair, which he accused her for producing with her stubbornness. She defended herself by saying that it was becoming increasingly difficult to produce reason enough for his begging sessions and the "gainful actions" that often followed. This quieted him with a nod of agreement and grin of appreciation.

The years were filled with love, family, and abundance. Mr. Bell's investment advice and the success of the mills, made the Thornton's one of the wealthiest families in the North—after the Watsons', that is.

Somehow, Mr. Watson was able to stay way above the line of wealth, even with all of Fanny's lavish spending and spoiling of their three children—all girls. Thankfully, Fanny became more practical in the naming of their children.

However, as Margaret predicted, fairy tale beginnings do not necessarily mean happiness and joy, thereafter. The lines of fear and sorrow were to be crossed.

While away on their tour in their second year of marriage, an infectious epidemic invaded all of Darkshire, and many perished, mostly the elderly and children. The Higgins were struck down, and

Clara barely survived. Tragically, two of the younger Boucher orphans found their way to their heavenly sleep.

After the difficult birth of the girls, she became dismayed that attempts to become with child were unsuccessful. By the end of the fourth year, they were discussing adopting. Not two months later, to their great joy, she was with child. John's son was born and his father's laugh lines increased.

Within months, Margaret became, surprisingly, with child again. It was most unexpected and welcomed. However, it was not to be. A three-fold tragedy was to strike sending in a period of great distress and grief.

Dixon and she was coming back from Milton when the horse spooked, flipping the carriage. Dixon's head struck a rock, breaking her neck. Samuel had lost his second wife, and the Thornton's lost an irreplaceable, treasured soul. A week after, still recovering from the accident, Margaret lost the baby at five months—it was a girl. The doctor then informed them that there would be no more children.

John's anxiety for his wife was heightened as she fell into a deep depression. Her husband's love and constancy, along with the smiles and laughter of their four children, eventually brought Margaret out of her deep mourning, as well as, the promise of adoption down the road. John had her smiling again, saying that he had to beat Higgins orphan tally but an expansion on the cottage may have to occur first. Margaret was sensible; she said half that count would suffice.

There were many years ahead, and as John had said, many chapters to still be written, and most likely, many divided lines to be crossed. Looking tenderly at her husband, Margaret knew that as long as they were together, they would endure until the end of their story. Their children would continue to write their own with the foundation of a loving, happy, and stable childhood. It was the new Thornton legacy.

Margaret's arm was wrapped protectively around the baby, as he bounced on strengthening legs on her lap. Moving her freed hand over to John's face, she brushed back some of his hair off his forehead.

Glancing at her affectionately, his expression had her drawing in breath, taking her back. The adoring look she received was the same as the one that he gave her on that life-altering day years ago. She would never forget.

"A long time back, I was nervously holding a rose in my hand while sitting on a bench," she said. "Now, I'm holding our son. Where would we be if we missed each other and fate took us down different paths?"

"Maggie, look at me." His deep unassailable voice lured her to focus on him intently. "With Lennox's wedding last week, and Higgins now owner of Hamper's, we have come full circle, but I have no hesitation in saying that we had to happen." Reaching out he took her hand into his. "I am certain that all roads would have eventually led to one explicable conclusion…us finding each other."

"Yes, I know you are right," she said with eyes now shining with surfacing emotion. "I love you, John Thornton," she said plainly.

Striking blue eyes smiled. Remembering, he brought up her hand up to his lips, speaking, low and deep, on her skin, "Now, what have I said about actions speaking for words?"

Margaret's expression was one of gentle reflection, as her hand reached behind his head, fingers threading in his hair, drawing him forward into a selfish, passionate kiss, not caring who saw. There was no fear of impropriety in their intimate display of affection as their mouths moved purposefully together.

However, a merry protest was raised, as a pudgy little hand intervened, walloping his parent's enjoined faces while gurgling out happy, jabbering sounds.

Breaking their connection, they laughed at the child's intervention. John grabbed up his namesake, lifting him up in the air, chiding him playfully for interrupting his attentions to his mother. Baby belly laughs sounded loudly, coercing smiles out of nearby, transitory passengers.

The announcement of the departure to Milton became drowned out by the shrill of the train's whistle. Standing, with son perched securely on one arm, John held out his hand to Margaret.

"Come on, Love, let's go home."

Eyes lifting up to him, with a slight lift of her mouth, she put her hand into his. ☙

End

About the Author

Mary Jo Schrauben is a confessed "Period Drama Junkie" currently living in lower Michigan, with her beloved "herd" of pets. She has a deep love for the Lord's beautiful creations and the great outdoors. Her passion is her fiction writing, history, and international travel.

She works as an Office Professional and volunteers as Webmaster and pet foster caregiver for a local pet rescue group. She is an Original Christian who dismisses all man-made doctrines, customs and traditions, and lives as Christ and His apostles taught and demonstrated in their own lives.

To contact, please email her at Mary.Jo.Schrauben@gmail.com

Printed in Great Britain
by Amazon.co.uk, Ltd.,
Marston Gate.